OUT OF THE WRECK

AND OTHER NAUTICAL TALES FROM THE PULPS

WILDSIDE PULP CLASSICS

The Blind Spot, by Austin Hall and Homer Eon Flint
Far Below & Other Horrors, edited by Robert Weinberg
The Golden Dolphin, by J. Allan Dunn
The Grand Cham, by Harold Lamb
Murgunstruum and Others, by Hugh B. Cave
Out of the Wreck, by Captain A.E. Dingle

BY JOHNSTON MCCULLEY

Black Star
The Mark of Zorro
The Spider Strain and Other Tales
Tales of Thubway Tham

BY ROBERT E. HOWARD

The Complete Action Stories
Gates of Empire
Graveyard Rats
Treasures of Tartary
Waterfront Fists

PULP MAGAZINE FACSIMILES

Strange Tales #7 (January 1933)
Ghost Stories (June 1931)
Spicy Mystery Stories (August 1935)
Spicy Mystery Stories (February 1937)

THE MYSTERIOUS WU FANG

The Case of the Suicide Tomb, by Robert J. Hogan

OPERATOR #5

Blood Reign of the Dictator, by Curtis Steele

SECRET AGENT "X"

Legion of the Living Dead, by Brant House

OUT OF THE WRECK

AND OTHER NAUTICAL TALES FROM THE PULPS

CAPTAIN A.E. DINGLE

WILDSIDE PRESS

**OUT OF THE WRECK
AND OTHER NAUTICAL TALES FROM THE PULPS**

Published by:

Wildside Press
www.wildsidepress.com

First Wildside Press edition: 2004

CONTENTS

OUT OF THE WRECK

A SEA fog with wind, and intermittent flurries of snow; a deep, ancient, and ill-manned three-masted schooner charging lumberingly across the Northern steam lanes, spouting gray torrents from reeling scuppers to the grumbling clank of laboring pumps; a mate at odds with the skipper, and a skipper at odds with the world: thus the *Centurion*, mahogany laden from Africa, groping blindly toward Boston.

"There it is again!" snarled Captain Gedge, swinging around to the mate. "A steamer's whistle — and you can't hear it! What use are you, anyhow?"

"It's no steamer, sir," returned Mr. Howse, doggedly. "I hear it all right — it's the three blasts of a windjammer in succession — and it's at one minute intervals, not two minute. That quinine you're doping yourself with is making you deaf as an anchor, Captain Gedge."

Three blasts on a sailing-ship's foghorn meant a ship running before the wind. So far as rule of the road went, the *Centurion* had right of way equally over such a vessel as over a steamer — if the running vessel gave it to her. The schooner's own wheezy hand-pump foghorn ground out two blasts to indicate that she was on the port tack, and eyes and ears strained through the murk of fog and snow and night to catch the reply from the unseen stranger.

With her three seamen to a watch, an only mate, and a single-handed cook-steward, the *Centurion* was poorly manned; with a skipper hard bitten by the money bug, and in whose veins flowed a mixture of mean blood and utter selfishness, her emergence from the tropics into the raw Northern Winter was a shivering nightmare to all hands — except Captain Gedge.

Long months of stewing on the blazing Gold Coast had thinned the blood and softened the endurance of unaccustomed seamen; fever had already diminished their number; the cook, a derelict from the Coast whose earlier life had obviously been cast in less unpleasant places, had never found his galley too hot even with a vertical sun at noon. And the money bug had bitten the skipper with such virulent effect that the ship's slop-chest had been emptied at the last moment to a trader ashore at five times the price his poorly paid crew could have paid him for the necessary comforts it contained.

7

And now, with swirling snow stinging the face, and dank fog saturating clear through to quaking bones, the scanty crew cursed the skipper for a stonyhearted Shylock. Each seaman's trick at the wheel was a horror to anticipate; the cook's thin face grew haggard and blue; his bloodless fingers clamped frigidly on to his dishes the moment he left the warmth of the stove. That alone saved him from a visitation of wrath for broken platters: his hands were too coldly stiff to drop them.

"Take the wheel, Mr. Howse, and send the helmsman for the steward," ordered the skipper, surlily. "I want some coffee."

"No need to haul that poor devil of a steward out of his bunk at midnight for coffee, sir," retorted the mate. "It's all ready in the galley. I'll get it myself."

"You do as I tell you!" returned Captain Gedge, with vicious emphasis. "By — ! Who's captain o' this vessel?"

Mr. Howse stepped over to the wheel with a shrug of his wide shoulders, and sent the seaman forward to the steward's bleak and coverless bunk. It was but the culmination of a series of petty cruelties on the part of the skipper; cruel not because of the orders given, but because the hardships of the crew might easily have been softened by a little common humanity.

The mate knew full well that only the nearness of the home port restrained the scanty crew from attempting reprisals in line with the threats he had heard; threats which his sense of right had impelled him to ignore in spite of his sense of duty.

The three blasts of the unseen ship to windward came down to the schooner again, much nearer now, and again the shivering seaman on the forecastle replied with the *Centurion's* two wheezy barks. Captain Gedge showed his uneasiness, for the direction of the sound indicated no change of course on the part of the stranger.

Then, up from the fog and sleet of the main deck, stumbled the steward, scalding coffee slopping over from the mug gripped in his shaking hands. The fellow's teeth chattered with a chill that reached to his bones, and the shivering of his ill-clad body must have induced pity in any humane man. But Captain Gedge was not in that class. He snatched the hot beverage, and, as the steward turned in haste to run back to the poor shelter of his bed, snarled:

"Stay here! Wait for the mug, you white-livered rat!"

The helmsman resumed the wheel, having loitered forward for a whiff of his pipe, and the mate stepped up beside the skipper, placing himself to windward of the quaking steward with the kind intention of intercepting some of the night's bitterness. His nostrils sniffed longingly at the aroma of the hot coffee; all his other senses were keenly attuned to the confused sounds to windward. Somewhere behind the blinding curtain of fog and snow Fate foamed down with shearing stem.

That the skipper was rattled Mr. Howse more than suspected. In between noisy gulps of his coffee, Captain Gedge turned toward the wheel with a gesture which almost became an order to change the schooner's course. That alone, in a vessel having right of way, proved uneasiness.

Suddenly through the swishing of seas and the hollow snoring of wind in the canvas came a deeper, heavier sound — the unmistakable thunder of an out-falling bow-wave; in the same instant a shrill note high up told of running gear in a squealing sheave: and with the whole blared those three horn blasts, so close that one might imagine he felt the breath of them.

"Up hellum! Up with it!" shrieked Captain Gedge.

His coffee mug clattered on the deck, the warm fluid sluicing gratefully over the steward's numbed toes.

"Hold your course!" roared the mate, springing to the wheel to stay the catastrophe.

He had detected the sounds which told him the stranger had sensed the danger, and was altering her course to pass astern of the schooner. To obey the skipper's command meant to place the *Centurion* fair in the course of the oncoming ship. But, as he had said, the skipper's hearing had suffered from quinine, and those vital sounds had escaped him.

"Up hellum, I say! Hard up!" bellowed Gedge, joining the other two at the wheel.

The helmsman yielded to the confusion of clashing orders, and relinquished the spokes to his superiors. Mr. Howse, after one furious attempt to overcome the skipper's frenzied strength, left the wheel and hurried forward, sending the seaman in haste to rouse out all hands. The steward still shivered at the poop-rail.

"Get below, Steward, and scoop all the blankets and grub you can find," the mate told him. "This smells like a boat job to me, son. Get a move on now."

The three seamen of the watch below were out on deck in a twinkling. Men clothed as they were, whose clothes were their only bed covering, slept lightly in such weather. Dumbly they peered aft and to windward, where as yet no definite menace appeared. The schooner fell off before the wind with a creaking of sheet-blocks and squeal of gooseneck as the skipper cast off the turns of the spanker-sheet and eased the after-pressure.

All the while in the ominous gloom chirruped the brace-blocks and parrels of the stranger; her bow-wave thundered nearer. Then a seaman of keen vision caught the blur against the fog, and screamed:

"Here she comes! Look out, Cap'n, she's right aboard yuh!"

Towering high in air, fair over the *Centurion's* poop, the jibs of a great square-rigged ship soared up into the nothingness of the swirling mist. Her long jib boom spiked across the poop and tore through the spanker; and like the Javelin of Wrath her spearheaded dolphin-striker smashed through the taffrail, made kindling of the wheel and binnacle, and flung Captain Gedge headlong the length of his after-deck.

The stranger was a steel ship of four times the wooden schooner's tonnage. The great steel stem crashed deep into the *Centurion's* stern, whirling the lighter craft broadside on to her own course by sheer weight; trimmed yards and sheets gave her added power; she tore loose from her victim, hurled her aside, and surged off into the night.

No need to order out the solitary seaworthy boat. Even as the mate raised his head from the prostrate skipper to issue the command, the six scared seamen swarmed about gripes and cradle, clearing away the raffle of a voyage by the simple method of kicking overboard everything in the way. Mr. Howse bent over the skipper again, fearful of what he should find on close examination.

Captain Gedge lay crumpled up in hideous shape, his face set and white. One leg was doubled under him, and his teeth shone out of tightly withdrawn lips. The boat-falls sang to the pull of desperate men, and the boat hung over the rail. Then up ran the steward, laden with a nondescript burden and to him the seamen shouted:

"Come on, Doctor! Shake a leg! Tumble in wi' th' junk and bear a hand, onless yuh want's a swim!"

"Wait, wait for the captain and Mr. Howse," cried the steward.

Somehow in the crisis his shivering had ceased; he moved with surety across the streaming deck.

"Mr. Howse kin come if he likes; tuh — wi' the skipper!" roared back a voice, and again the falls squealed through the blocks.

The boat dropped lower. A man saw the futility of lowering away with the schooner charging along before the wind in a lumpy sea, and the falls were belayed while hands hauled down the jibs and let go fore and main-halyards by the run. Then as the schooner swung up to the wind again, a hand hauled in the mizzen-sheet and righted the helm, leaving her to ride head-to-wind with a flat spanker to hold her.

"Comin', Mister Howse?" a seaman called. His mates were vociferously arguing with him to waste no more time. "Yes, boys, I'm with you," answered the mate, tugging at the prostrate skipper. "Give me a hand here; ain't going to leave a man like this, are you?"

"Yuh'll have tuh leave him or stay yerself!" came back the retort. "She ain't goin' to float much longer. She's mighty deep aft now. Comin'?"

The mate sprang to the rail, peering down into the boat tugging at the tackles with oars out all ready to cast off. The steward had jumped into the boat to stow the things he had brought up from the cabin, and now two men tried to prevent him climbing back on board.

"Come now, lads," urged Mr. Howse. "You won't feel very sweet afterward if you leave an injured man behind to drown. Lend a hand with the skipper. Do this for me."

There was a scuffle, and out of the swaying huddle of dim figures emerged the thin form of the steward, swarming up the after-fall in response to the appeal.

"Good lad, Doctor!" the mate said, clapping the volunteer heartily on the back. "We can manage to get him down, I guess. Come on."

He looked about for a line with which to lower Gedge's bulky form, calling all the while to the seamen to wait.

"Here, I'll drop the peak. Haul the gaff over with that vang, there; we'll ease him down on the end of the fall," he directed, running to the halyards and slacking away.

Then the skipper awoke to the situation, and cried querulously for news.

"All right, sir; we'll have you in the boat in a minute," the mate assured him. "Just hold on and lay quiet. Here, let me pass this line under your arms."

"What d'ye say? Boat?" queried Gedge, trying to see about him. "Is the schooner sinking then?"

"She's cut down to the keel aft, sir, and almost clear through to the mizzen-mast. But keep still. The boat's all ready."

And upon the skipper's ears smote the steward's husky cry —

"They've shoved off, sir — the boat's gone!"

As if in mockery, faintly, receding down the wind came the three blasts of the foghorn from the ship that had stricken the *Centurion.*

"You let 'em get away with the boat, and leave me!" snarled the skipper, raising himself to glare around the dismal prospect. "You've done this on purpose, Howse! It wouldn't have happened only you hollered cross-orders to the wheel! Here I am — all mashed up — and you let 'em leave me! Help me to my bunk, you murderer!"

The man was incoherent, raving; and the mate could have done real murder gladly at that moment but for the restraining thought. He beckoned to the steward, and they stooped over Gedge.

"Don't waste breath cussing me, Captain," said Mr. Howse. "You ought to have held your course. As for the men quitting you, seems to me you've asked for that all the trip. Come on now; we'll put you in the galley while we see what's to be done. It's warm in there, and dry; your bunk, and the cabin is awash by now."

"Who's the other lunkhead, him carrying my feet?" queried the skipper as they bore him down the short poop ladder. "Why ain't he gone? Is he paralyzed?"

"Ain't no credit to you if he ain't," growled the mate. "It's the steward, as you hauled out of his bunk and kept shivering in the fog and snow for spite."

"Huh! That white-livered rat!" was the muttered comment, spat out between a groan of pain and a curse. "Go easy, you butcherin' grub-spoiler! D'ye think I'm built o' concrete?"

The galley was cozy enough, once the doors were shut, and the lockers made a convenient couch. They laid the injured man down, taking off his heavy pilot jacket and folding it for a pillow. The steward piled coal on the stove while Mr. Howse examined the skipper to ascertain his damages, the patient cursing both impartially meanwhile. Luckily the galley coal-bunker had been filled from the main stock in the 'tween-decks the evening before.

"Plenty of coal here, sir — enough for two or three days," remarked the steward, lingering over his job to allow the heat to soak into his chilled bones. At the moment it mattered nothing to him that the schooner rolled more soggily every minute; warmth was immediate life — Death might howl its fiercest outside.

"That's fine, Steward," replied the mate, rising from his examination. "Nothing much the matter here, except a bad bruise or two and a strained knee. The schooner'll float on the lumber in her for a while, though Lord knows how long her own old timbers can stand battering from inside and out too. Come on out, son, till we see what can be done about leaving her."

He opened the door and stood waiting for the steward. That ague-smitten individual started, shivered at the damp gray night outside, and tried to drag himself away from the stove. Mr. Howse was wholly sympathetic.

"That's right, too," he said, coming inside again. "It isn't fit for a dog to be outside in those rags."

He peered into the galley corners, then at the skipper. Captain Gedge lay on his side, his face ruddy now in the firelight, his great bulk the embodiment of well-fleshed bones and pulsing blood. And since the mate's announcement of the slight nature of his injuries, his eyes gleamed with a sort of devilish satisfaction that he could lie there in dry warmth while others toiled in the fog and sleet for his benefit.

"Here you are — hand me that potato sack," said the mate. The steward handed up a coarse burlap bag, part full of potatoes. "Now raise his head," the mate went on, doubling the loose part of the bag over the full bulge.

"Hey, what's your game?" snapped the skipper, knocking away the steward's hands as they raised his head.

"Keep quiet!" growled the mate, seizing Gedge by the hair. "You be as good as you can, or by Godfrey we'll quit you too!"

The heavy, warm pilot jacket was taken away, and the potato bag replaced it.

"There you are, Steward, clap that onto your back," said the mate; and as the steward's eyes flashed in half-amused appreciation of the kindly thought, Mr. Howse added: "Now take his boots and stockin's. He won't need them in here!"

In a torrent of oaths from the despoiled skipper the steward was snugly clad, and he cheerfully followed the mate into the unpleasantness outside. The galley doors were shut, for there alone, so long as the schooner would float, was shelter and food for the laborers; and warmth must be conserved if coal was to last.

Morning brought no sunshine; instead, a whistling wind and driving rain dispelled the fog and raised a tumble of sea that racked the stricken schooner to the keel. Her decks thundered to the surging balks of timber in the hold; early in the morning the planks gaped in a dozen places; bulwarks went by the fathom, leaving gaunt stanchions to add to her forlorn aspect.

The mate looked at the result of their labors with misgiving. His first procedure had been to hoist the peak of the spanker again, in order to keep the comparatively high bows to the rising sea. That alone had kept the schooner from being swept and shattered in the gray hours of dawn. In the waist, between hatch-coamings and shattered bulwarks, a mass of miscellaneous lumber, spars, and casks had been gathered, each piece held against mishap by ends of loose halyards and sheets.

The lanyards of the fore and main rigging on both sides had been cut, in hope that the masts would fall and give them more stout spars for their projected raft. But the stoutest part of that ancient schooner was her spars and their steps; roll she did — giddily, sickeningly — but the masts stood defiantly, unstayed.

"Better get some grub now, Steward," said Mr. Howse, shaking his head at a swooping sea that buried the poop.

It passed, taking with it the main cabin skylight and both poop-ladders.

He flung open the upper half of the galley door, and surprised Captain Gedge in the act of replacing the coffeepot on the red-hot stove. The place was like an oven: a veritable snug harbor after the bleak hurly-burly of the decks; and there was little of the sick man in Gedge as he sat down on his locker with a sheepish grin. That grin heated the mate's blood; his hands twitched with the impulse to vent his bitter mood on the cause of their plight.

Yet, he considered, the skipper might really have made a tremendous effort to get that coffee. That was it! He could go on making such efforts: others were making efforts as tremendous in far less pleasant surroundings. The steward began to busy himself preparing food, and the mate stopped him.

"Leave that," he said. "We've got to hurry up with the raft if the sea's going to kick up any more. Get a mug o' coffee now, and" — he turned savagely to the skipper — "you're able to feed your own face, Cap'n, so you can feed us. I don't think you're man enough to do a man's part on deck; but you can rustle some grub for all hands."

"I'll see you both in hell first!" swore Gedge, starting to his feet with little appearance of disability, "Easy now, easy," warned the mate, shoving him back. "I don't believe you're hurt at all — and you've skulked in the warm here while I and the man you called a white-livered rat have wrenched our soul-cases trying to save your miserable life. You just get busy and make some hot grub. You can call when it's ready by hammering on the door with something —"

He flung out a hand to stay the skipper's furious objection.

"Oh yes you will! I'm going to fasten the doors outside, and they won't be opened until breakfast is ready. If there's no grub ready when the raft's finished — you stay here, and I mean it!"

A half hour of labor went toward the assembling of the raft materials, interrupted at swiftly lessening intervals by the boarding seas which all but undid the work. Then a clamor inside the galley reached the mate's ears above the racket of crashing timbers, and he seized the steward's arm.

"Come on, son; time to eat," he bawled.

The steward followed, stumbling blindly in the mate's wake, and reached the half-open galley door with a tottering rush.

"Hey, stand up, lad!" cried Mr. Howse, bracing himself as the steward crashed into him. "What's the matter? You hurt?"

The hardships of the voyage, the bitter chill of the past night, and the recent stupendous toil had sapped the steward's failing strength, and now, on the threshold of warmth and rest, he collapsed utterly. The mate snatched a steaming mug of coffee from the skipper's hand, and forced a few drops through the steward's blue lips. Then he pushed Gedge aside and laid the unconscious man on the lockers.

"Now you see how white-livered he is!" said Howse, intensely. "He's worked himself out for you — and God knows why. Now it's work or sink for yours, Gedge, and you'd better say work. I won't sink, or let the doctor sink, so long as there's a spar left to float us; but I'll leave you like a dog if you skulk. Where's the grub? Come out with it."

"There's nothing here but coffee and hard-tack," retorted the skipper, defiantly.

He had the appearance of a man who had fed on better fare, and the mate's keen nose refused to be satisfied that the barge of biscuit on top of the coalbunker could add the savor to coffee as he sniffed it.

"Help yourself," said Gedge, "There's the bread — and you'd better remember who's skipper of this ship."

"I'll take my chance about the skipper part, if we ever make shore, and as for the grub, you're a dirty liar!" said Howse, between set teeth.

He flung open the oven, and peered inside. Then he darted his hand in, and brought out a tin plate half full of dry hash, with a fork still in it. Dry hash had formed part of the previous evening's cabin supper. A sailor's nose could detect the savory smell of that dish in a sulfur storm. The mate stared from the food to the sneering skipper, then placed the dish between the bars of the stove-fiddles to keep it secure, and stepped forward crouching.

"You hid that on us, you skunk? Fed your hungry belly while we sweated for you, and offered us hardtack? Outside with you! I'm going to hammer you."

"Leave me alone! I'm a sick man, I tell you!" cried Gedge, backing away from the menacing figure of the mate, and paling before the eyes that blazed into his.

"I warn you not to strike me," Gedge went on, dragging heavily after Howse in response to the fierce grip on his arm. "I never told you fools to sweat out here. I know, and if you had any sense you'd know, that the schooner'll float on her cargo forever. Leave me alone; go look after your slinking pet on the lockers inside."

"So that's your notion, eh? That's why you've laid doggo while I got my fingers and toes smashed to jelly out here, eh? All snug and warm, while the white-livered rat proved himself such a man as you'll never be in a million years! And you're a Master Mariner! You're a rank disgrace to a fine profession. Listen to the planks ripping away from the ribs — how long will she hang together, d'ye think? Eh? Now put up your hands, you yellow dog!"

A long gray sea roared up through the smashed bulwarks and sluiced along the deck knee-high. It picked up the raffle of spars and casks in the waist and carried them heavily against the mizzenmast, making that sturdy piece of timber groan and crack. Mr. Howse got in one solid jolt to his skipper's jaw, and thrilled with the relish of it; then he noticed that though Gedge might be guilty of malingering, his knee was shaky. Regretfully he dropped his hands.

"I can't scrap with a cripple," he mourned, and Gedge sneered triumphantly. "But," Howse supplemented, "a half-crippled pup as mean as you is the same to me as a mean kid, and I'll handle you according. Come here!"

With a skill born of many a sailing-day battle, he seized Gedge by the hair and tripped him behind the knees, flinging him to the streaming deck, face downward. Then he knelt on the skipper's neck with one knee, put the other knee firmly upon one outflung arm, seized the other arm with his own left hand, and reached with his right for a snaking rope-end. Another swishing sea climbed aboard, and swept over them, but it lacked the weight of former seas, and only resulted in choking Gedge's frantic protest into a wet gurgle.

"Now you poor specimen of a sailor," grunted Howse, with a wet, stiff rope-end in his good right fist, "when you say 'Mr. Howse, I'll work,' I'll let you up!" and the flail descended with a whistle.

A wet rope applied to wet pants by a righteous arm amid the stress of a North Atlantic gale is stiff medicine. Captain Gedge squirmed under a half dozen lusty strokes before he could clear his mouth of salt water to shout. Then he heaped upon the mate and steward and ship and sea a copious torrent of virulent abuse that only added ginger to his punishment.

Another hungry gray sea surged up the bursting side and lollopped aboard ominous with lazy strength, and when it passed it had carried the two struggling men aft to the very edge of the jarring, tossing raft timbers. The mate fought to retain his advantage, and once more in position he applied the rope with renewed gusto. Gedge blinked the water from his eyes and saw the peril of those surging spars and casks. The rope swished down.

"Let me up — I'll help, blast you!" he howled.

The rope fell again, and again. The mate's knee lightened not a bit from the swelling neck.

"Let me up! D'ye want to drown me? We'll be smashed in that raffle in a minute."

Again the rope. And another sea, less in weight but full of portent.

"Mr. Howse, I'll work!" screamed Gedge, and lay still.

Mr. Howse stood up, cast away his rope, and helped the skipper to his feet. The grim visage relaxed, and his eyes shone with the light of justice satisfied.

"Get busy with the raft, now," he ordered, dashing the brine from his burning eyes. "Look out for your legs when the sea comes aboard, and pass the lashings good. I'll see what I can do for the doctor. I'll be right back with you."

Captain Gedge went silently to his task, all the tyrant, all the meanness whipped out of him. That terrible whipping at the mate's hands had more than bruised his flesh: it had cracked the crust of his soul.

His memory had to grope back many years for a similar sensation to that which now subtly began to steal through his being: straight back, in fact, to a time in adolescence when a thoughtless but cruel word to his over-indulgent mother had been promptly paid for through the medium of a horse-whip in the fist of a righteous father who believed implicitly in the "spare the rod, spoil the child" maxim. And the similarity of sensations in the two occasions engendered similar emotions.

As a chastised boy, Gedge had in time realized that meanness ought to be punished; now, a man, he was suddenly overwhelmed with a man's shame at the meanness he had allowed to grow within him. He shuddered at the thought that his own actions had warranted the desertion of his entire crew, leaving him to drown; and he knew that nothing except simple manhood, void of meanness, induced the mate and the steward to stand by him.

He could not at once throw off the heavy scowl from his face — his sheer physical anguish prevented that — but, as the mate entered the galley-door, Gedge shouted after him:

"There's a flask of rum in my monkey-jacket pocket. Maybe it'll help th' steward, Howse."

Then he went to work, as a seaman should, and the raft lost nothing on the score of sailorly lashings. Money greed was alone responsible for making Gedge over from a capable seaman into a grasping brute; and his money greed was useless to him now. As he worked, his seaman's sense, long allowed to become dull, cried out to him to notice signs that had been plain to the mate all the while.

With every sea that swept the decks the thunder of the timber in the hold increased; the ripping crash overside and aft could mean nothing less than stripping planking from the hull itself; if the ear left any doubt, the eye satisfied it when great masses of wood shot up alongside after every heavy plunge of the racked schooner.

The mate came out and nodded approvingly at the work done; then he noticed that Gedge, coatless and barefooted, shivered in the biting wind in spite of his toil.

"That drop of rum fetched the doctor round a bit," said Howse. "You'd better take your jacket and boots. He don't need 'em and we can't lose much more time."

"Oh, let him keep 'em," growled the skipper, plunging afresh at the raft. "I'll be warm enough before we get this pile o' lumber overside. And" — he added, after a momentary hesitation — "there's a lot o' canned meat in the locker under the steward, Howse. We'd better have it handy."

"We'll finish this job first," replied the mate, diving into the task. "The galley is coming adrift. About three more big seas will carry it away. I've shut the doors tight to keep the water out, but we'll have to get the doctor out as soon as we can, and the grub can come out at the same time."

"By God! If the galley goes, we can't help him!"

"Then work like blazes, and let's get him lashed to the raft," retorted Howse, grimly. "He's helpless, and the only safe places for him are the raft and the galley."

"And the galley's a trap!" cried Gedge, furiously.

Again the insistent sea climbed through the broken bulwarks, washing both men heavily into the midst of their raft timbers. A tearing crack from the galley told of a parted lashing, and the galley was a separate box-house, built apart from the ship of stout timbers, and lashed to ringbolts in the deck with six inches of clearance underneath to allow the water to run under it.

"Here, cut all the small line in reach and throw it on the raft," cried the skipper, unconsciously resuming command. "Make an end fast; we'll need all of it to lash with when she begins to part after we're afloat."

Mr. Howse grinned softly, and resumed his own rightful station as mate. He was no usurper, except in a righteous cause; and with the cause, the usurpation passed.

Now the raft was capable of bearing the three men and what provisions they could snatch. The mass of timbers lay on the deck, ready to float clear on a sea should the schooner suddenly break up or founder, and a line at one corner held it to the mainmast. Mr. Howse felt in his pockets until he found his knife, then, with a last scrutiny of their handiwork, suggested briefly:

"Better get the steward out now, sir. I don't like the way she's rolling."

The schooner lurched heavily to port, buried herself to the hatches, and slowly rolled back to the tune of tearing strakes. Her high bows dipped into the side of a roaring gray-back, and the torrent surged over the forecastle.

"Hold on for your life!" shouted Gedge, snatching a turn of a line about his own wrist. The mate seized the mainmast in a tight body-hug.

Aft roared the sea. Divided at the fore-hatch, the two parts rolled together again, received added power from a licking crest that poured over the lower side, and crashed against the tottering galley with the thunder of Doom.

"God! He's gone!" gasped Gedge.

The galley was swept through the shattered bulwarks, and now it careened dizzily on the top of a sea, leaning down to one side and showing the tiny skylight on its top. The after wash of the same sea carried the raft overside, but the rope held it within reach. The schooner's decks cracked and heaved up; the foremast went by the board; the deeply wounded stern gaped like a giant wedge.

For one breathless instant skipper looked at mate. Then Mr. Howse seized the raft painter and hauled in on it.

"There's only one chance for the doctor," he muttered. "We may edge the raft down to him. It's a slim chance, sir; but I can't swim a lick." And something very like a groan burst from the mate's deep chest. Together the two men hauled at the line, until the raft floated close in the disintegrating vessel's lee. Then both sprang on to it, and the mate slashed through the rope that held it as the mainmast fell and the *Centurion* fell apart like a house of cards. The galley floated lower, and as it tottered on the seas they could see the little skylight was smashed, and water poured in through it. The unwieldy raft was incapable of navigation in any given direction; but every sea that swept it carried it after the galley with its helpless inmate. Captain Gedge bent low on the raft, while the mate stared hopelessly at the galley.

"Hell! why can't I swim?" he muttered, fiercely.

"Here, bear a hand to knot this line," growled the skipper, flinging wet, tangled coils of small-stuff to him.

One end was knotted about his waist.

"You going after him? Oh, ginger! Can you make it, sir? By Godfrey, if you can I'll — but you can't! Your leg!" chattered Howse, in an ecstasy of doubt.

"Never mind my leg — knot the line!" growled Gedge. "I can swim with one leg through Niagara to get — to get the grub in that galley. Knot, you lunkhead!"

The mate's fingers flew. Length after length was bent on, and he dared not raise his head to look for the sinking galley. He was aroused by a shout, then a splash, and the line began to slip into the sea. He saw the skipper's head rise, and two mighty arms strike out in an overhand stroke, while one leg kicked out — the other trailed stiffly behind.

Now his attention was taken up in clearing the line and flinging it out in smooth coils; but he had time to watch that stubborn head as it sank and reappeared in the seas, ever nearing its goal.

Once the line fouled between two logs of the raft, and for ten seconds the skipper went out of sight, dragged under by the pull of the wet, heavy line. Howse worked like a madman to clear it; he saw the skipper emerge, strike out more desperately, then with a supreme effort grasp at the sloping roof of the galley and haul himself up on it. A hand waved limply, and the mate shouted:

"Oh Glory! the man's done it! By — — , I always said he was a real sailor!"

Then he hauled in on the line and slowly drew the two derelict floats together.

The sea was littered with wreckage, and among it darted great square mahogany logs as deadly as torpedoes to anything in their path. Such a log surged head-on into the crazy raft, bursting lashings, and flinging the mate on his face. A hand was nipped between the raft timbers; but with set teeth Mr. Howse hauled away with a hand and wrist grip on the line until the raft crashed into the half-submerged galley. Then he raised his head and noticed that the galley-top was bare.

"Poor old Gedge is gone too!" he breathed, chokingly.

But a shapeless something appeared at the little skylight, and Howse strove to reach it. The galley was perilously near capsizing as his knee gripped the edge; but the bundle still came further out, and the mate grabbed it. He saw it was the steward, closely wrapped in potato and coal sacks, white of face, with tight-shut eyes.

Another bundle appeared at the skylight. And a muffled voice inside shouted —

"Catch hold — it's grub!"

The voice gurgled and died away as if the speaker were submerged. Howse dragged the sack of food on to the raft, then called out to the skipper. The reply came faint and watery; the skipper's purple face appeared in the skylight, his eyes shot with the fear of death, and he uttered grimly —

"No use, Howse, I can't get my shoulders through!"

That was it. It was one thing for a big man to drop through a tight aperture: gravity and stretch aided him in that: it was an entirely different problem to get those wide shoulders back through the same hole when no foot-hold availed below and no handhold was to be got above.

The mate was stunned by the horror of the thing. A few hours earlier he would willingly have left Gedge on the sinking ship to drown like the dog he then appeared; but things were altered now — and Howse could not swim.

Then his own jaw jutted out, and his eyes glinted with the light of a forlorn hope. He tore off his coat, kicked off his boots, tied a line about his own waist, and shouted:

"Don't let go, Skipper! Hang on to the skylight and keep your head up!"

Then, awaiting no reply, he floundered off the edge of the raft and grasped desperately for the wooden wedge that fastened the iron batten of the galley door.

His weight sank the side of the galley completely under water. His fingers, mashed and bleeding from his labors on the raft, wrenched at the wedge, tight with the water-soaking. All the time he was under water; his lungs were a bursting torment; his fingers grew numb with the grip to hold his position; he swallowed water.

Whirling bubbles and streaks of fire tortured his brain; his fingers worked mechanically, without guidance. Dully he felt that he had succeeded, but it didn't matter. There was a feeling, as he dropped into a delicious sleep, that the galley door had burst open and wrenched his fingers loose. He cared nothing. He was tired.

Mr. Howse opened his eyes and looked blankly around. Still the same weltering sea, covered with a chaos of lumber. He shivered, and felt angry at being awakened from his soothing sleep to again face the stinging spray and the sweeping seas. Gradually he gathered his wits, and discovered that he was not drowned; the square-built figure of Captain Gedge stood erect on the raft, frantically waving a coat on a piece of hand-rail.

Something moved at his side, and he turned to look into the wide, inquiring eyes of the steward, chalky of face, but wholly alive. Then the skipper dropped his flag with a shout of relief, and knelt down by his two shipmates.

"Oh, boys, I'm tickled silly to see your eyes open again!" he howled, gripping a hand of each.

"Can't swim, eh, you old whale?" he whooped. "You're a blamed submarine, Howse! Got me out o' that rat-trap like a Gov'ment diver, you did — and look over there — to the eastward —"

He grinned as he paused, and rummaged in the pockets of his pilot jacket, still on the steward's back. He found his flask, half full, and pulled the cork.

"Here, boys," he said, "we'll splice the main-brace before that steamer picks us up. I drink to the best mate and steward a man ever sailed with."

"And," rejoined Mr. Howse, "Captain Gedge — white man!"

"Sign me on next voyage, sir," smiled the steward. And the steamer's boat, fifteen minutes later, picked up three quiet, thoughtful men.

DOC

IT WAS a queer friendship to develop in the pestilential river estuaries and surf ports of the Gold Coast, and not the least queer part about it was the fact that Captain Belfort was a man who had numbered, and might yet have numbered his friends by the score, while Doctor Ross possessed apparently only one friend in the wide world — the captain of the ship in which he served as surgeon.

That was what puzzled men, for of all the types that exist, it would be hard to find two so hopelessly opposite. Belfort was still young, though he had fallen from grace as a naval officer and was reduced to the command of a smelly, bug-infested little coastwise passenger steamer on a steamy, fever-soaked route; and he was of the strong, good-looking sort that never lacks friends of one sex or the other.

In Belfort's case the women deserted him first, chiefly because he wanted them to, and forced them to by his open and shameless dissipation in other things besides liquor. But he retained many of his men friends, for in his drug-free moments he was a jolly comrade and a good fellow.

Ross was as different as possible. A good bit older than Belfort, he was as coldly grim as his own Highland crags. Knowing him, it was easy to visualize those dour old Covenanters who stubbornly refused to swerve from their beliefs in spite of armies and threatened damnation.

"A mon's worrd is no t' be gi'en nor tak'n wi'out thocht!" was one of his queer sayings. And this: "Gin ye pairrmit a mon t' ca' ye friend, ye're bluid o' his bluid for aye; ye've no longer body or soul o' yer ain, but ye're his."

Men laughed at Doc's strange notions, and dubbed him The Granite Oracle, and yet there was a subtle strain of humor in him, as revealed to a jaundiced missionary taking passage along the Coast to take overseas ship on sick leave.

"Ye're sick, and ye come to me?" Doc uttered as he felt the man's pulse. The missionary was notorious wherever Coasters dwelt, for he was one of that meddlesome lot who cannot stick to their native flock, but ever and again drift into the white man's quarters and start a prayer meeting in which they piously pray for the sins of their hosts, which sins are rarely heavier than a little profanity and more or less indulgence in alcoholic beverages — both of small account as sins in such a country.

"No doot ye're vairry sick, parson," mused Doc, letting go the man's wrist and mixing up a bolus. "Tak' this. Ye'll notice, ma' friend, there's a wee bit difference in oor methods. I've hearrd that ye tell the benighted heathen to pray when they're sick o' some fever ye can't understand. I've hearrd that ye tell 'em yer prayers will cure them, and then ye give 'em a dose o' salts as a sort o' second string to yer prayers." Doc stopped stirring the deadly looking decoction and put it to the man's lips.

"Drink it all up, my manny. That's vairry good!" The missionary spluttered and all but choked as the vile mess passed down his gullet, and his eye looked reproachfully at the grim Scot, who went on piti-lessly —

"Ye see I do otherwise. I gi' ye a good physicking fairst, and leave ye to pray it worrks. I ask ye who's the better doctor, little man."

Yes, there was something queer in the friendship of Belfort and Doc Ross, and it was never more sharply in evidence as when they sat together in the little surgery on the evening of getting in to Sekondi, where the missionary man left them for a homeward-bound steamer.

There could scarcely be a greater contrast in two men. At Doc's elbow a tall tumbler stood, half full of good Scotch whisky and soda, for Doc was no despiser of the gifts of the gods. Belfort's glass was empty, unused. The bottle and siphon stood beside him, but he made no attempt to take a drink, and Ross watched him narrowly.

"Mon dear, I ha' doots o' yer wisdom in denying yersel' o' guid liquor entirely. A mon wants something oot on this — coast. Ye're no getting restless for the ither stuff again?"

Belfort laughed, with little mirth in his laughter, and his eyes shiftily avoided Doc's stern look.

"Oh, don't rake up that old stuff again, Doc!" he returned peevishly. "Didn't I give you my word? Where should I get dope if you shut down on me?"

"Aye, laddie, ye passed yer worrd," said Doc quietly, and his steady gaze searched the other man's pale face. "Ye passed yer worrd, and a mon disna gi' his worrd to a friend wi'oot guid will to keep it, I ken. Then tak' ye a dram, laddie. I prescribe it. Yer nairves are all in bights, like a Span-iard's riggin'."

He canted the bottle over Belfort's glass.

"No!" The captain stood up impatiently.

"Whisky tastes like bilge to me somehow. I'll take a walk out past town, that's all I need — exercise."

"Wait, then." Ross went into his inner den where he slept. Belfort's eyes glittered with cunning as he realized that he was left alone. Swiftly, as one who knows his ground, he opened a drawer in the surgical cabinet, took out a flat case and slipped it into his pocket as Doc returned.

"Here, laddie," smiled Doc, as indulgently as his grim features would permit. "Swallow a couple o' these pellets. I don't prescribe 'em. I keep 'em for my ain deesipation, y' ken. Twa won't hurt ye, an' they'll set yer nairves up brawly."

Belfort took them and put them into his mouth, but did not swallow them. Muttering thanks, he hurried out and went to his own room up on the bridge-deck, spitting out the pellets with a curse as he mounted the ladder. Then, laughing unpleasantly, he locked his door behind him.

It was fifteen minutes later that Doc watched him go ashore, and his step was jaunty and free-swinging, his face alight with vitality. The kindly Scot went back to his hammock and book entirely satisfied.

Belfort had not returned when the cabin dinner was served; but it occasioned no uneasiness in the officers, who were hard-bitten Coasters and knew a man's weaknesses. Doc alone knew that Belfort's weaknesses were not those of the run of men, and as the hours passed on towards midnight he became uneasy.

He was about to turn in, not to sleep, but to await the return of Belfort, when the mate, Mr. Braid, stepped in for a dose of quinine. Doc opened the cabinet and stiffened from head to toe; but he gave the mate his quinine, and closed the drawer again.

"The old man's ashore, isn't he, Doc?" remarked Braid with a knowing smile.

"Aye, Mister Braid, he's to some pairty or ither at the Club. I'm to go there to meet him in a minute or twa. Guid nicht, t' ye." Unmistakably he urged Braid outside; then, shutting fast the door, he hurriedly sought through every part of his surgery before standing up and reaching for his jacket again.

His face was set and gray as he hastened down the gangway and strode through the town. He passed the Club without a look inside, and struck off into the country beyond the stone buildings as if he knew quite well where Belfort was most likely to be found.

"Puir, puir laddie!" he muttered as he almost ran through the outskirts of the first native quarter. "He'll no be able to fecht it wi'out a shairp jolt to buck him up. I doot I'll ha' to gi' him one."

Suddenly he swung aside from the open path and entered a narrow crevice between two native houses. In one a dim light shone through the screens, and he darted inside, bowling aside a startled native who leaped up from a sleeping mat to bar the way.

Voiceless and resistless as a glacier, and as cold, he tore down a wall screen, burst into a squalid room, and glared around.

The place was empty. And all about him shrill voices chattered protests against his intrusion. He turned back.

"Awa' wi' ye, chattering loons!" he gritted, thrusting through them and emerging into the road again. He had drawn blank in a place which he had thought must surely hold the drug-enslaved Belfort.

Once before he had found him thus, after a fall from grace; and there were signs that the skipper had not only betaken himself to the natives to drug himself without interference, but had entered into the native under-life to an extent not good for a white man.

"Ah, weel, maybe I misjudge the laddie this time." He sighed heavily as he climbed the gangway and went to his room. Throwing off his jacket and cap, he passed on to the captain's room, hopeful, yet not sure of finding the erring one there.

He was shocked mildly to find Belfort asleep in his bunk, fully dressed. Listening to his breathing, Doc shook his head gravely.

He rolled up a sleeve and felt the pulse. Roughly he began to push the sleeve higher up the arm, his eyes glittering terribly. Belfort awoke with a start, realized what was going on, and sat up cursing.

"What the — are you up to?" he blared, snatching furiously at his sleeve. Doc went on pushing the cloth towards the elbow, peering steadily into the skipper's convulsed face. There were rings about Belfort's eyes, and a smear of white under one jaw, as if some unguent had been imperfectly wiped off.

"Belfort, what ha' ye done wi' my hypodermic case?" asked Doc quietly. In spite of the man's struggles he had now bared the arm to the elbow and was staring at two tiny punctures in the muscular forearm.

"Confound you, Doc! What d'you mean?"

"What ha' ye done wi' it, laddie?" persisted Doc. He let the arm fall, and shook his grim, gray head. "Ye're no a liar as weel as thief, are ye?"

Belfort leaped to the floor, misjudged his strength, and would have fallen but for Doc's arm thrown about him.

"By — Ross! I'll hammer you for that!" he stormed, making a wild pass at the impassive face bending over him.

"And so ye shall, laddie." Doc bent a searching look on Belfort's face, which was drawn and pallid for all his bluster. "An' if ye'll no say where ye've hidden yon hypodermic, I'll ha' to gi' ye a shot fra' my own case afore I let ye pummel me, or ye'll no be able to stand what I mean to gi' ye mysel'.

"Oh, Robbie Belfort, Robbie Belfort! 'Tis a sad man ye've made me this day. I ha' thocht ye foolish, an' a leetle weecked, but never was I ha' believed ye'd steal, an' then lie aboot it. Come along to my room."

Belfort followed him snarling savagely. His fingers ached to tear at his friend; his nerves refused to obey him. And his being cried out aloud for stimulant! Silently, ignoring all curses and threats, Doc injected a stout dose of heart and nerve stimulant, and carefully locked the outfit away.

Then he stood at the door and kept his eyes full on Belfort's face.

"Now, Robbie, we'll settle this," he said. "I'm goin' to hammer ye, as mon to mon, for ye've stole and lied. Gin ye cry 'enough,' I'm yer friend still. If ye whup me, ye can go yer ain way and be — to ye. But ye won't laddie, ye won't.

"I gave ye my friendship, and I'm yer friend for aye, so I needs must pummel ye. Come doon behint the funnel. We'll no be seen."

Belfort's nerves had steadied, his eye cleared. He stepped outside, and led the way to the place suggested. Arrived there, he flung aside jacket and shirt, and snarled while Doc stripped:

"Ross, I've had more than enough of your — nursing. I warn you now you're finished. For the few minutes I'll take to thrash you, I'm Belfort and you're Ross. Afterwards you'll find I'm captain of this steamer and you're a subordinate.

"You'll answer to me as your superior for insolence, intrusion, and insubordination. Now get busy!"

"Ah, manny, I weesh I was ten year younger!" sighed Doc, and hurled himself upon Belfort's driving fists. Sheer Scots impetuosity and righteous wrath enabled Doc, for all his years, to match Belfort's drug-stimulated strength and greater skill in contest.

For three minutes the fight was a real one. The lights on the wharf shone upon the battling men and showed them ever at close quarters, neither giving nor asking space for finesse.

Belfort sported a puffed eye which rapidly darkened. A trickle of crimson ran from his lips to his chest. On Doc's rugged face sat grim determination, made ghastly by reason of a cruel gash at the temple, from which blood flowed fast.

It was at this particularly gory stage that the quartermaster wandered that way. But neither saw him. He watched them pop-eyed for a full minute, saw Doc stagger hard against the stem of a boat, and totter forward into a flurry of punches — and fled to bring up Mr. Braid.

Mr. Braid arrived seething with excitement to find the boat-deck spotted with red, but no fight. He ran down and knocked on the captain's door, asking if anything was wrong.

"No, no! There's nothing the matter!" snapped Belfort viciously from within.

"But the quartermaster said Doc was —"

"Oh, go to blazes! The quartermaster's drunk! Don't come here bothering me, Mr. Braid. I'll send for you when I need you."

Mr. Braid was a man who was rarely beloved by his fellow officers, because of a certain habit of nosing into a mystery until he solved it. He might rise high as a commander for those very same faults, or, strictly, merits. However, he shook his head sagely, left the bridge, and proceeded straight to the surgery, which he entered without the formality of knocking, as was the right of an equal ranker.

"Asleep, Doc?" he whispered, in doubt, for the cabin and surgery were in darkness. Cautiously he switched on the electric light. Doc was standing by his bunk, half undressed, and when he turned to investigate the intruder Braid saw his battered face.

"Hullo! What's up?" he inquired. "Then it was right?"

"Richt? Up? Mon, ye're wool-gatherin'!" drawled Doc, slipping out of his clothes coolly. "Go to yer bed, and let honest and harrd worrkin' men sleep."

"But the scrap? Weren't you and the skipper — ?"

"Hech, hech! Wull ye no stop blatherin' and go to yer bed?" Doc cut in, gently shoving Braid toward the door.

The mate departed wagging his head. He decided that the matter deserved sleeping on anyhow, since neither Captain Belfort nor the Doctor was in a mood to talk just then.

He poured himself a stout peg of whisky and quinine, and slept the sleep of righteousness. At six his boy awakened him; at six-ten he went to the skipper's room for daily orders; at six-twelve he burst in upon Doc, who was bathing his bruised face.

"Doc! The Old Man's not in his room, and his bunk's not been slept in!" he announced, fired with excitement. He was well disposed towards Doc; but duty compelled him to see possibilities, and among these were the natural conclusions one would draw after hearing the quartermaster's report of that midnight conflict, and seeing with his own eyes that blood-spattered boat deck.

If the Old Man had met with foul play —

"Gone?" exclaimed Doc sharply. "Ha' ye looked in the saloon? The skipper's getting his morrning tea, likely, or he's in his bath. Ye're all jangled up, mon. Tak' yer quinine dose, and dinna starrt blatherin' so early in the morrn. 'Tis bad enough for ye to be blatherin' at midnight!"

The mate vanished hurriedly, but Doc was uneasy for all his show of indifference. He dressed swiftly and went to see for himself. The bunk had been undisturbed, as Braid said. There was no trace of even hurried departure.

The skipper's uniform lay on the settee, and his shore suit of white drill, and his sun helmet, were missing. The mate returned with the watchman while Doc was there.

He glanced keenly at the wide gash on Ross's temple. In the broader light of the upper bridge-deck it looked ghastly enough. The quartermaster grinned behind his hand at sight of it, too. It would give him something to babble about in mess for a long time.

"Well?" snapped Doc.

"He's gone ashore," said Braid, stupidly. "Quartermaster says he walked down the gangway dressed even to gloves and cane about one o'clock."

"Yussir, went t'wards back o' town, the skipper did, sir," the man cut in. "Dressed same as daytime, he wos. Says to me, he says 'Tell Mr. Braid — ' Then he run on down the gangway, an' never finished wot he was sayin', sir!"

"Was he — Did he look ill?" snapped Doc. "Did he walk as if his legs could carry him?"

"Ho, yus," grinned the sailor, knowingly. "'Is legs wos proper strong, no error! He run past them sheds faster 'n I could, sir."

Doc left them without a word. Later, while Mr. Braid went up to the office and reported the steamer ready for sea, but no captain on board, Doc took a policeman and turned the native village upside down and inside out, but to no effect.

In the den he had visited the previous night they found an ancient, hideous bit of withered humanity grotesquely bedecked with feathers and teeth, beads and paint — a near civilization travesty on the witch-doctors of the hinterland.

Powerless himself for harm, the old villain could still teach such white men as cared to learn enough of the secrets of Ju-ju to whet the appetite for more. And Doc knew that Belfort had visited the place before. But he returned to the ship empty-handed and void of heart — for he knew his friend, and feared that this last would prove, in truth, an outbreak.

Finding that the steamer was to wait for the outward-bound mail, due the next day, Doc enlisted the aid of two of the meanest ruffians in Sekondi and spent the whole twenty-four hours combing town and near-by villages.

His aides' meanness and ruffianism were merits in the circumstances, since no other sort of white men would possess their intimate acquaintance with the kind of places to be searched. But the search proved fruitless. Belfort seemed to have vanished as utterly, as if a transcontinental aeroplane had snatched him up.

Doc left word with a few of his most-to-be-trusted club acquaintances, who could be depended on to make quiet inquiries without spreading the news broadcast, and joined the ship in dismal spirits.

Braid took over the command, and carried the ship to sea. He showed his appreciation of the service Doc had rendered him in a manner that caused the Scot's grim visage to harden ominously.

"I'm not going to rake up old scores, Doc," Braid told him, "but I'll say I have to thank you for my promotion. It must have been a whale of a hiding you gave him, to make him run away like he did. Humiliation, I suppose. Well, it's too bad. I rather liked Belfort."

It took Doc three minutes to catch his breath before he answered Braid:

"Captain Braid, ye're my superior officer th' noo, and I ha' no doot whatever that ye merit the poseetion. But in regarrd to Robbie Belfort, ye know no more than yon anchor. I did na 'rayther like him', as ye did: he was my friend.

"I'll thank ye kindly, Captain Braid, if ye'll confine yer remarrks to ship's duty in future, unless ye can leave Belfort out o' yer conversation."

Braid departed in high indignation, for he considered he had shown Doc Ross great honor in continuing to treat him as an equal. Braid was a man who stood stiffly on the dignity of rank, though not by any means a bad sort of fellow at bottom. His fault was that he could not any more than other men, probe under the tough exterior of Doc Ross.

Doc was deep in a rummage of Belfort's effects a moment after Braid left him. The steamship agents in Sekondi had put the vanished skipper's affairs in his hands, as being his most intimate friend; and a first cursory examination of Belfort's papers did not even divulge the man's home address or the address of his people.

Yet Doc knew quite well that the Belforts were people of distinction, and he refused to believe that his friend's fall from grace in the navy had so utterly sent him to the bow-wows as to cause him to sever all home ties. Hence his fresh search.

The discovery of a flat case made Doc screw his lips tightly, for it reminded him poignantly of that other case that had precipitated all the trouble. But this one contained no drugs. Rather, it contained what should have taken the place of all stimulants forever; for it was Belfort's private hoard of secrets — the container of letters from the father and mother who still believed in him.

Doc read one of them, and felt no shame in thus prying into such secret matters.

It ran:

> So glad to know how well you are getting on, Robbie. Perhaps you were wise after all in resigning from the navy when you did, since your prospects in the passenger service are so splendid. Your mother is delighted every time we receive a letter from you — but, Robbie, don't make it too long before you let us see you. Mother said only today (she was feeling a bit blue, I think) that absence was as bad as death among loved ones. She said she could almost endure the thought that you were dead, and in an honorable grave, rather than that you were living in such a climate as we hear the Gold Coast is and never seeing you to satisfy herself that you are as well as you tell her you are. (That's mother's *love* for you, Rob! Did you ever see an old hen with her brood? All mothers are alike, I believe. Bless 'em!) —

Doc read no more. His gray eyes misted over, and he took a half-tumbler of good Scots' whisky to brace himself against the unpardonable sin of showing emotion. The letter had given him one thing greatly desired — Belfort's address at home — and the rest might wait.

Next time the steamer put into Sekondi, Doc Ross quit, much to the astonishment of everybody.

The astonishment was intensified tenfold when he volunteered as surgeon for a punitive expedition of W. A. A. F.'s about to proceed up country against the Adansis, who were making trouble around Coomassi. Rumor had been busy about that uprising.

The Adansis had achieved such stupendous successes against the small forces at first sent against them that it was deemed necessary to form a real force to go after them; and the men who had failed had queer tales to tell of tactics in play on the Adansi side which pointed to a master mind trained in a military or naval school of one of the great nations. The rumor decided Doc.

He wanted to be with the force that eventually solved this mystery of the Adansi leader. Hence the steamer lost a good surgeon, and the W. A. A. F.'s gained an enigma.

That force suffered as the first one had suffered, and returned to base sadder, not much wiser, and decimated by fever, field casualties and runaways among the more superstitious of the native troops; for their experiences had sufficiently bordered on the ghostly to instill into their woolly heads the fear that their early training had been more truthful than the later teaching of the white man after all: that there were, the white man's Bible to the contrary notwithstanding, Devils and Ju-jus, Fetishes with real power, and men who died and returned in the flesh to lead those who believed in them, and to destroy with ticks, flies, maggots and rotting of the bowels all who forsook them in life to follow the lure of clothes and hats and coffins for the feet.

The next expedition was formed on lines making for success at any cost, and volunteer irregulars were attached to the regular forces. Doc Ross was busy unpacking his medicine kit at the first bivouac beside the Prah River, when a volunteer saluted with clumsy precision and stood grinning at him.

"Kin I 'elp, Doctor Ross?" the man asked. Doc recognized that quartermaster who had last seen Belfort on the night he quit the ship.

"Hoot, mon! and whut are ye doin' hereabouts?" Doc returned in surprise. "Why are ye no wi' yer ship?"

"Volunteered f'r active service, sir. The ship ain't wot she used to be when Captain Belfort wos in 'er, sir. I'd like to be yer batman, doctor. 'Ow abart it? I ain't used to soldier ways, but I'd be all kushy alonga you, sir."

Doc had had a native soldier assigned to him as a servant, and already had experienced something of what he might expect when the real business of the march began.

A score of men in the camp writhed in torments of itch, for the doctor's boy had issued croton oil to them instead of the regular specific for mosquito bites, and mosquito bites are sufficiently unpleasant on a hot night in the jungle without the addition of a violent irritant.

"Vairy well," said Doc. "I'll have ye detailed to the medical branch o' the sairvice. Do ye drink?"

"Thenks, sir," the man grinned anticipatively. Doc poured out a draft of quinine tonic. It looked like whisky, and the man swallowed most of it before he realized what is was. He drained the tumbler, pulled his features straight with a great effort, and rinsed out the glass.

"Thenks, sir," he said quietly, and saluted, then marched back to his own part of the camp.

"Yon's likely to turrn oot a guid mon!" chuckled Doc, as he rolled up in his mosquito net. "He has the vairy necessary quality of a sense o' humor."

But humor was not Doc's own outstanding characteristic as the march proceeded.

It was a godsend to him when Rumble, the ex-quartermaster, appeared and offered himself for his servant. Doc still retained his grim, kindly ferocity toward men who came to him for treatment; and they preferred his type of ferocity to the smoother incapabilities of other field surgeons they had campaigned with.

But Doc's most secret thoughts were ever set upon Belfort and his disappearance. He had written to that home address taken from the letters, telling the trustful parents that their son had left his ship and gone up country upon a mission of great secrecy and, doubtless, importance, so suddenly that he had asked Doc to write telling them, since he was unable to do so himself.

"An' God forgie me for lyin'!" Doc had breathed as he sealed that letter. Now, with every mile the force traveled, came rumors which later grew into plain statements of fact, brought in by advance guards, captured rebels, fleeing traders, panicky natives, of the terrible being who led the Adansis to such complete triumphs.

Doc's face was haggard and gray, but his keen eyes had lost none of their glitter, when the column halted one sweltering noon to await the report of scouts sent out during the forenoon. The Prah River ran sluggishly, and straight as a canal for a mile from the halting place, through a flat plain covered with buffalo grass.

At the end of the flat straight, there rose a jungle-clad cliff, through which the stream meandered in the crazy convolutions of a locoed snake. Drinking water stank, and flies laid eggs in the sores left by mosquitoes on the bodies of the cursing soldiers.

"Bli' me!" gasped Rumble, sweating in streams. "I don't care a bleedin' ha'porth wot sort o' ruddy ghost is leadin' the niggers, if only the Old Man sez the word that takes us out o' this stinkin' 'ole!"

In mid-afternoon a scout came in, then another, and another. All bore signs of feverish haste, and one man was prostrated with rank fear. The reports, reduced to coherence, told of a big village five miles up in the crook of a half-mile elbow bend of the river, containing an army of natives camped in what amounted to an impregnable position.

"Making Ju-ju, the fellows say," remarked a young lieutenant delightedly. "Jove! I hope we capture the bally camp before the gory blighters destroy the witchdoctor stuff. What a rippin' souvenir to take home — the wishbone of a baby, or a necklace of dried fingers!"

Doc listened with stony face. He had seen the commanding officer organize a body of volunteers who had come from the sea, and the gang were busily constructing half a dozen light floats on the river, while the gun detachment made stays and blocks with which to steady their pieces on the rafts.

The coming attack would be no mere demonstration, but an attack to be maintained to a finish.

"Rumble, ye'll mak' yersel' ready to come wi' me," Doc said, when the last raft was afloat, manned, and loaded with one field gun fixed in position, with two cases of ammunition.

The force that was to make a land advance when the six rafted guns had started was striking camp, and, as an earnest of the determination of the C. O. to carry things to a finish, all impedimenta, even to spare ammunition, was left. Each man carried his belt full, his emergency ration and full water flask, and his bayoneted rifle.

"And if the blighters will stand, we'll try the strength of their witch medicine, by Jove!" announced the C. O., as he led the way into the forest.

Doc and his batman kept in the van of the advance.

"Ye'll need me up yon," he told the C. O. when it was hinted that he might do good work among the stragglers. "Any one o' yer young medicos can stay behind and care for funk or that tired feelin', but ye'll need a mon when ye see them bluidy braid spears a-flashin' oot th' jungle at ye."

So they marched until the out-flung scouts reported the village within touch. To emphasize the statement, and as if purposely designed by an uncannily keen brain to throw dismay into the attacking force, on the heels of the scout came a shower of flashing assegais which crumpled up the front ranks as if a blast of infernal wind had struck them, and a peal of fiendish yells out of the dark depths of the forest.

Yet, a madly courageous charge, led by the youngster who craved a necklace of dried fingers, resulted in the discovery of nothing human, and only the death of the impetuous leader, who was brought in with his brains drilled out cleanly by a high-power small caliber rifle bullet.

Doc stayed until he saw that the column was steady under this initial disaster, then he called Rumble.

"Ye'll travel light, Rumble. Shed all yer dunnage except yer arms and a double whack o' amuneetion. Ye'll follow me across the neck o' yon river bend, and we'll see whut we'll see, d'ye ken? Are ye scairt?"

"'Oo, me? Not much I ain't!" growled Rumble in disdain. "I ain't scared o' much, anyhow, sir; and the man as licked Cap'n Belfort's good enough for me to swing in with. I'm wi' yer. Go hon."

Doc swallowed the inclination to retort, and at the first opportunity slipped away into the forest and plunged on ahead of the scouts.

Rumble kept at his heels, and in fifteen minutes the pair had left behind them all sound of the troops, and had nothing ahead of them, apparently, but impenetrable undergrowth.

The troops had started out to follow a line nearer the river, keeping thereby in close touch with the rafted guns, and also, while lengthening the route somewhat, making faster progress in the less dense thicket. Doc struck straight across the neck of land within the river bend, and instinct guided him.

Very soon his keen eyes spied a twig set in the earth, festooned with chicken feathers and smeared with blood. A few yards farther on other similar twigs appeared, and now he saw that they formed a definite avenue. His time on the Coast had not been wasted. He knew those twigs were the outward and visible signs of the presence quite near of a big witch doctor.

Cautioning Rumble, Doc crept forward, keeping to one side of the path, until the forest opened out ahead into a wide grassy glade, in which sat a small village, and beyond which the river ran in a sluggish, yellow flood out of a vast marshy plain to disappear between the frowning jaws of a cleft hill.

"Bli' me, sir! Wot's that buzzin'?" gasped his man, standing as if stricken to stone, his head inclined forward, his usually wooden face awork with excitement. The forest glade seemed to be filled with a tremendous note: it could be called nothing else: and a low, circular hut in the middle of the village was the source of it, apparently.

"Yon buzzin' is likely to come fra the same beastie as carries a sting," replied Doc, quietly parting the last fringe of jungle and cautiously peering through. Not a human being was to be seen in the village; except for the vibrating hum coming from the hut, the silence would have been ghastly. But Doc guessed at the reason, and attuned his ears to the limit of their powers.

The sound was soon recognized as the hum of a multitude of men. At moments it swelled to a shriek, and again sank to a sobbing murmur; and like a prelude, before each swelling crescendo, a single voice could be heard raised in a passionate harangue — the voice of a white man, with the accent of a white man speaking the negro tongue, lashing human brutes to frenzy.

From somewhere back in the jungle a cry pealed out, and scattering shots. As if muted under a vast extinguisher the hum ceased in the big hut, the single voice screamed orders, and out poured the congregation at the instant that a score of runners appeared from the forest paths shouting warnings and brandishing spears and guns. Back still further bugles shrilled, and beyond the hill, from riverwards, a field gun boomed in answer.

The swarming natives sent up a devilish yell of defiance, and at the urging of that lone voice still issuing from the center hut the entire army darted into the thick jungle and vanished so swiftly that Doc and his man were all but surprised before they reached the shelter of the branches of a giant baobab.

"Mon, but that was near!" panted Doc, peering down through the dense foliage and watching the last of the blacks running past. "Stay where ye are now, until ye see the floats on yon river, or the troops begin drivin' the benighted heathen back. I'll tak' a look yon."

Before Rumble had a chance to reply, Doc had dropped to earth, and was running swiftly across the glade. As he ran, he took his revolver from the holster, and transferred a handful of cartridges from his belt to his loose pocket. Then he reached the building, and, with every nerve tingling in anticipation of what he would find within, was abruptly halted by the outrush of a body-guard of six gigantic blacks, painted and feathered to the point of fiendish hideousness.

But Doc Ross had entered upon this expedition from motives born of the fear that Robbie Belfort and the mysterious leader of the rebel blacks might well prove to be identical, and the fear had become conviction since hearing that terrible voice within the hut, urging the rebels to fury.

No six men, black or any color, could stay him at the point of entry.

With a cold curse on his lips that took the place of a prayer, Doc shot down the foremost guard, fired again, and advanced shooting, while from within the lone voice shrieked demands for news, and from the baobab came the yell of Rumble as he dropped from his tree, ignoring orders, and started on the dead run to his officer's assistance.

Seizing a spear dropped by his first assailant, Doc fought doggedly, parrying thrusts with his spear, and shooting as he got a clear aim in the dim entrance. Back by the river he heard the cheers of the landing gunners, and nearer, the shouts of the fighting forces who were at grips with the blacks.

Rumble's lusty yell reached him at the moment when, stepping forward as he fired the last cartridge in his pistol, and seeing small chance to reload, he came abruptly before the high platform in the middle of the circular house and saw upon it that which turned his heart cold.

"Lord help ye!" he panted, and braced himself to fight more furiously against the attacking guards. Stabbing and parrying with the spear he had snatched up, Doc fought stubbornly to reach that evil Thing on the platform, and opening the breech of his revolver with a thumb, he slipped the weapon into his pocket, the pocket holding the loose cartridges, and loaded the cylinder with blind fingers.

Far out across the village square the forest rang with the sounds of conflict. Nearer at hand Rumble's shrill Cockney oaths poured damnation upon the benighted souls of the blacks who suddenly materialized out of the gloomy jungle to cut him off from his doctor.

And on the platform the Thing chuckled horribly. At intervals it sent out a piercing note not to be likened to anything human, and invariably at the sound of it the savage cries of the blacks fighting in the forest redoubled.

As Doc fought, sorely sapped as to strength by a score of cruel spear wounds, he strove ever to reach the platform, and when he tottered, and all but fell under the terrific attack of the two remaining guards, to his ears came the low, wicked, maniacal voice which was unmistakably the voice of Belfort:

"Join us, white man! Come back to Mother Nature! We are the chosen people, and the men of clothes and trade shall replenish our altars, their women —"

Rumble had been brought to a stop. He could see Doc stubbornly battling against a host of foes to reach that gibbering Thing in the great hut, and behind him the troops surged forward with a shout. The rafted guns began to vomit iron and flame.

"Hold on, sir! Back out!" yelled Rumble. "The lads'll get 'im in a jiffy now!"

Doc might have heard; probably he did not. His pistol again contained but one cartridge; his foes gave him no time to reload, and into the four entrances to the great hut poured retreating blacks to defend their chief.

A shell whined over the ridgepole and exploded with a crash in a tree just beyond. The huzzas of winning troops came closer, and Rumble shrieked jubilant encouragement to the master he could no longer see.

Doc let his pistol swing from the sling, grabbed his spear in both hands and plunged forward again, sobbing with weakness, terrible with purpose, and literally hurled himself at last upon the platform where a low, devilish chuckle greeted him.

Through the red mist that gathered before his eyes Doc gazed upon his friend — upon a creature from which all human semblance had vanished, a Thing slobbering bestially, filthy with unnamable vices and utterly dead as to soul. Doc hurled his spear into the breast of a black giant reaching up for him, then gripped his revolver arid lurched to Belfort's side.

"Lord help me, Robbie," he muttered. "An' ye'll forgi'e me, puir manny, for I canna let them tak' ye back where men'll know ye!"

His pistol cracked and Belfort's brains splashed the great center pole of the hut as a shell ripped the roof off and a last desperate charge of the attacking forces carried the entrances.

"Bli' me!" Rumble exclaimed to his shipmates when the little war was over, and he returned to his true work. "I'll never forgit old Doc! I never see a bloke like 'im. I seen a part o' the scrap he 'ad wiv Cap'n Belfort, and I'd 'v put a bit o' brass on the Doc winnin' in the end, for 'e didn't seem to care a farden for wot the Old Man wos a-givin' 'im, and that wos aplenty, my word! But Belfort must ha' put it on 'im rough while I wos fetchin' the mate, and Doc didn't forgit it, neither.

"You orter a seen 'im tear through them niggers! I thought he wos tryin' to git the chief alive and cop the credit. But not 'im! 'E gets in there, all on 'is lonesome, an' blows the bleedin' 'ead orf o' the big chief, as I 'eard some orficers sayin' they s'spected might turn out to be Belfort, wot 'ad disappeared months ago and who wos known to have 'ad a likin' fer the black fellers.

"O' course, that give me my idea about Doc gettin' even for that beatin', but he wos fooled arter all, for I seen 'im examinin' the chap 'e'd shot, and you couldn't see who it wos arter his shot in the 'ead, but it wos a fat, flabby elephunt of a chap, as much like Belfort as I'm like Wenus.

"So Doc wos fooled proper. Funny bloke, though. Never seen another like 'im. Takes me wiv a couple o' sapper's shovels, he do, and we digs a grave for the fat chief, and 'e sticks up a blessed board at the 'ead and takes a photo of it!

"'Onner to a fallen' enemy, Rumble!' 'e sez, and, blast me, if 'e wosn't a-pipin' 'is heye!"

At base hospital, as soon as his wounds healed sufficiently to permit the exertion, Doc enclosed a little Kodak picture in a short letter which ran in part:

> I have lost a friend, but you have lost a son. It will not lessen your bereavement, but it may soften it, to know that Robbie died in action and the world is better for his sacrifice. I send you a picture, taken by a brother officer, and you will see that your son was well thought of — —

RED SAUNDERS' PROTEGE

"YOU'D BETTER leave that cash-box behind in the bank if you're adopting this here yaller-belly, cap'n," grumbled Tod Carter, mate of the *Black Pearl* trading-schooner.

"Red" Saunders laughed quietly, good humor and utter lack of apprehension in every line of his strong, bronzed features. He was known throughout the seven seas, and some others not included in the seven, was this big, fearless skipper with the close-trading propensities of the hard-bitten commercialist, the nattiness of a naval officer in his person and his navigation, and the manners and carriage — when he chose — of a gentleman. And no man had ever been able to say that a danger or a difficulty could affect the big redheaded skipper in any way unless it was to set him more stubbornly on the scent of whatever he went after.

"They don't give medals for worrying, Carter," he said; "otherwise that bread-chest of yours would look like a picture of a ribbon-counter on bargain day. The boy goes with us; so does the cash-box. I have taken a fancy to the one, and have always had a sneaking regard for the other.

"Go ahead and get your anchor, old chap, and let's get away from this putrid pestuary as soon as possible. I've a hunch that our first trip to Timor will produce results."

It did. But it's good seamanship to get the anchor up before piling on canvas, and while the anchor comes up it will be well to go over the situation as it stood when the *Black Pearl* left her steamy anchorage a bit to the southward of Macassar in Celebes, bound for Lifou in Timor.

Saunders was a stormy petrel of trade. When he quit a port it was long odds that his next stamping-ground might be in a far-distant part of the wide ocean. Therefore he preferred his own strong-box to all the banks in the world; and in order to accommodate his growing store without building a bigger ship he had a habit of converting first his trade into cash, and then his cash into less bulky gems of various kinds.

From time to time he heard of rich finds of precious stones or pearls; finds of individual gems of such vastly enhanced value over mere carat appraisal as still further to reduce the space required for stowage, if he could secure them. So his little steel box contained in the space of a cheese-cutter cap or so wealth which in any other form would have occupied many times the room.

His visit to Macassar had resulted in the exchange of half a pint of mixed rubies, pearls and turquoises for half a dozen flawless black pearls, a few dazzling pink ones and two hybrids, pink and black combined, which left his box loosely packed but caused his smile to broaden like the sun at noon.

And in Macassar he shipped the pale, yellow youth to whom grim old Tod Carter had taken exception. A man who could take a beating and still fight always found a sympathizer in Saunders; and when on his way to the boat on the Macassar coast he stumbled upon a street-fight in which a slim, lemon-tinted native of variegated parentage was going down under many blouses, squealing like a coward but fighting back like a hero, the burly skipper took a hand in his defense. A couple of swipes of his big fists scattered the mob; and when he picked up a fallen attacker and hurled him bodily among his fellows like a ball at alley-pins the rumpus was over.

"Here, quit that foolery, buddy!" he laughed when the yellow youth fawned at his knees like a big dog. "Stand up, lad; I'll see you clear."

"I come wid you, sar," the man panted, glaring around in obvious terror. "I stay here I git kill, sar."

"But you can't come with me, sonny. I'm bound to sea."

"Orright. I go sea too."

Taking no rebuff, the little native elected himself body-servant to the skipper, and by accepting the more or less unwelcome service Red Saunders was the gainer. Tod Carter made his protest, and repeated it as already set forth, but Parchelly, as the youth called himself, was a member of the *Black Pearl's* crew when the coast of Celebes became a gray blur merging into the night mists astern.

"He's all right, Carter; don't worry," the skipper smiled when the mate relieved him for supper and was still grumbling about the liberty accorded to Parchelly.

Tod Carter had been right-hand man and close companion to Saunders in innumerable exploits all through the Far East, the Pacific and the East African seaboard for many years, and a deep affection existed between the men, only to be understood by those who have lived a similar life and have been lucky enough to meet up with one sterling soul in harmony with their own. Except for sheer physical strength the two men were entirely dissimilar; and even in strength Saunders was too greatly Carter's master for them ever to regard each other with jealousy. In other ways they differed so widely that it was undoubtedly the sheer contrast which welded them so closely together in comradeship.

Where the skipper refused to see trouble until he bumped into it, Carter smelled it as far off as he could sniff bad weather; where the mate doubted, Saunders radiated assurance; if terrific odds suddenly rolled up against them — Yes, that was one other point where they agreed; both would face odds, and both would fight the harder as the odds multiplied; and each had yet to see the other let go a hold when he had it.

Tod Carter would grumble and complain right up to the point of conflict, and go into and through a scrap still grumbling, but fighting like a Highlander after prayers. Saunders rarely permitted a foe to wipe the smile from his handsome face; in fact, one man who had the nerve to face him a second time had suddenly gone panicky at seeing the skipper's smile brighten and broaden, and had run away without shame, fearful for his life. That yarn still goes around certain ports in Northern Queensland.

The smile of Red Saunders was a thing to be noticed. It could mean a friendship as wide and deep as the ocean, or it might simply mean that a presumptuous antagonist was about to peek in through the Pearly Gates, even if he did not actually enter.

"Don't lose sleep over Parchelly," the skipper told Carter. "The lad's grateful to me for saving his yellow skin. He's a queer mixture; most of these Timor chaps are, with the Dutch and Portuguese strains —"

"Ho, and he's a Timor scut, is he?" grunted Carter, peering hard into the skipper's laughing face, "And, if I may ask, is there any connection between findin' this here yaller-belly and us goin' to Timor, where he belongs? Not as it's any o' my business, o' course."

"There's a connection surely, Carter. I'd never have given Timor a thought if Parchelly hadn't told me in gratitude that there are rich pickings to be had by the first trader to see the old chief of —"

"And off you go like a country slob tryin' to find the little pea under the walnut-shells, to git us into another o' them woolly messes wi' a swarm o' niggers, just on a yaller swab's say-so! Maybe I'm gettin' too old, cap'n. I don't see no fun in such Flyin' Dutchman cruises no more. I better quit soon's we get back to some four-square port."

Saunders laughed softly and let his mate go on. He knew well enough that when old Tod Carter quit there would remain no unexploited fields within the *Black Pearl's* scope; either that, or Tod Carter would be dead.

When the grizzled old grumbler finished his growl Saunders again gave him the schooner's course, added a hint about currents and turned to go to his supper, pausing to add as he half-drew the companion-slide:

"Give the lad a chance, Tod. He's either the most grateful little cuss I've met, or the best actor. If what he says is right there's a haul to be made in Lifou that'll put us all on Easy Street for life."

"Queer Street, you mean!" grunted the mate, and turned aft, at once to become the alert, seamanly watch officer and to forget all about Timor, Parchelly, and Queer or Easy Streets until his watch was done.

Certainly the little Timor hybrid appeared sincere in his affection for Saunders. Tomba, the Fiji steward, found plenty of time on his hands because Parchelly assumed charge of Saunders' body-service, and seemed ready to fight for the privilege too.

Yet there were times when Red Saunders harbored a faint doubt about his new valet; a suspicion that after all old Tod Carter might have weighed the little yellow man up correctly. Parchelly was certainly a strange mixture of sobbing, whimpering, fighting frenzy and cringing cowardice. Had the skipper not witnessed how he could fight for his skin, he would have kicked him over the side in sheer disgust when the Jap cook beat the oakum out of him with a skillet without drawing any retaliation.

Then again there was Tomba. Frizzy-haired Tomba was no weakling; there was no room for such in the *Black Pearl*; but in a matter of trifling concern touching on the cleaning of the skipper's cabin Parchelly gave the old Fijian a fright which ever after forestalled interference from that source.

All things considered, it was a caution which ruled Saunders at last, when he dropped anchor in a jungle-fringed creek five miles outside Lifou town and prepared to go ashore to look over the prospect for trade. He took his case of pearls out of the strongbox and secured them in his inside pocket in full view of Parchelly. He grinned when he detected in the little yellow man's eyes a glint of intense interest; and he chuckled happily as he entered his cabin again, ostensibly to get some shells for his gun, and replaced the gems in their proper hiding-place.

"That's drawing a red herring over the trail," he muttered. "Perhaps the boy's all right. If he is, there's no harm done. If he's wrong, he won't bother this chest while he thinks I have the things on me. So that's that."

At the gangway he paused a minute before stepping into his boat, and surveyed the blue mountains beyond the tangled jungle. No sign of human habitation appeared; neither could he discern anything which hinted at a trail leading town-ward or back into the forest. Yet Parchelly had indicated this spot as the best from which to interview Sadrash, the head man — sultan he called himself — of all that portion of Portuguese

Timor outside the town itself.

It was advisable to anchor out of sight of Lifou. The Portuguese authorities had found it cheaper, and less bother, to leave native affairs in Sadrash's hands; but they had no suspicion to what extent the old rascal actually saved them work and worry in matters closely concerning revenue. So it was out of the question to deal with him direct from Lifou. Saunders finally nodded his head to Carter.

"I'll go look-see, Tod. Keep your eyes skinned, and don't let any natives come on board unless they show good credentials from the old Pooh-Bah himself. Keep an eye on your friend Parchelly, too," he smiled, lowering his tone.

Parchelly was hovering near with an expression on his face which might have been agitation, doubt or impatience.

"He's home now, you know, and it's now or never he'll prove whether you or I have him sized up right. If I'm not back by sundown clap a strong guard at the rails and bring half a dozen boys to see what I've tumbled into. But I'll be back, I expect.

"Another thing. Watch your ground tackle. Keep all clear in case it's a quick hop out."

The skipper sent his boat back to the schooner as soon as he stepped ashore, and straightway plunged into the gloomy jungle at the only spot which seemed to offer ingress. At first the path was all but non-existent; but just as the forest grew black with shadow and appeared to thicken to impenetrability he emerged into a wide glade in the midst of scattered, rotting tree-trunks, and a track of wagon-width opened before him. To all appearances the jungle might have been devoid of human life, though teeming with birds and small beasts, insects and slithering reptiles. Yet there was a vague suggestion ever present of lurking bodies and peering eyes, in no way connected with the swinging monkeys; and as Saunders strode forward he held himself alert, using every precaution against surprise without showing outwardly that he felt uneasy.

It was with something of a shock that he presently emerged from the forest and came upon a closely huddled village enclosed within a wattle-and-daub wall. As he paused for a moment in search of the entrance, he could have sworn that several figures hurried past him some distance away, out of the jungle, and disappeared through the wall.

But when he approached, and pushed in through a wicket door which he found open, he experienced no opposition; he saw a few natives, women and children as well as men, and as he neared the center of the huddled huts and came up beside a large, pretentious bungalow with glass windows he was mildly surprised to see several men who might have been white once. Of all breeds they seemed, and all bore the stamp of rascality, but white undoubtedly, except for the coloring of sun and weather.

"Here, you whiskers," he hailed, "take me to old Sadrash, will you?"

The man accosted turned slowly and flung an insolent glance at Saunders.

"The sultan is asleep," he retorted, and promptly turned away again.

That was not Saunders' idea of getting business done. He overtook the fellow in half a dozen long strides, and swung him around as easily as he would turn a wheel.

"Listen, buddy, you wake him up. I've come all the way to Lifou to talk trade with his nibs, and my time's as precious as his."

"We know all about you," the man returned. "It's part of our business to get to know things in advance. And it ain't healthy to go waking the sultan out of his after-dinner nap, old codger. If you want to see him today you wait until he sends for you. He'll know you're here the minute he wakes. You might as well go back to your schooner, though, for he won't talk trade with you until he gets his report from the officers he's sent down to inspect your outfit."

Though expecting something of the kind, Saunders felt a trifle uneasy at the suggestion of native or half-breed officials making free of his little ship in his absence. Tod Carter was sound and safe, but he lacked that saving sense of humor possessed by Saunders, which would enable him to endure patiently the petty insolence of intruding visitors. He might easily make a break which would ruin all chance of successful trading, especially if the visiting officials were of the same type as this be-whiskered, hybrid ruffian who treated the skipper so offhandedly.

"So that's the game, is it?" he retorted. "All right, my ugly friend; I'll take a look at those officials first, to be sure they're honest, then I'll come back with them and interview the old chap."

The man laughed harshly, placing himself before the skipper as he turned to retrace his track.

"Not so fast, old-timer," he said, and swung his belt around so that a heavy holster came near to hand. "Orders is to hold you here. P'raps you won't have to go back to the ship at all; see? Sadrash decides them things for himself. If he wants anything you've got, he'll take it P'raps he'll feel good and give ye some coconuts or somethin' for what he takes, and p'raps —"

"Perhaps not," the skipper broke in with one of his sunniest smiles.

Like a streak of light he pounced upon the man, flung him aside from the path into the jungle and snatched his revolver from the heavy holster.

"Now stand up," he snapped. "I don't do business the way you say. You plod on ahead of me, and feel this."

He jabbed the pistol-muzzle into the man's back.

"You know best whether it's loaded. It's your own. So march. Hold me here, hey? Not an army like you."

They started forward, and Saunders forced his unwilling guide to keep aside from the trail. He also forced him to hail a couple of curious women who peered after them, telling them that all was well.

And as he trod in the guide's steps the thought of Tod Carter's outspoken distrust of Parchelly recurred to him sharply. For the first time he really believed that he had made one of his rare mistakes in the little Timor man. He felt sore to madness, for his mistakes in human nature, as his failures in his undertakings, were amazingly few.

The pistol prodded viciously into the fellow ahead.

"So I am to be held here, hey? Sort of expected me, did you?" Saunders remarked. "Perhaps that little snake Parchelly has been smarter than I thought, and sent on word by bush telegraph?"

The man half-swung around, his evil face working curiously.

"Parchelly?" he grinned, showing yellow teeth. "Ho, so you got him, did you? Well, maybe he did let the sultan know about you. Y'see, Sadrash had Parchelly flogged 'most to death and sewed him up in a cowskin for gettin' sassy. You bet Parchelly wouldn't come back here unless he could bring a offering to square hisself. Ho, that's a good one, mister!"

Chuckling, the fellow resumed his way, and not another word would he utter, but ever he kept up a running chuckle of deeply rooted mirth which set Saunders to figuring closely just how much of a tangle he had ventured into this time. Not that it made much difference. His complete self-confidence was not to be broken by mere possibilities. But he began to see something far less simple than a desire to trade in the methods of this old Timor sultan.

Tales had not been wanting of such vessels as his own being unaccountably lost in the Flores and Banda Seas, and nearly always the missing ships had been self-owned by their masters, and making just one more clean-up voyage before quitting the seas for markets of disposal. And Parchelly might easily be an ultra-cunning decoy, willing to stage a street fracas and to accept a personal beating in order to attract the attention of the shipmaster he was sent out for.

"What confounded nonsense!"

Saunders laughed aloud at the thought.

"Theatrical stuff like that is only done in films. I don't believe Parchelly could do it. Anyway —"

They were nearing the shore, and he was willing to let the event decide. Then they were on the edge of the creek. The schooner's boat was there with two wide-eyed Gilbert Islanders waiting, and the schooner herself lay in apparent quiet, with only a couple of heads visible above her rails.

"Everything all right, Sammy?" the skipper hailed.

One of the boatmen grinned without mirth.

"No, sar; he all wrong. Massa Ca'ter he go look for dat Parchelly fella. He —"

"What?" snapped Saunders, suddenly smitten with foreboding.

"Parchelly he bus' open de safe, cap'n, an' run fas' ashore. Den Massa Ca'ter he say to plenty ob mans dat come on board from de sultan, 'Yo' git off dis ship, I got bodder ob my own,' an' dey no go, so he tell us to t'row 'em in de ribber. When dey git to land, dey holler very loud dat de sultan come back soon an' burn we up, sar."

"So that's how it stands, hey?" mused Saunders, darkly scanning the river and its encroaching jungle fringe.

Soon he came to a decision.

"Sammy," he said, "take charge of this fellow. If he gives you trouble you may cook him and eat him. Take him on board, and lock him up.

"And listen. Don't let another man climb over that schooner's rail unless it's one of our own men. Keep your eyes open, now."

Taking a whistle from his pocket, he blew a series of shrill blasts that echoed through the gloomy forest and awakened the rivalry of hosts of feathered things. Twice the call was repeated before Tod Carter plunged out of the bush, looking as black as thunder, with a sore and savage crew of Kingsmillers and Gilbert Islanders at his heels.

"Find him?" snapped the skipper.

The party's blank looks answered him.

"Find him!" growled the mate, spitting emphatically into the river. "'Course we didn't find him! Darned good thing, I say, that you was sensible enough to put them pearls in your pocket before goin' ashore. He cleaned out the safe of all the rest o' the stuff."

"And, by Godfrey, he got the pearls too!" the skipper rejoined. "You were right, Carter. I was foolish. Now let's go and straighten things out and make my foolishness profitable."

"That'll take some doin'," grumbled old Tod.

"Oh, go ahead just the same, cap'n," he hastened to add, catching the hard glint in the skipper's gray eyes. "You ain't got to ask or order me or the boys. Where you goes we goes, foolish or not. But —" his voice rumbled off in a low, earnest growl — "I'd surely like to get my hooks on to that Parchelly!"

As they marched back along the route already traversed twice by the skipper the gloom of the forest deepened with waning day, and there descended again a subtle suggestion of human presence which brought out all the half-dormant primitive bush instinct of the *Black Pearl's* native crew. Lithe Gilbert Islanders became silent, stealthy shapes among the dense tangle of jungle; shining brown faces assumed stern lines of predatory keenness; coal-black eyes glittered metallically.

Yet no human obstacle confronted them. Even the beasts and creeping things of the forest appeared to have withdrawn before their advance. Presently, in response to an involuntary oath from Carter following a headlong stumble over a root, Saunders laughed softly as if the mate's mishap had broken a tension, and remarked:

"Tod, old horse, you must have given the sultan's emissaries a rough handling to make you so darned taut-strung now. What did ye do to 'em?"

"Do?" echoed Tod, grinning in spite of his intense devotion to the job of keeping his feet clear and his eyes free of brushing leaves and swinging vines, "Do? Why, blast 'em, that mob o' yaller-ocher fakers pulled some yarn on me that they was reg'lar customs guys and showed a bit o' dirty parchment signed by a spider-crawl signature which they said was old Sadrash's, and said they was come to rummage the ship.

"I told 'em they could stay alongside until you come back, and they said you wouldn't come back until they took their report to Sadrash, and they all grinned like monkeys. Said you was being held — they'd heard about your reputation — " here Tod Carter indulged in a grim chuckle —"and Sadrash wasn't takin' no chances on the safety of his officers.

"So I gives the boys a wink to keep their eyes peeled and let the gang on board. They peeped down the hatch, but that wasn't what they was after. No, sir! They wanted to see the cabin.

"Then when I'd about decided to show 'em everything but keep tabs of 'em that blasted Parchelly runs up, dodges when I wasn't lookin' and was overboard and half-way to shore before I twigged him. I run below, and be darned if he hadn't opened your safe with a skiliton-key or something, and there we was, robbed by a yeller-bellied shipmate as ought never to have been aboard, and boarded by a lot o' dirty scuts o' fake officers as was more like pirates than customs men — not as there's much difference."

"Yes; but what did you do to them?" chuckled Saunders.

"Dumped 'em into the river, and lit out after Parchelly."

"Well, well; patience, old chap. You'll catch up with him when we come before the Sultan Sadrash, never fear," the skipper returned, and strode along in the wake of his leading man.

Again, and more insistently, came the suggestion of a lurking presence surrounding them, and the jungle had become dark with a cold gloom by the time they broke, shivering with chill and taut nerves, through the last cane barrier and into the stockaded village.

"Deserted!" Carter ejaculated, wiping cold sweat from his eyes. "Thought you said —"

"Shut up!" the skipper rejoined, irritably for a wonder. "This place is deserted like — — 's deserted. Two of you boys hide yourselves outside the gate here. Come on, the rest of you. Straight to the big hut."

The queer, brooding quiet increased as they stamped across the floor of a wide veranda, making their steps echo and reecho jarringly. Inside the big hut Saunders saw that it was almost dark, yet with sufficient glow from some hidden lamp to suggest that people might be inside and awake. The nostrils, too, were assailed rather than soothed with odors so richly sensuous as to render breathing difficult.

Impatiently the big skipper seized a heavy floating curtain at the doorway and tore it down; then he strode into a vast, shadowy chamber, his men close at his heels, and strove against the blinding gloom with straining eyes.

"I want to see the chief, Sadrash; where is he?" Saunders demanded sharply.

The only reply he received was the sudden heavy jarring crash of a door slamming behind him, a low, cunning laugh before, and the metallic sound of a score of rifles being cocked or charged all about his little party.

"You shall see the Sultan Sadrash when your eyes grow as keen in the dark as mine," mocked a voice.

Something hard touched his breast. His hand, involuntarily seeking, touched the cold barrel of a rifle.

"Trapped!" quoth Tod Carter, in a tone which said plainly, "I told you so!"

"Stand fast, and don't make any breaks," Saunders ordered imperatively. "Mark time until we can see. Use your eyes, boys."

Soon the gloom seemed to lighten. In recesses all about the chamber lamps burned, and their wicks were being turned up gradually. As soon as eyes might see clearly the skipper and his men saw this:

On a low, thickly cushioned platform, more than a dais but scarcely a throne, sat a thin little creature having an enormous head, dressed like some gorgeous pantomime travesty on royalty. His great skull was covered with a huge turban, jeweled and befeathered; his face was hidden, except for a pair of evilly brilliant eyes and an arched beak of a nose, in a beard of many hues which stuck out around him like a lion's mane.

A great curved scimitar lay across his knees, naked and gleaming; in his eyes glittered cruelty and greed; maned like a lion, he made one shudder with the resemblance he bore to a hyena possessed of a devil.

And the dozen or so of nondescript white men standing around him were quite obviously scared to death of the little creature. There were a score of natives, too; and these were standing by like so many terrified sheep, trembling to be on the jump at the sultan's least word; and this might have been expected in a place like Timor, where sultans and slave-owning chiefs probably flourished when China was struggling to learn its first ideograph.

But for white men, beach-combers, adventurers, rascals undoubtedly, to serve a native sultan and stand frankly in fear of him was something so utterly unexpected that Saunders gave the little potentate more than a passing glance before he addressed him.

"You're Sadrash, I suppose," he said at length. "I'm Saunders, of the *Black Pearl* schooner. I want my boy, Parchelly, and the contents of my safe. Out with 'em."

A concerted gasp of horror filled the chamber, the horror of the sultan's men at the effrontery of the captive who refused to accept his position but addressed their chief rather like a captor. The sultan himself appeared to swell with fury. His eyes shot sparks, and his great beard bristled. With nervous hands clutching the handle of his scimitar, and trembling with passion, he screamed in shrill, broken English:

"Parchelly is my slave! It is you who shall give him up! Your ship shall burn, and you shall burn too, if Parchelly is not before me this night."

"Burn?" laughed the skipper contemptuously. "You're hot stuff, old boy, to talk of burning me. I came here to trade with you. You sent men to board my ship in my absence, and your Parchelly, who lured me to come to your pestilential creek, stole the contents of my safe and brought 'em to you. Now you produce or it's you who'll sizzle, no mistake!"

"You lie! Parchelly came not to me!" the little sultan screamed, purple with fury.

Then, half-rising, laying down his scimitar the better to help himself up, he commanded:

"Seize them! Bind them! Out with you and fire their ship!"

Scowling men, white and yellow and brown, closed in about the *Black Pearl's* men, and Tod Carter spat on his hands. A rifle-barrel knocked his hands down as he involuntarily felt for his revolver; a Gilbert Islander stumbled under a blow on the head, dealt to persuade him to quit fighting. It seemed as if at last Red Saunders had ventured into an inescapable trap, for his men were outnumbered two to one, and the two were armed. But what success he had achieved had not been won by slow wits.

Like a flash the thought crossed his mind that perhaps he had misjudged Parchelly after all; that the boy had not come to the sultan with his stolen loot. But the thought only induced the equally bitter one that his protégé could in that case only have stolen the pearls for himself.

All this passed through his brain with the speed of light. As swiftly came the decision to prove the truth.

"Stand by, Tod!" he snapped in his islanders' native tongue.

With the words he hurled two men aside who held his arms and leaped straight forward to pounce upon the half-risen sultan. So swift, so decided, was he in action that he had taken an unbreakable grip on the sultan's beard with one hand and snatched up the great scimitar with the other before even his own men had fairly grasped his intention. Then with the gleaming blade held across the hairy throat of the chief he barked out:

"Stand back, you scum, unless you want to see the old boy's throat cut. Tell 'em to drop their guns, Sadrash."

The keen edge touched the skin; the great bush of whiskers stood out straight as Saunders tugged the huge head backward to tighten the withered neck; and Sadrash squealed in terror to his men to do as they were ordered. The weapons fell to the floor with a crash, and then the skipper laughed grimly.

"Herd 'em up, lads! Keep a lookout at the door, while I have a little chat with this old monkey."

That first application of the keen edge of Sadrash's big scimitar to its owner's throat had been so intimate as to leave hairs upon the blade. As the skipper put question after question to the ancient rascal he idly shaved more hairs from the withered neck, and as question after question brought unsatisfactory replies, so insistent as almost to convince, and the sultan's befooled bodyguard remained staring in genuine terror, a grimly humorous notion brought a sunny smile to the skipper's face. He deliberately made a sweeping cut and sheared off a thick mass of bristly hair.

"Be brave, little man," he laughed while the sultan squealed shrilly with the excruciating rasp of the dry shave.

Another sweep of the blade sheared a bigger patch, and another squeal announced it.

"Now you tell up, Sadrash, old dear. Sure you know where Parchelly is. Didn't he fetch you my jewel-case? No? Very well. The shave won't cost you a darned cent."

Tugging Sadrash's head back painfully, Saunders set to work to shear him in earnest.

"Kill them! Kill them!" screamed the sultan in frenzy.

A deep murmur rose from his men, and they involuntarily moved forward, forgetting their own plight in their inherent fear of their chief.

"Steady!" the skipper warned. "Stay where you are unless you want me to toss his ugly head among you for a football. Now, Sadrash, for the last time, are you going to produce my boy and my valuables?"

Swiftly he sliced away mass after mass of the terrifying whiskers, making the sultan writhe in real agony. For a minute Sadrash was stubborn. Then when he was all but shaved clean he began to whine:

"Your boy is not here. He has not come back. He is a slave who has run away. Go to your ship, and go away! Go away!"

Sincerity rang in every word, and Saunders released the big head and stood back in momentary perplexity. And as he regarded his handiwork he laughed amusedly, and the laugh found echo in all his own men and at least one of the white bodyguard of Sadrash.

The reason was plain, even in the imperfect light of the interior. Every bit of Sadrash's terrifying aspect had been due to that monstrous beard, which, emphasizing vividly the black eagle eyes and the hooked eagle nose, hid entirely the weak, all but toothless mouth and the chinless lower jaw.

But there was another side to the situation now. The sultan raved, and he might rave, at his mongrel crew to destroy the insolent intruder; and his men, no longer holding him in the awe that he inspired a few moments before, might ignore his ravings; but Saunders realized in a flash that any threat he held over the sultan's head now could not prevent that gang of nondescript white men from taking a hand for themselves if he and his crew gave the least opportunity.

"Carter, take this," he said quickly, handing the mate Sadrash's scimitar. "Two of you boys come with me; the rest keep this gang in order. I'll soon see if this place holds anything worth while to pay us for our trip."

Two islanders followed silently; they passed out by the two lookouts Saunders had posted when he entered, and searched rapidly for anything in the nature of a storehouse. There was a long, low go-down in the rear of the big chamber, whose barred door and grated windows seemed to indicate that the contents might be worth investigating.

Toward the door they ran; but while the skipper's hands were on the massive wooden door-bar the distant forest rang with growing human sound, an answering howl pealed up from a mob of women who came running from the holes they had hidden in, and Sammy, one of the lookouts, appeared in haste.

"Cap'n!" he announced. "De woods he full ob mans wif gun an' spear, sar! One, two thousand, sure. What can do?"

Inured as he was to facing odds, Saunders was no scatter-brained fool to throw his men away needlessly. He remembered the threat that his schooner would be burned. He recalled the scanty numbers of the ship-guard left on board.

And against them, in face of imminent trouble, was a sun-scorched go-down of uncertain contents, a rapidly lowering jungle night, a hostile village and the conviction that he had forced the truth from the sultan's unwilling throat — in short, that his pearls and other effects were irrecoverably lost, and that he stood fair to lose his schooner and the lives of his men. As for his own life, he never let that sway him in any conceivable event. That was Red Saunders.

"Begins to look as if we've backed a loser, Sammy," he replied briskly. "Come along boys."

Reentering the chamber, he took hold of Sadrash, tucking him under one powerful arm.

"Scat, Carter!" he snapped. "Have the boys gather up these guns, or break 'em, and follow me. Looks like a fight on hand before we sail from this place!"

Then he swung his captive off his feet and plunged out and into the forest. Carter followed, swinging the great scimitar.

The fight turned from a prospect to a certainty. Out of the jungle swarmed a small army of dark shapes, and in answer to the howls of their released but disarmed fellows guns began to spit, and the swarm converged upon the little band of retreating *Black Pearl* boys. And highest of all the urging squeals was the thin pipe of the terrified Sadrash, desperation forcing his vocal cords to rebel against the bodily fears inspired by that awful grip about his squirming form.

"Got to stop that, old-timer," grunted Saunders, stumbling heavily in the darkness as the old reprobate kicked like a boy under parental coercion.

He shifted his pistol to the hand holding Sadrash and drew his knife, jabbing the point persuasively into the skinny ribs.

"Now, you runt, squeal all you want," he gritted. "But squeal right, and keep your dogs at heel, or I'll let your withered tripes out."

The sailors, at Carter's heels, were fighting with grim ferocity when Saunders plowed forward again; and many of them bore hurts sore enough to constitute a warning that they had a long way to go yet. But Sadrash proved a potent talisman to those of his men who had not yet seen him closely in his shaven state, even if his bodyguard had laughed at sight of him; and as the forest was penetrated deeper toward the night-blanketed creek only the rearguard of the schooner's men were forced to turn to fight their pursuers every few yards.

It was within sound of the sea and sight of the dim creek that Sadrash's body-guard managed to convince their mates of the sultan's fall from majesty in their eyes, and by that time Red Saunders was right in his element — in sight of his own good little ship, with the knowledge, imparted by lantern signals, that she was still intact and her small gang of watchmen yet complete.

His whistle shrilled a summons for the boats to hasten, and he led his boys in a last desperate charge which was to scatter his foes back far enough to permit them all to embark. He heard the rattle of oars, and relief seemed very near.

But the old chief had reached the limit of his usefulness as a talisman. Shriek as he might, his rascals ignored both entreaties and threats and surged forward with bitter insistence. Saunders dropped his knife, seized Sadrash in both hands and hove him high in the air above his head.

"All right," he roared. "If you want him, here he comes." He pitched the old villain headlong into the midst of his gang, and turned to meet the boats.

But the darkness which impeded the boats among the half-submerged jungle roots aided Sadrash's men. When he tumbled among them, whimpering with rage, even the white men who had seen him changed by a dry shave from a terrifying old villain into a mean-faced, impotent, skinny image, rallied to back him and stand off the sailors from embarking. And the boats were yet struggling with the mangrove barrier. The overwhelming army of enraged whites and Timoreans came on again, their growling and cursing resounding through the black jungle.

"Stand fast, bullies!" gritted the skipper, himself snatching the great scimitar out of Carter's hands and sweeping it about his head.

It whistled and sang as he plied it, and for a breath men fell back before its awful menace. But numbers were potent; the gang caught the full significance of the boats' predicament and surged forward resistlessly. Two of the *Black Pearl's* men were down.

"Fight 'em, boys; fight 'em!" panted Red, fighting like one possessed himself.

Inevitably the rush came on. The boats were coming too late this time.

Then out upon the discord of battle shrilled another, keener voice — a voice like that of a minor devilene — and between the fighting bands leaped a figure of appalling gesture, sobbing hysterically, shrieking of sudden death, whirling a murderous Dyak blade about his bowed head.

Straight for Sadrash he went. The blade sang and chopped, and Sadrash's shorn head flew from his shoulders into the face of his nearest adherent, his blood bespattering a score of others who shrank back from the shower.

And the skipper seized the Heaven-sent chance, willing to wait for explanations. His men rallied once more, and the boats grated on the shore as the last of the attackers vanished into the forest.

Then the strange apparition crept up to the skipper and fawned at his feet. There was a bundle tied about his neck, and this he nervously untied.

"Hey, Carter, look here," cried Saunders triumphantly. "It's Parchelly! I told you he was all right."

"Huh! Wait till he chucks that ruddy big knife away," retorted Tod Carter, still unconvinced.

Parchelly got his bundle free, handed it to Saunders, and flashed a strangely indulgent smile at the grim old mate as he told the skipper what had happened.

"I see you put dis pearls in yo' pocket, sar, and I was go to foller you 'shore. Den I watch you an' you put dem in iron box ag'in. So I watch fo' you. I know dis bad peoples here; oh, yis, very mooch, sar.

"Den come Sadrash's men, an' I know dey come fo' rob dis ship. I oppen box wid piecee wire like de bad white man show Sadrash when he want to open iron box from steamer he burn, an' swim 'shore an' hide in de jungle.

"I see Misser Carter t'row de men into de river, an' I wait fo' git on board ag'in. But oder mans see me, an' many mile I run, very fas', before I can git back here ag'in. Den I hear de fight, an' I kill one o' Sadrash's guard wid a beeg stone, and steal him sword. Dat's all, sar. I very glad see you ag'in, sar."

Saunders laughed softly, patting Parchelly's curly head. He glanced toward Carter; but that dour and disgruntled worthy was already stepping into a boat, growling back over his shoulder:

"Might as well pull out o' here. Call it a failure, cap'n, for once, and darn lucky we are that you didn't lose what you brought here with you too."

"Not quite a failure either, Tod," the skipper chuckled, "It's something to have found that I was not mistaken when I took Parchelly aboard and rated him a man. And what the lad's just hinted about a steamer being burned here and looted, gives me an idea that the authorities in Lifou town might welcome the news and be inclined to stump up a bit toward our expenses for wiping out old Sadrash."

"Now yer hollering!" quoth Carter cheerfully. "Another honest man won't annoy us, and he won't be no novelty either, in the *Black Pearl*; but while praisin' honesty, cap'n, don't ever forget it takes freight to stiffen the schooner. Let's go."

SKIMPS, SHIP'S BOY

SKIMPS WAS not reared in luxury's lazy lap. At the tender age of two days he was picked up on the doorstep of the Foundling Hospital, and the first seven years of his life were spent in perpetual wonder why human beings were considered superior animals.

For his part, he was in everybody's way — everybody told him so, some with a heavy hand, others with only a sharp tongue, and he deeply envied the lot of the ragged cat that howled on the roof just above his tiny window, and the gloriously care-free existence of the sleek rat that gnawed a full stomach from the wainscot while listening to the feline love-song overhead.

From his window he could hear mysterious voices, too, which did not belong to anything of fur and claws. Tugboat whistles, the sirens of big ships, the clattering of winches — all these whispered to him of happenings outside the four walls of his home, which he looked upon as his prison.

He wondered more and more why other urchins were free to scamper over ash-heaps, and roll happily in muddy gutters: these things he saw on the rare occasions when he was marching out to take the air, keeping step, like a soldier, with another pitiful mite of human forlornness, at the tail-end of a long procession of institute-reared orphans.

One day he broke from line twice, and was twice pulled and slapped back into his place.

The Gorgon in charge was looking the other way the third time, and Skimps spent a palpitating, adventurous night with a company of strange, tremendous rats, among piles of outgoing freight on a nearby wharf.

Up to the day of his emancipation a too-full stomach had never been one of his troubles. His early training in that respect fitted him excellently for the next five years of his existence, during which he fed himself largely by robbing stray dogs of flavorsome scraps, or sometimes — and these were events — creeping past some somnolent ship-keeper at night and foraging a full meal of hearty sea-provender.

He grew uncannily expert in eluding policemen and watchmen. His bed might be either a heap of sacks, or a crevice between cotton bales; but his sleep was never so deep as to befog his wits; the wisest old rat on the wharf never whisked out of sight any quicker or more completely than did Skimps on the approach of the softest footstep.

Gradually he began to take the shape that would characterize him in manhood; as yet, he retained a cherubic innocence of facial expression, which might change later on; his weedy, shallow-chested frame covered a spirit of bestial cunning, hatred of truth where a lie would serve, and distrust of mankind, which might change but was far more likely to develop.

Finally, Skimps learned to take his own part. The life he led tended naturally toward getting him more kicks than kopeks, and his skinny body was never clear of bruises. But while often beaten, he was never whipped. A heavy blow might send him running; but invariably the last blow was delivered by him, even though he had to wait a month to put it over.

It occupied a policemen and two lightermen the better part of an hour to bring back animation to one man who had kicked Skimps. A tight string between two bollards on the wharf-edge, a rock in a discarded coat-sleeve, and the resulting plunge into a January tide, repaid that man for his thoughtless kick.

But with all the hazards of his own small existence, Skimps had a warm fellow-feeling for the lesser atoms of the brute creation. His companions, friends in fact, were found among warehouse rodents, homeless cats, the kind of dogs that other boys tie cans to for sport; and for these the barefoot, ragged waif entertained a sympathetic comradeship that was as near affection as could be expected to dwell in such a shriveled, bedeviled soul. The ferocity of a Great Dane dog, which had been set upon him by a sour-hearted schooner skipper one evening, evaporated in ponderous tail-waggings, and the dog had to be dragged away from the new-found chum.

Skimps might never have realized his ambition to see what fairyland lay beyond the limits of vision where the outgoing ships vanished but for the pet monkey of the bark *Olinda*, then reloading freight for Brazil at the wharf which was for the time being Skimps's home.

The monkey belonged to the bark's skipper, and during the daytime was permitted to frolic in the sunshine on the poop; but always a chain held him prisoner to a staple in the mizzenmast. At meal-times, while the ship's people were below, Skimps stole near to the vessel's side and tried to open up communications with the monkey; and after the second attempt the animal's curiosity was only restrained by the chain about its waist.

One warm night, when the ship-keeper had sneaked off up the wharf in search of a cooling beverage, and the ship was deserted, Skimps slipped aboard by way of the stem-fasts and sought his new acquaintance.

Disappointed by reason of an impregnably fastened cabin-scuttle, and in momentary fear of the watchman's return, Skimps's sharp wits nevertheless found a solution of the problem. He made a swift examination of the staple in the mast, tried it with all his puny strength, and eventually loosened it with the help of a belaying pin taken from the pin-rail above it.

He watched anxiously enough the next morning, fearing that the monkey's custodian would notice the loosened staple. He breathed freely again when it passed undiscovered, and crouched out of sight to wait patiently for the dinner hour.

The hour arrived, the bark's poop was deserted except for the monkey, and Skimps stole to the edge of the wharf and called in the voice he had seen the monkey respond to before. There came back an excited chattering and rattling of chain; then the chattering ceased abruptly as the staple fell out with a noisy clatter.

Skimps called again, and small, swift feet padded across the deck; a chain rustled metallically after them, and right over Skimps's head peered out between the poop-rails the working visage and glittering eyes of the monkey.

For an instant each eyed the other; then the simian sensed the odor of brotherhood emanating from his seducer, and clambered down to Skimps's arms with a sigh of content almost human. Skimps vanished with his new friend, and the wharf knew him not for many days.

He neither knew nor cared that the bark's skipper was frantic at his loss, and consequently made life a burden for all about the ship; he retreated with his monkey to a snug hole on the next wharf, where, after trying vainly for a whole evening to get the chain off, he devoted his efforts to the improvement of their mutual acquaintance. He found a willing pupil, and a warm response to his overtures of comradeship. The monkey could all but talk in twenty-four hours.

Still might Skimps have never fared beyond the mystic horizon of his daydreams had the monkey's appetite been less nice. On the second day of his new possession he saw a pitiful expression settle in his pet's wrinkled face; all that day he had foraged for scraps, to offer the choicest to his chum.

But somehow the contents of garbage tubs and cast-out butcher's scraps failed to tempt the pampered simian taste. Sorrowfully Skimps turned the monkey loose on the wharf where the bark lay, willing that his pet should return home rather than starve.

The fellowship that had grown up between those two pals was stronger than hunger: the monkey stuck to Skimps like a barnacle to a buoy. One more day the monkey hungered, its eyes growing brighter as its face grew more and more pitiful, and toward evening the waif made the first great decision of his life. He took the monkey in his arms, and walked solemnly aboard the bark.

Captain Baker, dressed to go ashore, stood at the head of the gangway, scowlingly giving some orders to his chief mate. Attracted by a shrill chattering, he looked down and saw Skimps, and the scowl on his usually good-natured face was routed by an ear-wide grin of joy at the return of his lost pet.

"Gosh! Look who's here!" he shouted, leaving the mate and running forward with all the grace of an elderly sea-cow. "Where'd ye find him, boy? Here, come below, an' I'll give you a dollar. Gosh!"

He snatched the monkey to him, cuddling it in his arms as a mother would a lost and found child. He started down the cabin companionway, obviously expecting Skimps to follow. But Skimps was wary of mankind; he stayed where he was, looking wistfully after his departing chum.

The mate stepped to his side, gave him a shove, and told him to hurry: that shove brought results. For Skimps bared his teeth in a vicious snarl at the touch of the mate's hand, and darted aside, his eyes shining with hate and fear. In his experience, when a man laid hands on him it was generally to hurt him.

With the resultant volley of strange oaths from the mate, and the chattering rage of the boy, came yet another unlooked-for issue; chain-links tinkled on the stairs, and straight into the boy's arms flew the monkey, a spitting, grimacing, furious bunch of gray and brown fur. Hard after came a deep-throated expletive, and Captain Baker ran on deck again, dabbing at a long scratch on his cheek, and glaring open-mouthed at the astonishing tableau.

The result was that, after a long half hour of coaxing, and promises, and wheedling, the monkey once more became the *Olinda's* pet, and Skimps was entered on the ship's books as deck boy. On no other terms could the matter be adjusted, for when the ragged fragments of the boy's shirt-sleeve gave way and the monkey was torn loose, the angry little creature turned his attention to the skipper's hair, nor would he let go until Skimps spoke to him in the crooning voice he had got to know so well.

Skimps wanted to see the country where such animals lived, anyhow. The skipper had promised him he might even see parrots flying wild.

THE END of a week saw the *Olinda* spanking away to the southward, her prosaic commercial form made resplendent by flashing rainbows of fine weather spray. The wonder of it kept Skimps's eyes and mouth on a taut stretch: nothing he had ever seen of harbor craft, crushing through wind-whipped harbor chops, had prepared him for the glories of the great, wholesome ocean.

It had been a week of trial to the waif. The first day of his shipboard life had come near being his last; for Captain Baker had left his dinner to wrench Skimps from the shoulders of a seaman who had been teasing the monkey, and the skipper's interference was only just in time to save the fellow's precious eyesight from the boy's groping fingers.

And so far nothing could impress Skimps with the idea that he now had a job, that to eat he must work. The mate gave him up as hopeless after the skipper forbade him to apply the customary laying on of hands. The boy was of a strange breed, anyway, the mate considered; he would soon come to time when he was hungry; if he did not, it was the skipper's affair, that was all.

But Skimps cared nothing for mealtimes: he could not remember ever having one. When he got hungry, that first day on board the Olinda, he simply waited until the cook left his galley to carry the cabin dishes aft, then he walked in and helped himself to the first edible he saw, which chanced to be the tidbit set aside for the cook's own meal.

Skimps escaped detection, vanishing with the skill and stealth acquired in his years of vagabondage; but the cook swore to keep his eyes on that boy in future. That night the monkey, too, was missing, and Captain Baker lent a sympathetic ear to the growling of his chief mate and the suspicions of the cook.

The bark was going to sea in the early morning, and it looked as if she must after all sail without that monkey. But Skimps and his chum came to light when the hands were called, as if nothing were the matter, having spent the night in the lazaret. A broken box of raisins proved later that the boy had progressed in his knowledge of a monkey's food preferences.

By the time the *Olinda* had cast off her tug and had spread her broad, snowy canvas to the strong breeze, the ship's company realized that such a ship's boy as Skimps was neither useful nor ornamental, but simply another burden on the backs of hard-working sailors.

The skipper persuaded the boy to work by giving him the custody of the monkey; but Skimps had never known work; he simply didn't know how to use his hands, except to fight or steal, and the part he played in the scheme of things aboard the bark was such that the watch who enjoyed his assistance was rather at a disadvantage.

And, bitterest cup of all, the forecastle crowd and the cook knew they must keep their hard hands off the skipper's protégé, openly at least; until their superiors gave them a lead, they must grin and bear the urchin's obnoxious presence in their midst.

After the oldest A. B. had cleaned out the flourishing colony of rats which Skimps had attracted to his bunk in the dark eyes of the ship, and had managed to refrain from cuffing the ears of the budding naturalist while doing so, there seemed to be no excuse for his mates to exercise less restraint themselves.

Captain Baker, from the sacred aloofness of his position, found a sort of grim humor in watching the progress of Skimps and the perplexities of the crew. He well knew that he was establishing a dangerous precedent in allowing a street gamin the unrestrained run of the ship; but he had a feeling deep down in his heart that this weedy-bodied, warped-souled speck of humanity was, through the fault of somebody unknown to him, teetering on the border line between boy and brute.

He had seen that the brute was predominant; he hoped by leaving the boy alone to instill confidence that might prove the first step in his reclamation.

Skimps's duties gradually dwindled, through sheer inability or refusal to master others, to trifling services rendered the cook. He chopped firewood once only: the mate declined to have his spotless decks scarred and splintered by an inexpert ax. Potatoes after he had peeled them were practically non-existent; the doctor peeled them himself after that horrible first attempt, for the *Olinda* was a windjammer on a long passage, and potatoes don't grow at sea.

The one job that Skimps never fell down on was carrying buckets of coal to the galley bunker; that became his sole duty in time, and his skinny arms grew sensibly harder for the exercise.

The *Olinda* was loaded with coal for Porto Alegre; a small space against the after bulkhead, set apart for the captain's private venture, according to the custom of the line, was filled with the less bulky but costlier articles of commerce, mostly table delicacies for South American gourmands.

Entry to this small compartment was by way of a sliding hatch just forward of the poop; at the foot of the ladder was the small square aper-

ture through which Skimps had access to the coal for the galley. A ventilator cowl screwed into the deck above admitted air to keep the skipper's
goods sweet and free from noxious bilge odors.

Just before she crossed the Tropic of Cancer, the bark ran into a confused, oily sea, beneath massed coppery clouds that gave warning of
troubled weather, and Skimps was told off to fill the galley coal-bunker to
its full capacity. It might become necessary to batten down all hatches,
and the cook must be sure of his fuel supply.

Obediently the boy toiled, with the monkey perched on his shoulder,
until the doctor cried enough.

Then Skimps went forward to his berth to clean himself, and the
monkey went with him. The men were all on deck, busy with preparations for the threatened breeze of wind; there was none to notice the dis-
tended condition of the monkey's pouches.

One lesson the youngster had already learned; that stealing was
unaccountably held to be wrong, and that a thief in a forecastle was sure
to find trouble. He knew the lesson, though he could not understand why
it should be so.

So now he peered cautiously about the dingy forecastle before going
to his bunk; he made quite sure that nobody but himself was there; then
he swiftly whipped a bundle from under his shirt and slipped it beneath
his straw mattress.

Then he took his towel, of a beautiful chocolate hue, and a lump of
salt-water soap, and went outside to wash. The men, having finished
their tasks, trooped forward as he dipped a bucket of water from over the
side, and they too performed their ablutions.

Skimps was a rapid washer. He had never found washing necessary
before he came into the *Olinda*; he would not have commenced now,
except for the fact that the men refused to have him in the forecastle until
he made at least a pretense of cleanliness. He toweled himself now, and
emptied his bucket, stepping across the forecastle doorsill as the merry
Norwegian, Andreas, came out.

"Hollo! Vy you don't vash youself, Skimps?" roared Andreas, shaking with laughter at the boy's face, streaked black and gray.

"I'm washed, yuh fat-faced squarehead!" snarled Skimps, trying to
push past. "You'se leave me alone, see!"

The men stared at Skimps open-mouthed. Their horror at such a
reply from a boy to an able seaman slowly changed to uncouth mirth at
his queer appearance. He looked like a leprous Nubian — black, with
white patches.

Old Jensen, the patriarchal Swede, whose whiskers were the wonder of the forecastle, and who had held command under his own country's flag, had simmered in silence since the ship had been at sea at the unheard of immunity of Skimps. The boys of his day, as he always took occasion to remark when the youngster fired off a particularly staggering retort at the men, never dared to give back talk to able seamen. Skimps, in any of those ancient vessels of the old Swede's recollection, would have been dead or dumb inside a week.

Jensen boiled over at the boy's last effort, and, shoving Andreas aside, he seized the half-washed youth by the arm, growling:

"Ju vash juself, or I git vun 'oly-stone an' go ofer ju!"

The next instant he released Skimps, howling with pain, for the young savage sunk his teeth into Jensen's hand, kicked out viciously, and broke away.

"Keep yer hands off me, see! That goes fer all of yer, too," screamed Skimps, quivering with fury, the coal patches rendering his features grotesque in their working.

A roar of laughter went up from the seamen, in which the two mates joined more quietly aft, as Jensen recalled all the profanity of his youth and bolted into the forecastle jabbering strange oaths.

Andreas was more pertinacious. Still smiling, he laid powerful hands on Skimps, out of reach of his teeth, and called to a shipmate to hand him soap and swab as he required them. Then ensued a brief session of intense action.

Skimps saved his breath for the struggle; he was less inclined to talk, too, by reason of the unpleasant taste of saltwater mixed with salt-water soap. But his puny strength was futile against Andreas's great hands and arms; his face was scrubbed and rubbed, and polished, until the skin glowed pink and clean, and the inside of his ears revealed pretty shell-tints that now saw the light for the first time in years.

"Now we got a clean boy," smiled Andreas, letting Skimps get up, and standing back to regard his handiwork. "Vunce a veek shall I give a vash to Skimps after dis, und he shall be clean."

Skimps stood in a circle of grinning seamen, and his small body was fury incarnate. His teeth chattered with the torrent of abuse that surged up, and out of his incoherence pealed the warning:

"You look out, you big tough! I'll fix you fer dat, an' old rusty whiskers, too! You don't git away wid no rough stuff on me, so mind yer eye!"

Then the urchin darted into the forecastle and threw himself into his bunk in a paroxysm of dry weeping. There was only one man in the crew forward with whom Skimps found anything in common.

Micky Daveron, at twenty-five, had risen no higher in his shipboard value than ordinary seaman; and his mind was on a par with Skimps's. He at any time preferred stealing to working; but in his case it was due to native vice; he had not the excuse that the boy might well plead, that hitherto he had known nothing better than to either steal or starve.

Daveron was full of petty meanness, and the men in his watch departed from time-honored sea usage so far as to lock their sea-chests when they went on deck. It was Daveron who went over to Skimps now, and comforted him with suggestions for retaliation. The suggestions were sufficiently horrible to satisfy even Skimps's raging sense of wrong, and presently the boy's agitation was calmed and he settled down to quietly plan his revenge.

Through the dog-watches the crooning of the wind in the maze of the bark's tall rigging rose gradually to a deep howl accentuated by occasional long shrieks that became more frequent toward night.

The carpenter went around and battened down the hatches, and the men having the first watch below lost no time in getting to sleep, for the night promised to be one of hurry calls. And in the black den of the ship's bows the chain-cable began to clank solemnly to the heavier plunges, and the pouring seas outside filled the gloomy forecastle with muttering thunder.

Skimps occupied the upper berth farthest forward, and below him lived Micky Daveron. Next abaft were the two bunks occupied by Andreas and old Jensen, both of whom were already snoring rustily before one bell in the first watch.

Daveron carried on a whispered conversation with Skimps long after the others slept, for the boy had returned his one chum's doubtful championship by slipping down to him a big bunch of muscatel raisins, looted from the skipper's private store as a treat for the monkey. The monkey had of late taken up permanent quarters with Skimps, and the skipper ceased to object when he saw the little animal grow so tame under the boy's care as to behave quite respectably without having to be chained up.

The first call for all hands came at the change of watches at midnight, when topgallantsails were finally stowed. The call did not include the boy, who slept peacefully through the racket; but Daveron turned out with the others, and for half an hour the only open eyes in the dim forecastle were the monkey's.

That alert little creature lay curled up in the crook of the boy's arm, and the beady eyes shone like a rat's. They followed the stealthy motions of Daveron when that useless and unpopular ordinary seaman stole below to skulk until sure that enough other men had started on the unpleasant climb into the howling darkness aloft, and that a soft job of coiling down would fall to his share.

The monkey saw the seaman take something from beneath his own pillow and slip it under the mattress of Jensen. He did the same with the bunk of Andreas, then went out of the forecastle.

The monkey saw possibilities of discovering a new trick, and immediately Daveron had gone, the agile animal clambered down and investigated the three bunks. He found nothing in Daveron's bunk; but he drew no blank in the other two beds.

He crept away, chattering softly, and darted into the black recess forward of the hawsepipes. He was back in a moment, and his little arms were loaded. Swift as a flickering shadow, the monkey divided his burden into three, placed one moiety beneath each of the three bunks, and crept back to his own sleeping quarters as the watch came trooping below.

DURING THREE ensuing days the *Olinda* slogged through a teasing gale under the merest ribbons of reefed topsails. Men slept in wet clothes when they got a chance to rest at all; the forecastle reeked and dripped with oozing moisture that became noisome steam when the watch were below and the hatch closed tight.

On the streaming decks the carpenter and his temporary mates watched for smooths and gave the holds a little sorely needed ventilation as they could snatch the chance, for a cargo of coal when battened down tight becomes a source of danger.

The monkey shivered and whimpered in the wet, foul forecastle during the breeze, and Skimps was kept employed at first in carrying the little beast aft to the cabin.

Captain Baker insisted on having his pet in the pleasanter quarters under the poop until the weather should break, but the monkey refused to be parted from his chum. As often as he was carried aft, back he flew forward, until he was again fettered with the hateful chain. Then he decided to pine away, and became so miserable that the skipper was forced to liberate him again and allow Skimps to carry him into the forecastle.

Luckily the weather eased, and soon the forecastle scuttle was opened to dry out the den, so the monkey speedily recovered his spirits.

Skimps started in to replenish the cook's coal-bunker as soon as the small after hatch was opened, and the carpenter received orders to open up the main hatch as soon as the bark was under full sail.

Skimps groped through the small compartment that gave access to the coal, and found the cases and bales of the skipper's private venture thrown about pretty badly. It called for restowing before he could reach the bulkhead in which was the door into the hold.

To his request for assistance Daveron was sent into the small hold with him, and as soon as that worthy's eyes grew accustomed to the half-light down there they opened wide in wicked glee. Broken cases here and there revealed treasures of preserved edibles: sardines, salmon, milk, canned boneless chicken, and endless other things calculated to bring water to the mouth of a hungry sailor. There were bottles, too, that did not hold grape juice.

"Hey, Skimps, we gotta have a light here," said Daveron, rummaging among the loose litter with itching fingers. "I'll go an' get one."

"All right then," agreed Skimps, who was busy, too. "Take these to the monkey," he added, slipping a bunch of raisins to Daveron.

While awaiting the return of Daveron with his lantern, Skimps fell to collecting up the scattered contents of broken cases, and failed to notice the passage of time. He was puzzled at the number of cases which lacked some of their contents, but thought they had rolled out of sight and would come to light when the lantern arrived.

As he worked he was conscious of the heavy atmosphere that had arisen from days of closed hatches; the reek of violently disturbed bilge-water made him shudder at first; but, stronger than bilge, there was a queer, catching tang that he did not recognize, something that bit at his lungs and made his eyes run water.

He had almost reached the small aperture in the bulkhead, which lifted up like the door of a chicken run to give access to the hold, and was seriously thinking of going outside for a breath of fresh air when a thunderous bellow roared his name from the hatchway, calling him on deck in a hurry.

Skimps stayed a moment to drag the last box away from the small slide, then ran up the ladder and found himself propelled into the midst of a crowd of officers and men grouped about the waist and plainly laboring under subdued excitement. The carpenter and his helpers stood irresolutely at the main-hatch, as if waiting for further orders; and all hands were looking expectantly toward the forecastle doors.

The chief mate curtly ordered Skimps to stand by, and the boy obeyed through sheer inability to think of rebelling in face of the solemnity of the men around him.

And soon from the forecastle door issued the rest of the ship's company. Captain Baker came first, and his usually kindly expression had changed to a black frown; at his heels stalked Andreas and old Jensen, their arms full of canned and bottled luxuries, their faces, like the skipper's, dark and angry.

As they came aft, Skimps looked around inquiringly, wondering at the persistence of that acrid, lung-biting tang of the after hold, which seemed to hang about the deck in invisible waves. He saw the mates and the carpenter exchange anxious glances, and a shifting uneasiness possessed the men. Micky Daveron stood, lantern in hand, close beside the second mate, who kept a keen eye on him; and when any man's eye switched from the officers, it was to fasten on Daveron in a lowering scowl.

Captain Baker paused at the hatch and exchanged a swift question and report with the carpenter; then, followed by the two laden able seamen, he strode into the middle of the greater group and ordered the provisions to be laid before Skimps. Before making any explanation, the skipper dashed aft and down to the small hold where his own freight was stowed. Returning immediately, he ordered the carpenter to close the small hatch and batten it down, then came and took Skimps by the arm.

"Skimps," he began, and a harassed look settled on his ruddy face; "Skimps, these cans and bottles were found by Andreas and Jensen in their bunks. The men swear they don't know anything about the stuff! you're the only one who's been allowed down among my stuff, except Daveron today; and I hear that you have threatened to get even with these two men for handling you roughly. What about it, Skimps?"

"Huh, g'wan!" burst out Skimps furiously. "I ain't never took nothin' but a few o' them raisins fer the monk. That ain't nothin' to make a row about, is it? It wuz fer the monk, an' he's yours, ain't he?"

"This is more than stealing, Skimps," returned the skipper, quietly, peering straight into the small face of his protégé. "The fellow who slipped this stuff into other men's bunks meant to get those men into serious trouble. Don't you see that, Skimps? Daveron says it must be you —"

"Daveron says that?" screamed Skimps, his clawlike fingers working nervously, and his ratlike eyes gleaming with hate. "Why, 'twas him as told me to —" Skimps stopped short, biting his nether lip, and he refused to go on. A deep grumbling rolled among the men, and feet shuffled noisily as the group shifted to bring Daveron into full view.

The carpenter moved across the deck and spoke to the skipper, who gave orders to have the looted provisions carried into the cabin, and for the mates and seamen to join the carpenter. Captain Baker dropped the information as he passed Skimps that the men's charge against him would be taken up later, and Daveron and the boy were left alone for a moment.

Skimps swung around fiercely upon the ordinary seaman, maddened at what he had heard. Micky looked uncomfortable; big as he was, he feared the kicking, biting fury of the boy; he backed away, dropping his lantern.

Suddenly he saw Skimps's eyes flash past him, and he turned. The monkey was stealing swiftly along the lee side from the forecastle, and edging toward his chum. Daveron, who hated the monkey, saw a chance to placate Skimps, and darted over to pick the monkey up. But the monkey was wise; with a shrill chattering, and fierce grimaces, he flew past, and never stopped until he reached the after hatch. Only Skimps saw where his chum went: he considered him safe.

Now it was borne in upon the boy's mind that the present operations of the crew meant more than simply cleaning up after the gale. As he wandered from group to group, though he was not permitted to help, he learned the truth to the growing terror of his soul. He learned now what that awful, biting reek was that had nearly choked him while below.

During the gale, while hatches were all tight, fire had started somewhere among the coal. He heard, in fragments, that this was not uncommon with coal cargoes; but the *Olinda* had plunged so violently that the treacherous, shifting mass in her hold had been thrown and packed into spaces which had been purposely left clear in stowing against just such an emergency as this. So that now, when the smoldering fire was found to be too far down in the mass to be reached by hose from the deck, it was impossible to get down to the specially fitted sea-cocks to admit water from outside.

And the man who had discovered this reported that the iron collision bulkhead, which could be reached by way of the fore-peak and chain-locker, but which had no door, was already nearly red-hot.

"Only Skimps, or the monkey, could get down to the sea-cock," concluded the seaman who made the ominous report.

Skimps was abruptly reminded of the disappearance of his chum, and horrid visions of a roasted monkey rose before his mental vision. He listened eagerly until he caught the words he wanted to hear, then slipped from the group and disappeared after the monkey.

ON THE poop Captain Baker and his mates held a consultation. The nearest port lay dead to leeward as the wind then was, but it was not the steady wind of the trades. While the officers pored over the chart, calculating distances and the possibilities of striking a steady slant of wind, men worked feverishly under the carpenter's orders, trying to cut through the forward bulkhead and gain access to the fire that way.

Ten minutes may have elapsed since Skimp's disappearance, which had been unnoticed; then, red-faced from his labors, and panting with excitement, the carpenter burst from the forepeak and dashed aft to the poop.

"The for'ard bulkhead's sizzlin'!" he gasped. "She's fizzin' and crackin' like a dryin' boiler! We're leakin' like blazes!"

"Sound the well, you idiot!" snapped the skipper.

The mate jumped to the after ventilator, which had been shut off by means of a turntable disk in the cowl, and flung it open, sticking his head inside. The carpenter ran forward and dropped his sounding-rod down the sounding pipe.

"Smells mighty like steam, sir," reported the mate, from the ventilator. Then the carpenter came aft.

"There's four foot o' watter in her, an' it's sluicin' in, sir!" he shouted, brandishing his jointed sounding-iron in a frenzy. The imminent danger of roasting, complicated now by the fear of drowning, had shattered the poise of the doughty Chips.

Sparing but a moment to bethink him of Skimps, Captain Baker ran to the main-hatch, calling men to follow. He caught sight of his monkey, scampering over the doorsill of the forecastle, and felt relief, as he figured that where the monkey was, near by would be Skimps.

The hardest task of his eventful life had been to arraign the pitiful waif before the men that day. He held a deep-rooted conviction that great good lay somewhere hidden in Skimps's ill-used body; his strongest hope was that he might see it brought to the surface.

But his ship business demanded all his attention just now. He had a corner of the hatch lifted; a cloud of steam burst forth shot with heavier swirls of sooty smoke, and his face lighted with the knowledge that the greater the leak, from whatever cause, the surer the control of the fiery menace; and he knew that his powerful pumps could handle any leak that had developed as suddenly as had this one.

The pumps were tried, to make quite sure that the wells were not choked; then the hatch was replaced, the carpenter stood by the sounding pipe, rod in hand, taking frequent casts, and impatiently the men awaited the skipper's word that they might get busy. Inaction in such a dilemma chafes the boldest spirit.

Soon from every ventilator steam gushed untainted by smoke. Thin spirals and puffs seeped through mast-coats and under hatch-tarpaulins, and the mate, with his keen nose over the lip of a ventilator cowl, sang out:

"Pure steam now, sir! Fire's out, I think."

"Start the pumps, then!" shouted the skipper. "And you" — to the second mate — "get your watch below with shovels. Try to reach the sea-cocks first; I think you'll find the shifting coal must have battered one of them open. Now, boys, round with those pumps!"

For half an hour the steady clank-clank of the pump-brakes mingled with the slicing swish of shovels in the bowels of the bark until the iron hull rang again. The *Olinda* had been put back on her proper course, and Captain Baker and the mate stood together on the poop, discussing the matter of the stolen or broached cargo with which Skimps was concerned. Just as soon as the men were free, the matter would be taken up again.

Then came the second mate, black as a coal-trimmer, and knocked out of their heads all thought of petty thievery. In his arms he bore a small, singed, blackened figure that moaned piteously.

"Skimps!" gasped the skipper.

"Yessir. Found him down at the port sea-cock, half drowned, and nearly the other half suffocated. Where shall I put him?" asked the second mate, holding Skimps as he might handle a new-born baby.

"Put him in the cabin companionway, where he'll get the air," ordered the skipper, and went below for his first-aid outfit. Skimps opened his pain-drawn eyes some time later, and saw around him a circle of faces that comprised almost every man aboard. Even the cook was there, and none of the officers cared to send one man away.

"Wot yer all a buzzin' round fer?" demanded Skimps with his first words. "Yer waitin' fer me to git up, so's you kin hammer me, I s'pose. I tell yer I ain't done nothin' like you said. Daveron is a liar if he ses I did."

"No, sonny," replied the skipper soothingly. "We know who put that stuff in those bunks. That blamed monkey started it again as soon as he'd coughed the smoke out of his lungs. Daveron admitted pinching the stuff when he heard you were almost a goner, and the monk was seen stealing it from his bunk and poking it under the other mattresses.

"You've probably saved all hands from roasting. That's why they all want to see you now."

"Huh! Fergit it," said Skimps peevishly. "I just went down the ventilator after the monkey. I couldn't find him, so while I was there I thought I'd see if I could find that big tap wot the men said 'ud let water in on the fire. They said nobody else on board wuz small enough to do it.

"Youse tell ole rusty whiskers, an' dat big squarehead, that all I wuz agoin' to do tuh git hunk wit' 'em wuz to put some raisins an' biskit in their beds so's th' rats 'ud worry 'em, an' I'm sorry I couldn't do it, that's all."

A little brown, furry bunch of mischief stole in and climbed onto the settee where Skimps lay, and the boy's eyes brightened as he snuggled the monkey into his arm. Then he closed his eyes and dropped peacefully to sleep.

"Huh! Dot boy aind't det yet! Hooray!" said old Jensen, huskily.

Skimps stirred once in his sleep as the men trooped outside and, with big, merry Andreas as a cheerleader, made the old bark ring to the gilded trucks of her with a chantey voice, deep-sea "Hooroar!"

Captain Baker gazed down upon the sleeping figures — the monkey slept now — and with the old, good-natured grin suffusing his ruddy face, whispered to the mate:

"I thought I couldn't make a mistake. Look at 'em! There isn't a mite of mischief in the pair of 'em!"

HARD-SHELL CLAMMERS

THE CLAMS are hard, outwardly; so are the men who catch them. Underneath the flinty exterior the clam is no softer than the clammer.

Danielson's saloon, opposite the tip of Crook's Point, was full of fumes, fog, and fishermen. Outside, the delayed equinoctial gale threshed the Kills and the wider bay beyond into surly, snapping little seas; every building, pole, or pump-frame sang a shrill, windy song that sent a shiver to the bones in spite of sweater and boots.

But inside was comfort, unless a too fastidious taste demanded a clear atmosphere for breathing purposes. The barroom doors were closed against the gale; a great wood-stove reeked with piney aromas; eight corn pipes erupted volumes of Ivanhoe smoke, and the boss was using powerful Copenhagen snuff.

A little red whisky, and a lot of yellow beer added their share to the tremendous flavor, and contentment hovered around the poker table in the middle of the room.

It was bad weather for the clam sloops; and none of the hardy fishermen around the stove gave a second glance outside. If the gale wanted to howl, let her howl, they said; if clams could not be caught, it was no use going out after them.

The stove felt very good; big Carl Danielson sold very good whisky — real fisherman's booze, with a sea-boot kick to it.

> *"If you're inside, you can't be outside,*
> *If you're outside, you can't be inside — "*

Tippy Kanute roared the doggerel verse, running over a poker hand as bad as the weather. Nickels and dimes scraped across the table, and the smoke thickened.

"Play cards!" boomed Stub. Stub was a stocky little sailor with a true deep-water boson's voice. "Who's shy here? It's you, Louie, I think."

"Th' hellyusay!" retorted big Louie, reaching out for a battered nickel from the heap. "That's mine! I got it frum the buyer, th' sawed-off little robber!"

"Then it's a bad one. Put up another," growled Charlie Nelson, impatient to try out two small pairs.

Cards were slapped down with harmless temper or boisterous joviality, according to temperament, and more than one chair scraped back from the table.

"To Amboy wit' th' cards — let's have a drink!" suggested old Charlie, who never played poker. "Got to do something to keep us alive, boys."

A noisy trooping up to the bar mellowed away into a cheerful gurgle of liquids, and the atmosphere thickened again. Old Charlie — he was known by no other name, though he had the honorable one of Olson — old Charlie, the dean of Great Kills clammers, moved back to his warm chair nearest the big stove, and smiled indulgently upon the younger and thirstier members of the crowd.

"If you're outside, you can't be inside, by a damn-sight!"

"Haw, haw!" roared Tippy, and the bunch made it unanimous with a chorused "Haw, haw!"

"Put more wood in the stove, and we'll play a little freeze-out," suggested big Carl. He shoved bottles along the bar, took a hooker of whisky with a beer chaser, and rattled the change-drawer of the cash register alluringly.

The door burst open with a windy screech, and a short, foxy little man came into the barroom in a whirl of wet sand.

"Howly smoke, lads, it's cowld!" he stuttered, slamming the door shut and clapping his hands to the stove. The man's eye was red-rimmed, and he looked like a dressed-up ferret.

At his entrance the fishermen glanced at each other with side grins, and ostentatiously presently their broad backs to the newcomer. He saw, and appreciated the action. His keen face wrinkled in a smirk of contempt.

"Have something on me, boys," he invited carelessly. There was nothing spontaneous in the response. One man called for his drink, and paid for it, and the little foxy man darkened at the slight. He was the buyer, and the clammers' opinion of him might have been estimated by the little poker incident of Louie's bad nickel. He has departed now, but his memory survives.

"What's the matter wid youse guys?" he demanded spitefully. "Something wrong when a clammer won't either work or drink, I bet you. What's th' big idea? Come on up wid you an' take a drink."

There was a shuffling response, a halfhearted acceptance of unwanted hospitality, and for the space necessary for the swallowing of the beverages there was an awkward silence. One by one, as each man emptied his glass, the fishermen returned to the stove, leaving the buyer isolated. And he sneered at their backs.

"A lot o' fine weather fishermen, youse are! Get a breeze o' wind that a duck-boat could sail in, and it's round th' barroom stove fer youse. Why ain't youse out today? I got a order fer a hundred bushel o' clams, and there ain't one o' youse game enough to h'ist yer mains'l."

"Aw, give us a rest!" growled Stub, looking up sharply. "I'm game enough to h'ist you outside, you spike-nosed hoodlum. What do we want to haul rakes for you for? We're going South next week."

"You'll be mighty glad to haul rakes fer me next spring," retorted the unpopular middleman. "Youse'll be stuck fer fair if I shut youse out, won't you?"

"You shut us out?" echoed big Louie, leaning forward menacingly. "You try it once, and we'll all come to your wake!"

"Come on, play cards!" shouted Tippy at the table. "I wouldn't haul a rake for you, Mr. Man, if the price was ten dollars a dozen today, I'm my own boss, and you don't hire me; and you ain't no judge of weather either; you never see the water except from your old stinkin' little pilothouse."

"Sure, let's play cards. I got a dollar left yet," chimed in Nelson. "To Halifax with the clams; it's good weather in here!"

The buyer took another tack.

"Aw, come on, lads, and talk sense. I gotta have them clams. You can't let me down like this. There ain't a clam to be got, and the price is up, too. You ain't going to tell me you're quittin' fer th' season? Plenty o' time to go South. Come on; I'll raise the price another quarter if you'll let me have them clams. Have a drink, and start out, won't youse?"

"You go to —" came the response. Old Charlie, hitherto silent, added: "Besides, none of us would sell to you again, if you doubled the price. We're through with you. You're no good. There's nobody but old Joe, of the *Polly*, who'll stick with you; and he won't much longer if we can help it."

"Old Joe can't help it!" snarled the buyer viciously. "Old Joe will sell to me as long as I choose to buy. An' he'll go out today, too, if I can find him. I'll fix youse wit' the hull market, you betcha!"

The buyer slammed out as he had slammed in, and he left a trail of vitriolic abuse behind him that threatened to bring retribution close in his wake.

"Let him go, boys," soothed big Carl. "Don't let a little scab like him upset you. Shuffle the cards, we'll cut for deal."

"Bust the cards!" exploded Nelson, glaring out of the fogged window. "What's he mean about old Joe? Tell me that."

"Forget it; forget it. It's none of my business, anyhow. Let him go."

"Let go nothing!" cried another. "He got no right to talk as if he's bought the *Polly* out. I'm going out to bring that little pup back —"

"Sit down, and quiet yourself," the saloonkeeper insisted. "You mustn't believe everything you hear, and only half what you see. Besides, I don't want trouble with that fellow."

"Then what do you know about old Joe?" demanded Stub. "He never fell in love with that buyer that I know of."

"I don't know anything, in a way, Stub. I only heard that when Joe's missus was almost dying that time, and there was a lot of money needed to pay the specialist who could save her, that buyer advanced the cash, and took a bill o' sale on the *Polly* as security."

"Took th' *Polly* as security! She's worth eight hundred, Carl. How much was the loan?"

"About hundred and fifty, I think."

"Hundred and fifty!" rejoined Louie. "Must be a thousand and fifty! Joe told me a long time ago he was payin' somebody a hundred a month."

"I can't tell about that, Louie. I only know that if Joe misses a payment once he stands to lose the *Polly*, and that's —"

"That's why he's out every day, storm or fine, with a mate or without!" interjected old Charlie, warmly. "We been calling him tightwad, and other fine names, because he don't take a day off wit' us sometimes. And that's what that little runt of a buyer meant when he said Joe must sell to him. By Christmas, he ought to be filled full of kerosene and set light to!"

A muttered consultation was going on in a corner. Presently Tippy, Louie, and Stub moved to the door, admitted a roaring gust of wet wind, and shouting: "We're all going out, boys! Get ready to start; we'll be right back," plowed off along the beach after the common enemy.

The vague announcement sent all the others crowding to windows and doorglass to follow the movements of the departed three. Leaning against the gale they could be seen stubbornly fighting their way through the sand and shells toward where a lone figure stood, disheveled, staring out toward the idle sloops.

Soon clammers and buyer formed a little crowd of their own, and apparently a few words were immediately followed by angry rejoinders; then suddenly the little group surged back toward the saloon, three determined men dragging a very unwilling one.

On the porch the buyer shrieked:

"I'll have th' bunch o' youse pinched! I won't buy a blessed clam if you git a t'ousand bushel an' offer 'em at fifty cents a bushel!"

"You won't have us pinched, neither, and you'll buy every clam we get, at top price, too," growled Louie, hauling the captive inside.

"If you don't buy 'em, you'll eat 'em!" boomed Stub, reeving three fingers into the buyer's neckband.

"And that goes — shell and all!" chimed in Tippy Kanute, slamming the door shut and slouching forward. "Let's go, boys," he urged the rest. "This rat says old Joe's got to pay him ninety dollars by tonight, or he'll take the *Polly*. We'll get that ninety easy if the spars stand up; then we'll kick this little hoodlum off the beach for the good of his health. Give us a pint o' steam apiece, Carl, and we'll pull out."

"Sure! that's the stuff," roared the crowd, just glimpsing the idea. "Make the son of a gun pull rakes, too, and buy his own clams!" They trooped to the bar, swallowed each a stiff boson's nip of red rye, and pocketed the flasks big Carl passed out. The great, good-natured Swede was counting noses to figure his charges, and he saw a discrepancy in the number.

"How about old Charlie?" he questioned. "He's got no mate."

"That's so, too," agreed another. "Maybe we can find old Joe."

"No, you can't find Joe," cried the buyer, choking with viperish temper. "He ain't aboard, and he'll lose out for all yer schemin'!"

"Don't worry about me," rejoined old Charlie. "I can take the *Jessie* out alone for that matter. But I don't mean to. I'll take this sawed-off little runt along, an' make him work, too!"

Old Charlie went to Carl's tool-locker, took out a fifteen-inch steel marlinespike, and slipped it ostentatiously into one of his sea-boots. The intended victim snarled afresh; but in spite of his temper his lip quivered when he met old Charlie's eyes. Not for nothing were those eyes called the sharpest in the fleet.

"Aw, fellers, have a heart!" the buyer protested. The clammers surged out into the storm, and splashed toward the bateaux lying at the edge of the tide.

"Say, fellers, I ain't got any rubber-boots, or oilskins, or anything. I'll be killed wit' th' cowld. Don't play the goat, lads; I'll buy yer clams when youse come in."

"Sure you will," growled old Charlie, urging him toward the *Jessie's* bateau. "You'll help get 'em, too. A while ago you were calling us all kinds of names for not goin' out in this gale. Never mind if we froze or not. I'll see that you don't get killed wit' the cold, 'either; I'll keep you good and warm. Get aboard now. No monkey business!" And Charlie lifted three inches of marlinespike from his boot. Working out of the harbor was a wet, bone-racking job. The screaming sou'easter and a strong half-flood tide gave the sloops a dead beat out, with little chance to gather headway between boards.

Old Charlie's unwilling mate was convinced of the impossibility of his death from cold long before he succeeded in getting the heavy anchor aboard. Just once, for a moment he approached mutiny; when the weight of the anchor fell upon his solitary strength, he let the chain surge and turned aft with a vicious curse; but grim old Charlie put his helm down swiftly, and gave his man a wallop on the skull with the foresail-boom.

Afterward there was no hitch to fishing the anchor.

Once outside the Point the sloops lined out according to their speed, and stretched away close-hauled for the hook buoy. And the man who, an hour before, bore himself like a dealer in men's labor and gloried in his profession, was glad now to get a job cooking dinner in the warmth of the cabin. One by one, as they made the range, the sloops doused jibs, slacked off mainsheets, and lay to, making a first drift with a screaming wind blowing straight down the tide. One by one the rakes splashed overboard, and the *Jessie* commenced her own operations well to windward of the rest.

"Come up, you, and get busy!" shouted old Charlie, poking his smiling old face down the cabin-hatch. "You're going to learn what work is now."

The kidnapped mate crawled on deck, shivering violently as the breeze bit into him. In the cabin he had escaped the flying spray; for half an hour warmth had seeped into his bones; he had almost forgotten a gale was blowing.

This man was not of the sailor-fisherman type at all; falling heir to a little money, he had always taken the easy side of the business, leaving others to bring grist to his mill.

Even that side never tempted him when winter or late autumn gales whipped the bay into unpleasant tantrums. Aboard his own big, capable powerboat, his paid hands had learned what it was to be left a man short when the boss's chilly feet forced one of their number to take his vacant place in the pilothouse.

He cringed now, when the skipper sharply bade him get the rakes ready.

"Aw, Charlie, I can't do this," he protested, helplessly. "I'll only git yer lines all snarled up. Besides, I gotta be back in th' Kills at two o'clock, to meet my boat comin' from Keyport. Let's go back, I'll make it all right wit' youse. Them other lads kin git plenty o' clams wit'out youse."

Charlie gave him one warning look, hauled his marlinespike into sight, and uttered:

"Rakes, I said!"

The stout manila rake lines cracked under the terrific strain, and muscles cracked in unison. The toil was tremendous to seasoned arms; it was heart-breaking to the novice. But clams came up at every haul, and in satisfying numbers.

The *Jessie* made her first drift in silence as to speech, and the shellfish were showing above water in the tubs when Cap'n Charlie ordered the jib set and hauled his mainsheet to beat back for another trial.

As the sloop threshed up the wind the buyer had chances to ponder over the situation while resuming his cooking duties; and gradually his foxy face took on a cunning grin and he peered through the hatch at old Charlie, standing at his wheel like a grim old Norseman.

"Yuh durn fools!" muttered the temporary cook under his breath. "I'll git them clams after all; an' yuh'll git stuck. Think I'm goin' tuh let go o' that bill o' sale? Not much! I'll pay yer price fer clams — an' that's all."

He finished peeling potatoes, and put on the pot with a great appearance of contentment. His watchful skipper let nothing escape him; smart as his captive thought himself, the old clammer was smarter, and he knew well enough that trickery lay under that contented exterior.

He wore a grin himself as he prepared to round-to on the drift again.

"Up wit' you!" he shouted. "Take in th' jib, an' get busy again."

The sloop ran under the stern of the *Emma*, and across the bows of the *Ida*, old Charlie exchanging a hail with each that transmitted news of the catch. Clams were coming plentifully; the information was accompanied by gurgling swigs from half-empty flasks, in which all but the unwilling recruit shared.

"Can't youse ask a feller to drink?" shivered the buyer, enviously. "It's cowld, an' I ain't got much clothes on,"

"Sure," returned the skipper, replacing the cork. "This is sailor's medicine. It'd choke you. Water's good stuff to drink, and them rakes will warm you up. Get busy."

A hail carried down the wind from Tippy:

"Hey, Charlie, who's that beatin' out from the Kills?"

Charlie took a long look, picked up a slanting sliver of sail, and roared back with a grin at his shivering mate:

"That's Joe with th' *Polly*, ain't it?"

"Sure! Must be alone, I think."

Down the drift again the sloops sagged, rakes coming up full, haul after haul; the bins grew fuller and fuller; even the foxy buyer's eyes glistened with the growth of the catch. That hundred bushels began to look sure, and after all it was clams he wanted.

So the work went on. But it was hard, cruelly hard. Time after time the gale gathered force and whistled down athwart the sloops with a force that buried their lee-rails though their mainsails were spilled.

Gear cracked and masts complained; anxious eyes watched for the moment when something must part; and the parting of a rope in that breeze meant work — real sailorman's work — with more than a trifle of genuine danger.

Luck sailed with these men who had put to sea against their judgment for the purpose of helping a fellow fisherman. Time after time the danger-point was reached; as often it was passed with nothing worse than an extra thrill; and at three o'clock when the sloops came within hail at the end of a drift, the word was passed that each had topped the twenty-bushel mark. And foaming up into the fleet came the *Polly*, Skipper Joe handling her alone, hauling two rakes, sturdy and capable, but mad.

"What did you come out alone for?" roared Louie, hauling savagely on his mainsheet. "You'll have one high old time beating back."

"I know it," Joe roared back, and shook his fist at old Charlie's companion. "I heard in Danielson's what that rat was after. I had to come out. He'll get paid — two ways!"

"You betcha!" growled the others, and one by one they squared away for home.

The gale stiffened before half the distance was covered. It was the climax of a series of heavy gusts that first brought real trouble.

The *Jessie*, lying on the weather quarter of the fleet, plunged sturdily along, her keen-eyed skipper taking advantage of every let-up in the furious wind to edge nearer his mark. He had no time to watch his foxy mate; but that sorely offended individual had something of his own to watch, and his face wrinkled with anticipation as he stared long and intently at a white blur against the gray of sea and sky to leeward. A slap of the leg and a shout of jubilation brought old Charlie's attention to him at the moment when a screaming blast hove the *Ida* down and only let her up when her masthead snapped off short in the band.

The peak of her big mainsail dropped, and before she could be met with the helm her head ran off and the great boom jibed with a crash that parted the sheet.

"You laugh at that, you rat-faced pup!" swore Charlie, with glistening eyes. "By Christmas, I'll —"

"Sure I laugh at that," retorted the foxy one, grinning. "Why wouldn't I? It'll be my turn now, me lad. See that white boat? There, bound into the Kills — that's my boat — she's late — but she'll be in time to tow Tippy in, and that'll be one more of youse smart Alecks I'll have the pull on!"

He rubbed his hands, and chuckled with glee, but he had underestimated his men. Even as he spoke, the *Emma* hove to, her bateau splashed overboard, and stout Stub was pulling toward the Ida to lend a hand. And the next moment the *Jessie* came to the wind, and old Charlie growled:

"Into the bateau wit' you! Over wit' you, lively! You go and help, too, you laughing jackass! The boys will teach you seamanship properly now. Laugh, will you?"

"Aw, Charlie —"

"Over wit' you!"

The marlinespike appeared persuasively. The buyer went, his boat half full of water before he won away from the plunging side of the sloop.

A man was already at the broken masthead of the *Ida*; swinging aloft dizzily, the spar working dangerously, the man stubbornly reached the eyes of the rigging and hammered at the lower band to force it down tightly enough to carry the peak halyards.

And other able seamen attacked the broken gear, careless of the sweeping seas, oblivious of the laboring bateau painfully nearing them until old Charlie hailed them. Then Charlie Nelson got the idea.

The bateau reached within five fathoms of the sloop, her sweating oarsman pallid with fright at the seas, and out from the *Ida* flashed a clam rake on its line, to fasten with a clang on the bateau's gunwale. Some of the prongs pierced the buyer's trousers, and pinched the skin; for all his fright he was not wise enough to refrain from passing his opinion on the man who hove that rake: the next moment the rake was freed, another cast was made, and Nelson hauled the furious man in bodily with the rake.

The *Jessie* stood in close, and just astern of her came *Polly*, old Joe, single-handed though he was, eager to do his share.

Such is the way with these men: Lend an open hand to a mate; and a tight shut one to an enemy. And coming up ahead, foam to her stem-head, came the powerboat the buyer had sighted, smelling trouble and willing to be in it, at her price. She swept round in a wide arc, and as she passed the *Jessie* the pilothouse door opened a crack and the helmsman hailed:

"Got trouble, ain't she? Guess she's wanting a tow in, eh?"

"All the trouble she's in we can get her out of," roared back Charlie, gruffly. "She don't want none of your kind of help."

The man laughed harshly and shut his door, the powerboat standing on to hail the *Ida*.

Jessie and *Polly* stood after her, lines ready in case of need. But the fishermen on the disabled sloop needed no help other than their own good arms and seasoned skill; the masthead band was in place again; the peak halyards went aloft to their new station as the powerboat stopped her engine.

And the vision of more money earned by another's misfortune began to fade from the foxy little man, whose enforced labor had been brightened by the hope. All chance of a towing bill gone, his waspish temper rose again, and with the appearance of his own stout vessel his spleen burst all bonds.

"Come on, boys, an' git me out o' this!" he screamed, flinging both hands out toward the powerboat and dancing frantically at the rail. "These hoodlums have got me out here by force! Come alongside. I'll show 'em!"

The pilothouse door swung wide open, and the four men on the powerboat ran to the side to see what the trouble was. They had no deep love for their boss; but their boss he was, and he paid their wages. Still their brains could not grasp such a situation as this.

"What yuh waitin' fer?" shrieked the boss, dancing again. "I tell youse I'm a prisoner here. Come an' git —"

"Sit down quiet, you!" growled Stub, dropping out of the rigging and sitting astride the little man's neck. The buyer had lost all control now; his blood boiled, bringing all the bitter scum to the top. He struggled up fighting, and again he screamed:

"They're murderin' me, I tell youse! Pile in here an' git me out!"

The powerboat men understood at last that their boss was in real trouble. The engines were started, and the big boat nosed alongside the *Ida*. She stopped again as the boats met with a crash, and two men leaped aboard the sloop.

Now with real foes to handle Tippy and Nelson joined battle, and the *Ida's* deck was crowded with surging men. The clammers were still too many for their invaders; they took the fight as a good joke, handling the powerboat's men like children.

The buyer fought like a cat, but he was met with gibes and stiff arms like oaken beams, and he squealed orders for the other two men to jump in.

"Sure! All of youse!" he shrilled. "Never mind th' boat. She'll hurt nothin' unless it's this old ballyhoo! Come on wid youse!"

Coming up on the other side was the *Emma*; big Louie crazy to get into the frolic. And with the appearance of the full crew of the powerboat, he ranged his sloop alongside, grappled her with two rakes, and leaped aboard.

The numbers were now unequal, five against the four clammers; but the four were more than capable of holding their own, and keen old Charlie saw the opening that changed the course of the day's happenings.

The boats hung together with heavy thumps that meant no good to their timbers; the window went out of the powerboat's pilothouse with the first crash; and the scuffling men, hard put to keep their feet, threw all thoughts of the boats to the wind in the ecstasy of the fight which was already turning to the clammers' side.

Old Joe in the *Polly* hung alongside the *Jessie's* weather beam, and he ducked and scraped under his boom to try to get a sight of the scramble on the *Ida*. He had no eyes for possibilities either, until old Charlie flung at him:

"Here's your chance of a lifetime, Joe! Jam your wheel down and let *Polly* lay there. Then get your bateau, and go over and take charge of that powerboat. She's adrift, abandoned, and she's legal salvage! Beat it, Joe! I'll throw a rake into her and haul her clear."

Joe caught the idea in a flash, and as swiftly as the rake darted from the *Jessie's* side to fasten on the powerboat's rail, his bateau was hauled alongside, and he was pulling away around the seaward side of his sloop.

All in ignorance of what was being cooked for them, the powerboat's men still fought their losing fight. The buyer had been dropped into the *Ida's* hold by Louie's strong arm, and Stub kept his own particular opponent in grips on the hatch cover to keep the prisoner below. The *Jessie* gathered way by cunningly governed jerks, and wide water soon showed between sloop and powerboat.

And immediately the stretch of water was wide enough to forbid any attempt at jumping, the *Jessie* cast off, and Charlie howled to Joe;

"Now go to it, Joe! Start her up, and take her home. Well take care of these fellows who boarded the *Ida* like pirates!"

The shout drew the attention of all hands on the *Ida*, and the fight stopped. Then other shouts burst on the wind: shouts of jubilation from the clammers; howls of rage and discomfiture from the checkmated crew of the abandoned boat.

"Oh, Boy!" roared Tippy, flinging off the hatch cover. "Come up here, Mister Man, and see how you're making out!"

The buyer scrambled up, took a long look at his boat, and at the brisk figure of old Joe, even then entering the pilothouse, and sat down with a bump on the cabin-roof jabbering in helpless fury.

"Send my man back!" bawled old Charlie with a wide grin. "If you've finished wit' him, I can use him some more."

"Sure, in you go, Mister Man," urged Tippy, hoisting the buyer into the half-sinking bateau. "You go, too, Nelson, and see that he goes to the right ship. Then you may as well board the *Polly*, and take her in for Joe."

But Joe had his own notions about the *Polly*. As soon as Nelson was on board, the power-boat swung around and slipped past to take a line from the sloop; and it was Joe's tandem team that led the way back home. After having caused its share of damage, too, the gale slackened as the boats lined out, and it was no more than a good stiff working breeze that carried the fishermen into harbor with their passengers.

A wild attempt to get back with his own men brought the buyer a broken head, and when the *Jessie's* anchor was let go in the Kills, he was subdued and amenable to reason. The rest of his crew, divided among the other two sloops, were easily persuaded that they had no further business that day with clams or clammers; and one by one they were landed on the beach and departed for the village, bound for their own homes in a "foreign" port. All men not Killers or Jerseymen are foreigners.

Then old Charlie permitted his fuming mate to enter the bateau again, and together they pulled ashore and went direct to big Carl's saloon. Persuasion was needed to urge the buyer that way; but Charlie had plenty left in his bootleg, and one broken head a day is enough even for a waspish little interloper in the clam business. Besides, a marline-spike doesn't get any softer with use.

The buyer cast a last longing look at his own boat, now swinging to an anchor, deserted except for old Joe, who could be seen with his face glued against the pilothouse window gazing shoreward. Then he followed Charlie inside, and faced a crowd of grinning clammers grouped around the poker table on which lay paper, ink and a pen.

"Come up, you!" growled Stub, making a place for him. Big Carl at the bar looked on with a fat smile. "First of all bring out that bill o' sale on the *Polly!*"

"See youse further first!" snapped the buyer furiously. "What d'ye think I am anyway?"

"Come up with that paper!" urged old Charlie, playfully dropping his marlinespike for effect. The effect was good.

"Aw, honest, lads, I ain't got it. I don't carry it wit' me, an' that's true."

"You wouldn't leave it home today, when you expected to use it, yuh scab. Come up wit' it!" The marlinespike was again in sight.

"There it is!" snarled the buyer, slapping a folded paper on the table. "An' I'll have the bunch o' youse pinched if youse play any monkey business on me. I warn youse — youse, too, Danielson."

"Go ahead, boys, he can't hurt me," said big Carl, enjoying the fun.

"Nobody's goin' to get pinched," said Louie. "Here's a paper for you to sign, and that lets you out and us, too."

"I'll sign nothing!"

"Hold him, Stub," remarked old Charlie, carelessly rolling up his sleeve and gripping his spike. "Read that paper to him once, and if he don't write his name under it in five minutes I'm going to give his brain more room to grow!"

Tippy read the paper, which was a statement to the effect that the buyer relinquished all further claim on the *Polly* in consideration of services rendered to his powerboat, picked up adrift by Joe's sloop in a gale in the bay. In addition the paper stated that the buyer had made the trip in the *Jessie* of his own free will, and that all charges for his work were herewith settled by payment of one dollar in hand given.

There was a moment of mental conflict, then the pen was taken and the buyer scrawled his signature to the document, cowed by the faces about him. But in his defeat he saw a gleam of light, and he sneered up at his tormentors;

"Youse guys t'ink you're smart, don't youse? Well, let me tell youse this t'ing ain't legal. It ain't wort' two cents wuth o' crab-bait. Youse'll be stung yet."

"No we won't neither," growled Louie, itching for old Charlie's job at that marlinespike. "If ther's any question raised about this paper, you'll find there'll be a question raised about the rate of interest you charged poor old Joe. Savvee?"

"That's right, boys," agreed big Carl, beginning to set out bottles. "I know something about lending money; and that shark's got his back a dozen times."

"All right, boys, you win," smirked the foxy little man with a fine show of accepting defeat gracefully. He had still one hope of pulling at least some of his chestnuts from the cinders. "Let's all have a drink, then we'll go out and put out them clams. I'll take all youse got at the price I said."

"You can go, as soon as you like. We ain't selling to you no more," replied Tippy. And the crowd chimed in:

"No, sir!"

"Why, what's up now? Youse promised me them clams, and I'm offering top price. Come on, now, don't be hard, boys; youse have winned every t'ing else."

"We win here, too, Mister Man. There ain't no room fer th' likes o' you on a white man's beach. Better beat it."

The foxy little man turned red, then green, and looked helplessly from face to face. Then he turned to the bar, choking down his anger, and said:

"Well, no use partin' bad friends. Give us a drink, Carl."

"No drink. You've had enough," said Carl.

"Enough! Why I ain't had any! What's th' idea?"

"Not any's quite enough for th' likes of you."

"Come along, little man," advised Stub, leading him to the door by one arm. Tippy joined in, and they put the little man gently outside to a chorus:

"When you're inside, you can't be outside, When you're outside, you can't be in; When you're outside, you can't be in by a damn sight — Haw-haw!"

The foxy little loser outside turned his face toward the beach; seeking his own boat, and in his burning ears rang a roaring, triumphant —

"Haw, haw!"

MEAN AND USELESS

FROM THE moment he stepped aboard the *Wanderer* he was called useless, and there is scant indulgence shown toward the useless forecastle hand in a big windjammer. Except on the ship's articles, therefore, he possessed no other name but Useless.

The meanness was developed in him through the constant hurling in his teeth of his uselessness. Even the captain so far forgot the dignity of station as to refer to the lad, whenever he did so at all, as Useless. As for the men, his mates, if they ever hailed him by another name, it was as a son-of-a-something-or-other which was not nearly so pleasant as Useless.

"One hand for yourself, the other for the ship," is a rule born when the first yard was crossed. It may not always be adhered to; some men can never be persuaded to use a hand for themselves when two for the ship are needed aloft; but a sailor is within his rights if he holds on to a jackstay with one hand while he hauls up his portion of sail with the other, and his mates will only chaff him for it, never blame him.

But to take both hands for personal safety, while his mates sweat blood fighting a badly clewed-up sail that threatens to hurl them backward off the yard, is the crime unpardonable, and so Useless discovered now, when the weary watch came below after a bitter all-hands bout with the heavy foresail.

"Yo're useless an' a snoozer!" roared old Ted Barmer, shaking a tarry fist under the glowering delinquent's nose.

"Yus, an' dirty an' tired," added Lambeth Ike, with the indifference to accuracy often exhibited by his kind when a fellow man was being baited. Any charge, however untrue or ridiculous, was a fair weapon so long as it touched the victim on the raw.

And Useless was neither dirty nor lazy; therefore he began to chatter with rage. Another peevish able seaman, arm-weary and torn as to fingernails, growled from his corner spitefully:

"An' a bloomin' thief an' a bloody liar, too! Else where's my bacca plug gone?" There was a rasping sound, an inarticulate mouthing like the challenge of a lung-wounded but fighting ape, and Useless charged head-down upon his latest and most untruthful accuser. He was met by a sea-booted kick in the stomach which brought him up standing for a second, but failed to stop him entirely; and he rebounded from the kick and reached his man, quite unaware of the sly, hard punches and kicks bestowed upon him by the other men as he passed.

"Say, chaps," old Ted put in dryly, "y'don't want to go for to kill him afore Cardiff puts a head on him, do y' now?" He reached out a long arm which terminated in a hand like a steel claw, and hauled back an enthusiastic ordinary seaman who was taking out on Useless's unconscious back some of the discontent induced by the knowledge of his own actual superiority and his apparent inferiority as shown on the articles.

Another pair of back-slammers found old Ted's interference putting a stop to their fun, and the old chap cleared the fighting floor in time to let Useless and Cardiff get to close quarters before the young and unsatisfactory one was lammed from behind.

"That's better," growled Ted, crouching to watch. "Give th' lad a show, boys. Maybe he ain't yeller, f'r all his other complaints. Give him a chance, I says. Fair field, no favor."

Such fights are for daylight. In the murkiness of the close forecastle, dripping with steam from beams and plates, wet of floor and bunk and bag with the pervading wet of heaping seas over a battened-down interior, dancing with odorous shadows cast by a single smoky coal-oil lamp, and, above all, in the queer chill that comes with the morning watch, there was something jarring in the spectacle of a weary watch below foregoing the scanty period for sleep remaining to them in order to howl and curse at a pair of suddenly murderous fellow men.

Murderous indeed they seemed. As for Cardiff, his was simply the ferocity of the attacked loose-mouthed talker, who was ever in the habit of uttering charges and oaths without motive, never expecting to be brought to account; but Useless was fighting with the blind hate of an honest man called thief, and he beat at Cardiff's scowling face with both hands, muttering under his breath through clenched teeth, heedless of the fists and knees that hammered heavily at his own nervous body.

"By Cripes! th' lad's game!" chuckled old Ted.

Cardiff had smashed a fist into his foe's tight-lipped mouth, hurling him violently against the heel of the great steel bowsprit; and Useless came again, more ferociously than ever, silent now, seeing red, only to meet a vicious jolt that sent him headlong across a bunk into the midst of the occupant's little stores collection. A tobacco tin half full of black sugar spilled itself over the damp blanket; a bully beef tin holding a smear of oily butter helped to complete the mess; a stone jar contributed a streak of marmalade; and the fragments of the shattered vessel resounded with a clang against the ship's unsheathed skin.

The tumult of shouting and cursing suddenly stopped with the fall of Useless; men started to climb into their bunks; old Ted stepped to the lamp to turn it down; but the fight was not over. Out of the mess he had created crawled Useless, a fleck of foam at his lips, his eyes glassy and unwinking. In his hand he gripped a ragged shard of pottery, part of the marmalade jar, and like a jungle beast he leaped upon Cardiff as that conquering hero bent down to arrange his bed.

Before the fearsome weapon fell Useless's arms were pinned to his sides, and in his ringing ears old Ted's voice shrilled:

"Hey! None o' that, my buckaroo! Drop it, quick! Blast yer mean hide, but I almost thought y'd make a man yet, th' way y' was scrappin', an' now y' got to try to murder a man wi' a pottery dagger, by Jasus!"

"Let me go!" screamed the maddened Useless. "I'll kill him!"

"Yes, y' won't," grunted Ted, throwing the lad with an old-time crossbuttock. Swiftly and expertly he took the piece of broken jar from the lad, rolled him over, and lifted him into his bunk. Then, leaning down with his grizzled head close to the other's face, he told him in scathing terms exactly where he had placed himself in the eyes of men.

"An' for the future, me boy, you eat by y'rself, see?" he concluded coldly. "Don't never try to butt in when men 're talkin', an' keep y'rself out o' my way, savvee? F'r a man I got use; f'r half a man I kin find excuses if so be he tries to act man-fashion; but f'r a dirty, low-down, murderin' broken-bottle scrapper I ain't got no more use than I have f'r a rotten gasket. Ye're outlawed, savvee?"

So the verdict went, and Useless, baited and bullied into that frenzy of fighting though he had been, began his period of suffering which was to nearly sap his reason before it ended.

At first he rebelled against the injustice of it all. He had not shipped as an able seaman of his own free will. Had he done that, his mates would have had complete reason for detesting him, for a man doing such a thing, knowing all the while his own incapacity for the work, deliberately places upon every one of his shipmates the burden of a share of the work he ought to do. And he draws pay for his inability at the same rate as they add his share to their own for.

Even Useless could see that, long before that eventful night when a call for all hands resulted in his humiliation. But he had been shipped at the hands of a shipping agent along with the rest of the crew, being supplied to the skipper as an able seaman of sail when all he expected, or sought, was a chance to work a passage in a steamer to any port offering better chances for work than his home afforded.

So he cared little when the mate took him aft one day to interview the captain, and he found himself disrated to ship's boy, at boy's wages.

"That's what I want, sir," he told the captain seriously, and went forward feeling glad that now perhaps his mates would admit him to their fellowship on his true basis, and leaving behind him two amazed superiors who stared first at each other, then after him, shaking heads gravely as at a lunatic.

"Said he wanted to be a boy, on boy's wages!" the mate told the second greaser when relieving him later on, and both enjoyed a chuckle; but altogether the result was that Useless was given real boy's work and left pretty much to himself by the officers thereafter.

But it made no difference forward. He now had to fetch and carry for the men, clean out the forecastle, and wait until every man had eaten before taking his share of the leavings; but all his willingness, his anxiety to please, his rigid cleanliness in the matter of mess-kids and floors, brought him no recognition beyond a curse or a wanton bespattering of his freshly scrubbed deck with tobacco juice. In desperation he made an advance against old Ted's armor of contempt, for the old man had been less brutal toward him before that unlucky episode of the broken jar.

"Son, me an' you don't savvee the same parleyvoo," was old Ted's retort, uttered with a steely glance of eye and a downward turn of the mouth. "Out where we're goin' now, in 'Paraiso, now, there's knifers an' bottle-throwers as might like your sort."

"I'm not that sort!" cried the tormented youngster. "You know they badgered me until — "

"Can't make a man use a broken bottle unless 't is in his natur, my bully," retorted Ted, with cutting emphasis, and left Useless where he stood, almost ready to take the rail for that vast depth of blue profundity over the side wherein he saw the peace denied him by his fellows.

But a time came when he no longer thought of those overside depths in such somber mood. As part of her cargo, the *Wanderer* carried two big discarded naval steam pinnaces, purchased by the harbor board of the port the ship was bound to. These craft were carried on deck, one on each side of the house, taking up rather too much of the deck room, but leaving sufficient room for handling the gear at the expense of a little profanity.

In the hot, all but windless days between trades, when the decks were baking torture to bare feet, and rails and rigging scorched the hands, the mate conceived the brilliant notion of putting Useless to work cleaning out and overhauling the two pinnaces. It was a piece of thoughtfulness likely, at first sight, to prove more gratifying to the owners of the craft than to Useless.

But, strangely enough, the lad found interest in the job which raised him far above the discomfort of heat and grease and dirt. His face assumed a glow and a smile for the first time in weeks when his first day's work was done and he scrubbed himself clean in salt water before carrying along the kid of dry hash for his watch-mates.

"There's a real electric plant in those boats," he told them eagerly, standing aside, as insisted upon, while they ate. The hungry jaws champed and chewed with ox-like stolidity; not a man gave him a glance; his electric plant might as well have been a century plant for the interest they took in his announcement.

Not a word was spoken in answer. He glanced down at slouching backs and hunched shoulders, at averted faces, and moved away to hide the flush of shame that rose to his cheeks.

He made no further attempt to break through the cruel barrier erected against him. His work in the two pinnaces kept him busy from turn-to until sweep-up; and after that hour, too, when the donkeyman, who was carried in the ship to take care of the hoisting engine and winches, began to amuse himself with the pinnaces' engines for lack of other essential work. Then hours were stretched without limit, for the donkeyman, Jaggers, was one of those rare creatures, a mechanical devotee without any mechanical instinct.

Work he could, work he did, according to book, strictly and unswervingly; but no trace of originality dwelt in his brain to advise him what to do when the machine refused to turn and all was apparently right with it. In Useless he found a surprising helpmate, the more surprising because of the perfectly well-known reason that had earned him his unpleasant name. It was Useless who by simply straightening the rod of an eccentric caused a pump to perform its duty after the donkeyman had spent a whole sizzling day futilely packing and repacking perfect gaskets. And it was Useless who, hidden away in the pinnace, collected batteries and wires, bits of brass and odds and ends of the small steamboat's lighting plant, and constructed a workable electric fan which he quietly installed in the reeking forecastle while his mates slept in perspiring uneasiness.

Not a word of notice did it bring him. At the change of the morning watch, when both watches were passing in and out of the dark den which his ingenuity had made endurable, he tinkered with the fan quietly, unobtrusively, with the unspoken pride of the creator in his work. A heavy blow on the ear bowled him over and upset his fan.

"Quit foolin' wi' that blarsted whirligig an' go git the hash!" howled Cardiff, and a booted foot doubled up the blades of the fan with a crash.

Dumbly, Useless obeyed. He ate no hash himself; but while the rest wolfed their breakfast he picked up the damaged fan, crept to his own bunk, and silently went to work to repair it. He forgot that he ought to be on deck; as boy, he worked from six to six, all day without a spell save for meals and the cleaning up after them; and a mate, sore and peevish from days of finicky breezes that barely kept the log-line straight, came to seek him. He found him, crouched in the dark corner where his squalid bed lay, athrill again to the soft whir of the repaired fan.

"Come out of that, you!" the officer growled, seizing Useless savagely. Then he noticed the fan, felt the cooler air, and peered closely into the vague dimness of the bunk.

"Oh! so that's the game, hey? A skulkin' thief! Here, fetch that gadget along to the captain. He'll be tickled to know why the donkeyman couldn't make them engines go."

Useless went aft in a daze, carrying his precious fan in hands that trembled with anger.

The skipper regarded him blackly.

"Been stealing fittings to make that plaything. Hmm!" he said. "Well, my man, you seem hopeless as well as useless. Stowed away below when you ought to be at your work, hey? Mr. Stokes," he suggested to the scowling mate, "take him on deck and tie him up to the mizzen sheerpole. A taste o' rope end may do him good!"

Useless was flogged. He made no whimper, offered no protest; when set free he resumed his work with the stolid patience of a laden mule, his lips close shut, his eyes burning, a ghastly chill creeping into his heart. Men jeered about him and his manner of taking a flogging, but not at him, only among themselves in his hearing.

His life in the forecastle was rather less bearable than that of a slave at a galley-oar. Even his work in the steam pinnaces was forbidden him, lest, as the mates took care to let him know, he steal the engines next.

For weeks he endured — weeks of equatorial misery, more weeks of biting winds and sweeping seas off the Falkland Isles — and he wondered if he would forget the art of speech before the deadly voyage was done. In the saloon he knew they had set his fan to work, and, while the hot weather lasted, he nursed the hope that he might be called aft to explain about storage batteries when the fan ceased revolving. But the cool days came just when the batteries ran out, and the fan was no longer needed. That brief interval when they would have to let him speak was denied him. There was not even a ship's pet, cat, dog, or monkey, to which he might whisper his troubles.

Then came the bitter gale which later settled down into the stubborn westerlies such as keep ships beating off the bleak Horn for weeks at a time. But Useless was fated never to experience the supreme misery of a forecastle under such conditions.

The gale struck down with a shrieking snow squall that blotted out sea and sky and made the ship a treacherous, slippery thing of horror. The snow fell wet, and froze where it lay, rendering rigging and sails, decks and ladders, a picture of cruel beauty. It did more. It froze clew lines and buntlines stiff, and transformed flapping canvas into crackling sheets of inflexible devilishness.

Men on the fore and main upper topsail-yards cursed and fought the malevolent devils that bad gotten into the sails; and on the poop an anxious captain watched nervously a blacker blast sweeping down from windward.

The mate was hoarse with cursing; the second mate was already where good second mates should be at such times — at the bunt of the main topsail. And the great sails, imperfectly clewed up by reason of rigidly frozen lines, billowed high above the yards, offering capacious bags, wide-mouthed, to the coming blast.

"My God!" yelled the skipper frantically. "Can't you get those sails rolled up?"

The mate leaped down the ladder and into the fore rigging. They needed a man aloft there. Useless, contemptuously left on deck with the cook and steward to give a pull on buntlines when howled at to do so, shivered with cold and sickness, hanging on to the fiferail with numbed hands.

"On deck there!" yelled the skipper suddenly. "Hang on for your lives! Up with you — into the rigging!"

Close aboard over the weather-rail roared the crest of a mile-long graybeard. It curled, hovered, then crashed down on the staggering deck, while aloft the main-topsail exploded with a crack and flew in streamers to leeward. At the same moment the foretopsail parted from the jackstay and flapped over downward like a cut eyebrow; a man's shriek was echoed by a hoarse chorus, and a body hurtled through the flying squall to crash in a huddled heap on the forecastle head.

Useless clung terrified to the mizzen-stay, his legs flung around the wire high above his head. At the cry from aloft he tried to make out what had happened; but the snow was flying thickly. He was permitted no time for idling then; the ship, relieved of the mighty pressure aloft, came slowly to the wind and was hove-to, and by the time he had got through hauling on braces, mid-deep in freezing water, he was barely able to slink forward to his cold, wet bunk along with the rest who were entitled to go below.

Then he was conscious of a terrific ache at his chest. Opening his shirt, he found his entire chest bruised black. The injury, got he knew not how, reminded him of that dark body he had seen hurled down from aloft, and then he realized that the men were talking of the accident in lowered, awed tones.

"Broke up like a mashed boat on the rocks, th' mate was," growled old Ted. "Felt like a shirt full o' bits, he did!"

"Dead?" Cardiff blared.

"Good as. Merrikle might mend him, but there don't no merrikles happen these days. Cap'n says to me, 'Lay 'im in 'is berth, Barmer, gentle as you can, me lad, for I doubt as he'll weather th' Horn this trip."

Useless listened with a shudder. So it was the mate, then, and as good as dead if not actually killed by his terrible fall. The pain at his own breast seemed paltry in face of the mate's injuries; he tried hard to ignore it; stifling his impulse to go to the captain for advice — he believed his breastbone must be broken at least — he suffered in silence, physically, just as he had mentally the whole voyage through.

But his determination could not blind him to the fact that, before dawn, his breath whistled and his lungs seemed to be stabbed by a hundred red-hot needles.

So unbearable did his agony grow toward noon that when the crew were ordered to stand by in what security they could find on deck, he crawled into the pinnace last finished, pulled the cover over again, and crouched down in the tiny fore-cabin to sob despairingly. Gradually numbness crept over him, and he dozed. He dozed through those wild hours when the ship was filled away again in the mad endeavor to boat up to the Falklands and land the mate; and the sleep did him good in a measure, for it gave his troubled brain a rest which it had been unable to secure in the cold and dreary atmosphere of the forecastle.

He awoke when the ship, going about in the teeth of the howling gale, flung him heavily against the restricted walls of his little retreat. When the ship seemed to be safely on the other tack, plunging madly but surging forward, he raised the cover and started to climb down to the deck.

Then he was aware of two men standing on the midship-house above him, and one was the second mate.

He drew back, and was forced to listen.

"We won't make it," the officer was saying. "It's decent of the old man to risk straining this ship to give Mr. Stokes a chance; but y' see where we got that last tack. The islands ain't more than twenty miles away, but it's dead thrashin' and we daren't carry sail enough to hold her to it. Might as well bear away."

"Don't find many skippers who'd try it, sir," said the other man, and the voice was old Ted's. "If so be there's a chance for th' mate's life, it's a shame to gi' up, I says. Them steamboats, now — ain't they *pukka* navy craft? Able to live in a sea? S'pose, now, as you was to git Donkey to fire one of 'em up, like? I reckon as I'd take a chance at makin' Stanley, if so be y' could hi'st her over with all of the crew aboard, an' Mr. Stokes snug in the little cabin, sir."

The second mate clawed his way aft along the monkey-bridge without replying, and old Ted followed him, his gruff voice rumbling like a bear's as he drove his argument home.

Useless hurried forward, for the darkness warned him that it was evening at any rate, and he had a meal to carry and a quite possible ragging for being late, no matter what excuse the vile weather gave him.

His lucky star shone out for once. He dumped the kid and kettle down exactly on time, and for once, too, he found himself unchecked when his throbbing chest urged him to take his pannikin of tea before his time.

The hot fluid soothed his pain, and the men were too weary, too sore, to notice him at all. So, not feeling hungry, and having drunk his tea as soon as any, Useless was first out of the forecastle when the slide was hammered lustily and old Ted's stormy bellow overwhelmed the wind:

"All hands! Tumble up, lads! Shake a leg!"

At his heels the men stumbled. He felt proud in his being first to answer the call. Then a fit of coughing seized him, and the men swept past, leaving him spitting blood on the streaming deck. But he fought off his spasm, and when the crew gathered in a huddled mob at the midship-house, around the second mate, Useless was with them.

"Men," the officer yelled, "I want one more volunteer to man this little steamboat. The donkeyman'll go to 'tend the fire and drive her, and Banner's willing to take her to Stanley to save the mate's life.

"It's only eighteen miles. It'll take the ship days to beat up that much to windward; the steamboat can make it in three hours at most. It's a hard trip. P'r'aps she won't make it; p'r'aps even if she does, the mate'll be dead when she gets there. But there's a chance, and I need one more man to spell Barmer and keep lookout. A volunteer. Who's man enough? You, Cardiff?"

"Me? Huh, I can't swim!" growled Cardiff, taking a less prominent position in the crowd.

The donkeyman was already in the little steamer, taking up coal which the cook handed him in buckets from the galley bunker. A thin streak of smoke whirled from the brass smokestack, and old Ted Barmer was busy rigging a span by which to hoist the boat overboard.

Useless involuntarily pushed forward; but the black, hungry seas roaring past the ship frightened him to sickness. The cold, wet darkness turned his blood to ice water. There was a moment of anxious waiting in which no man spoke.

Then old Ted finished his job with a furious tug. Finally he stepped forward and growled:

"Never mind more hands, sir! While these woolly lambs are screwin' up their pluck, Mr. Stokes is a dyin'. Donkey an' me'll go, sir, if you'll have Mr. Stokes put aboard. I'll get yard-an'-stay tackles ready to swing her out meantime, sir."

The ship was hove-to again, and lay almost broadside on to the seas. Her weather side was thundering with tons of icy water, but under her lee was a space of comparative smooth. Men aloft rigged tackles in a darkness which rendered them invisible from the deck. Old Ted was somewhere about the little steamboat, his presence known only by the hearty oaths with which he hurled out impedimenta which could only clog his movements when, if ever, he got clear of the swooping ship's side.

Then he leaped down to the deck, for a lantern bobbing along from aft showed the steward and the second mate, with two seamen, carrying the stricken mate to his last chance.

"Here," the old sailor shouted, seizing the nearest man; "hop up there and see th' fore-cabin's all clear for Mr. Stokes!"

Useless cringed under the fierce grip, and obeyed. He knew just where that little cabin was — right forward, entered by a tiny scuttle — for he had made it his snuggery that very day. It was black dark down there, dark and close; and he recalled with a pang that the vital parts of the boat's electric plant had gone to make that unlucky fan.

Groping, he placed the leather cushions on the floor between the lockers, and by so doing performed one of the few perfect acts of his seafaring career; for when the mate was laid there it was impossible for him to move sidewise; he was secured against the worst the boat could do in the way of rolling.

While busy, Useless heard men shouting for tackles to be lowered; he heard thudding feet overhead, on the deck of the small steamboat, he could hear the clang of the donkeyman's shovel in the little stoke-hole, then came the flickering lanterns, and the sea-booted legs of the foremost bearer of the sick man.

Useless stood on the side locker, crouching low under the beams, to allow the bearer to pass; he remained there, his head and shoulders above the circle of light, while Mr. Stokes was placed on his mattress; then the lantern was hung to a beam, the bearers mounted the narrow iron ladder, and Useless followed in a panic of fright, for old Ted's voice roared to the men at the tackles to sway away the moment his own feet touched the wheel-platform, leaving any others there might be to get out as best they could. To that extent had the hanging back of volunteers irritated the grim old seaman who was ready to take the chance himself.

In the bitter wind that beat upon his face as he rose through the scuttle, in the howling wilderness of the black night, Useless suddenly found his limbs fail him. Halfway in, halfway out, he swung by the elbows with his legs adrift in mid air, losing the ladder. His chest was a shooting agony; there was a definite streak of ice-cold flesh running from his heart direct to every one of his digit ends. He seemed to be suddenly stricken with paralysis. And high above him he heard the shrill squeal of the tackles; beneath him the pinnace swayed and bumped as it rose out of the stout wooden cradle in which it had been stowed.

Men yelled unintelligible words, which nevertheless meant something. Aft, the captain watched ship and launching with a keen, seamanly eye, megaphone in hand; and when the steamboat hung over the sweeping seas, in a moment of comparative smooth, his voice pealed out with a note not to be hesitated upon.

"Lower away handsomely! Stand by to cut the bridle! Lower — lower — lively! Let go!"

With a roar and a crash, the steamboat struck the water, and old Ted sprang to cut the rope. The ship swung dizzily above them, threatening destruction, and water spurted in a great columnar jet between the two craft, half filling the small one.

Then Useless found speech and movement through stark fright. He stumbled out on to the dizzy, narrow deck and yelled incoherently, reaching out his hands toward the streaming iron sides of the ship. Somebody reached down to him, put a knife into his hand, and bellowed at him encouragingly:

"Bully f'r you, old ship, whoever y' are! Here, cut loose, quick!"

And old Ted, slashing through the after bridle, staggered along to the wheel, and bawled at him too:

"That's you, old hoss! Cut her, quick!"

Into the tube to the engine-room he shrieked to the donkeyman:

"Full ahead, Donkey, an' give 'er 'ell!'"

Like an automaton Useless crawled forward and cut the remaining part of the rope bridle, and the steamboat moved away from the threatening ship's hull. The last thing Useless remembered was a tremendous voice — it was the skipper with his megaphone — warning old Ted to watch a northerly set of current.

"Keep her head at west by south, and that'll make the light!" was the last word. Then the pinnace plunged into the blackness of the wild night, her sharp stem burying her forward deck in the freezing seas, the bitter spray volleying like shot against old Ted's red face above the weathercloth.

Useless started instinctively to close down the slide over the forecabin. The boat dived deep, a sea swept him from his feet, leaving him hanging desperately by his fingers to the coaming, and shut the slide for him, smashing two fingers and wrenching his wrist. Dumbly he groped his way to where old Ted swayed grimly at the wheel, and as their bodies touched, and the old seaman glanced around, the faint light in the binnacle illumined Useless's pallid, frightened face.

"Oh, my Gawd! Is it you?"

The greeting was more than so many words, however punctuated. It expressed with terrible brevity old Ted's hope that his as yet unknown mate was a capable volunteer; it expressed his utter disappointment and deepest disgust; and if words can strike, that exclamation struck Useless between the eyes for his very uselessness.

Ted Banner never uttered another word in condemnation. He simply held fast to the wheel, disdaining to as much as ask the other man to spell him while he filled his covered pipe with plug. And mile by mile the boat battled onward, leaping half her length out of the water at times when she rose after a plunge into the breast of a comber which all but buried her. Grimly old Ted held her to her course, peering through the murk for a flash of the Falkland lights; and down in the sizzling belly of the boat the donkeyman battled as fiercely amid stinging cinders and scalding steam, flung from side to side, stifled with ashes, and all but roasted with the heat of the tiny, shut-down engine and stokehole in one. For the square hatch, left open for ventilation at first, he had shut perforce to keep the sea out. The cowls on deck he dare not turn to the wind, for the blast would have torn them out of their rings.

How the sick man was progressing down below, all alone, none knew, nor could find out. It was more than the lives of all were worth to open that scuttle now. And, as if to warn old Ted that his stubborn fight might prove futile even at that point, the gale shrieked afresh, the seas gathered savage weight. Once, twice, many times he met a roaring sea on the bow, and thus saved the boat from diving and sweeping her narrow decks. But there came one hissing comber which gave him no time to meet it. He saw it coming.

"Hold on, f'r Gawd's sake!" he roared, and gripped the wheel in desperation, bowing his head to the torrent about to crash down upon him. Where Useless was he didn't know. At that moment he didn't care much either. If the lad hadn't sense enough to hang on for himself, well —

Useless had crouched down just abaft the wheel grating, against the warm engine-room casing, where the hot iron sent a grateful glow to his chilled bones. He felt less frightened there, too, for he could not see the wild ocean rising ahead. When he caught sight of a sea it was roaring past him, all power for harm gone with it. But something in that yell of old Ted's warned him of the unusual, and he clung frantically to the edge of the hatch and waited breathlessly.

Down crashed the sea. Old Ted uttered a choking sputter that changed immediately to a howl of defiance as his grizzled old head emerged from the sea and he found the boat still unharmed. Behind him, Useless's cry of fright was drowned in the whirling sea that covered him. But both men, the useful and the useless, survived with equal immunity; thus is the sea impartial.

Something there was, however, which broke off Ted's yell in his throat. No man was farther from his thoughts that moment than Useless. The terrific fact that struck him to the roots of his stout old soul was the abrupt stopping of the engines. Inevitably the boat lost way, refused to answer her helm, threatened to roll broadside in the trough of the sea. Fiercely Ted howled down the engine-room tube; his ear caught no answer except a dull reverberation which might have been an angry man's soulful swearing, or the protest of machinery.

"Give us headway there, Donkey! F'r Gawd's own sake give —"

Then his alert eye caught sight of the elder brother to that great sea just passed, and, in despair of the boat ever surviving this new assault shorn of her vital power, he yelled again, instinctively:

"Hold on all! Hang on f'r y' lives!"

Vaguely, just as the sea covered his head, he heard the clang of the hatch behind him, and took a hand from his hold to wave a warning back to the donkeyman to keep below. Then the sea came.

The pinnace quivered like a stricken animal; for a full minute the sea rushed over her, loath to quit her unconquered. But she crept out from under the smothering weight again, and, if only she would move ahead, old Ted knew he could keep her afloat in spite of such seas. That was just what she would not do — move ahead. He yelled again down the tube.

"Just a minute!" came back the answer in a voice muffled as if by dense steam.

Ted glanced at the casing around the funnel; steam seeped up through every crack. But to his anxious ear, again clapped to the tube, came the assurance:

"Hold on just a minute, Ted. She'll go ahead in a minute."

"Get a move on then!" yelled Ted impatiently. "Ye're nigh as useless as that —"

He stopped abruptly, for suddenly came the thought that poor Useless had gone out on the crest of that last vicious sea.

"Hadn't no business to come to sea, 'e hadn't," he muttered, a little subdued. "Now 'e's gone, an' no bloomin' steam to go look f'r him even if we 'ad time, which we ain't."

He grew impatient again at thought of the injured man lying below, shut in, unable to help himself, unable to make himself heard however much he needed aid. And Falkland lights were still beyond that black veil ahead.

"Come on, Donkey!" Ted roared down the tube. "Give 's a kick ahead, man, 'less ye want th' blessed boat to rowl over wi' us all! Pore Useless is —"

Again his speech was halted abruptly, for underfoot he felt the quiver of the engines, in the darkness over the bows he saw spray flung aloft as the boat began to move again; and now he felt master of the sea and all its hosts of storm and current, for the steamboat gained speed, steered as he wanted her, and almost before he had straightened her out on the proper course he detected a faint white shaft of light against a blacker mass of darkness right ahead.

"Glory be!" he howled, defying the storm. "We'll save y' yet, Mr. Stokes!"

In an hour the pinnace glided swiftly over the sheltered waters of Port Stanley, and came to a halt with the last impulse of a speed which had imperceptibly slackened for half an hour past. She had just way enough to carry her alongside of the landing nearest the hospital, and old Ted wiped the spray from his eyes as an official stepped down to learn his errand.

"Poor old Donkey!" he muttered with a crooked grin, for he was tired himself. "Betcha it wasn't no bloomin' picnic down below f'r 'im, nei-ther!"

Then he turned to answer the official's inquiry, and in a few minutes more saw the mate carried on a stretcher toward the hospital.

Not till then did he think it queer that the donkeyman had not opened up the hatch for air. A fearful doubt assailed him. He opened the square hatch with a clang, was almost suffocated by the infernal reek of steam and ash and scorched clothes, and — and something which he could not place at once, but which sent fear direct to his heart.

He dropped down below, peered through the murk; and in a minute he was back on deck and his lusty roar went after the hospital men:

"Hi! Sawbones! You 'orspital chaps! Fetch back a doctor right quick! Yes, f'r me; an' send a *pukka* doctor, too!"

Then he dropped on to the floor plate of the tiny fire and engine room, the steam beginning to condense as the icy air rushed in, and knelt between two prostrate figures beside the engine.

Steam, leaking with diminishing volume from a steam-pipe, led his gaze toward the cause of that first stoppage of the engines and the reason for his ability to carry on. The main pipe had burst; around it now was a clumsy bandage of rags and canvas, waste and asbestos packing, just effi-cient enough to have carried the boat to her destination. And on the floor was the answer to the rest of the riddle.

Jaggers, the donkeyman, lay farthest from the open fire, his ban-daged head on his dungaree jacket. His arms, face, and breast were cov-ered with wads of waste dripping with oil; a corner, cautiously raised, showed old Ted great raw scalds and blistered flesh. But an anxious ear, placed at the raw chest, revealed a heartbeat strong enough to give hope.

Then there lay Useless, one hand clutching his shirt as if in intoler-able agony, the other fast gripped on the handle of a shovel, which, burned off at the blade, still lay red and cooling in the smoldering cinders of the fire.

The lad was fearfully disfigured with burns and scalds; two shape-less, bleeding fingers and a black, bruised wrist, and a terrible purple dis-coloration that covered his entire breast, told a story of dogged courage which opened the rimed eyes of old Ted Barmer.

How the lad got down there was a mystery to the seaman, who was satisfied that Useless had gone to his end far back along the roaring waste astern. But he detected a faint flutter of the eyelids, and a quiver of the drawn lips of the lad, just as the footsteps of the returning hospital medico sounded above him. Eagerly he bent low to Useless's lips.

"Don't blame me, Ted," the whisper came almost inaudibly. "I ran away from that last big sea. It scared me, Ted. I couldn't help it. It was so dark, so cold, and — so warm — down here."

The doctor dropped beside the old seaman, glanced down at the two prone figures, and stated briskly:

"That chap may pull around, thanks to whoever clapped those oily rags onto him; but this young chap's a gone goose, old man. Give me a hand. We'll take 'em both up to the hospital for you, and see to the burying of this one. You've brought us more work than we've had in a year, and with luck we can save two out of the three. Another twenty-four hours' delay, and Mr. Stokes would have been a box of bones, too. You saved his life, even though he may be a cripple."

He stooped to take up Jaggers's head, and nodded to Ted.

"Not so much hurry about the other one," he remarked. "What's his name, by the way? Have to register him for burial, I suppose."

Old Ted scratched his grizzled head. He laid down the donkeyman's feet, which he had lifted, and scowled darkly at the doctor whose greater experience with the Grim Reaper permitted him to refer to death so lightly.

"Mr. Sawbones, I be damned if I ever heared his name," he said slowly. "We called 'im by a name aboard th' *Wanderer* as I'll smash down th' throat o' th' next man as uses it, savvee? But this yere I knows: That young chap may ha' been useless as a bloomin' deck-hand, but soon's he dropped down yere among machinery he saved Donkey's worthless life fust, then he saved mine, saved th' blessed boat, and saved the life o' th' fust mate as flogged 'im, an' now goes an' slips 'is blessed cable in a Gawd-forgotten 'ole like this!"

The doctor looked mildly impressed; but such instances of humble heroism were not exactly rare in the coming and going of ships that fared Cape Hornwards, and, besides, there were two living men who might yet be kept alive.

"It's sometimes good to die with a record like that," he said, again lifting Jaggers and motioning to Ted to raise the other end. "But it's too bad we shall have to register and bury a plucky chap like that under a number."

"You wait, mister," growled Ted, lifting his burden at last. "You kin git his name from th' ship when she heaves-to off th' port to pick me an' th' steamboat up. If so be as you ain't got time, like, and Use — and you has to plant th' lad by number, just make it No.1, see? An' you see as there's a bit of a mark set at th' head, like — I'll send th' money for It from 'Paraiso — and 'ave this yere wrote on it, see?

"No.1 of ship *Wanderer*. A fust-class sailor, an' a bloomin' 'ero, an' Ted Barmer says so to all hands."

"I'll have it seen to," replied the doctor shortly, and shook his head gently at the old chap's bowed back as he strode ahead, as if smitten with doubts as to his sanity. But the albatross which carried the departed spirit of Useless, flying close overhead, heard and understood.

THE COOLIE SHIP

I

WHEN CARDS FALL WRONG

PAST FORT William rolled the Hugli, a turbid, inscrutable stream, bearing in its bosom the spiritual hopes of dead men's relatives and the hoped-to-be-forgotten secrets of dead men's murderers. Some of the secrets might by chance be revealed to the light of day on a sand-bar, before the waters were merged in the Bay of Bengal; the rest would be hidden by the God of Waters until the sea should give up its dead.

Douglas Sheldon, late captain in a Bengal regiment, brooded from the esplanade of the Citadel upon the mighty stream, for he saw therein a symbol of his own fortunes. His failure to meet a debt of honor contracted over the card table — not the first of its kind — had resulted in the cutting short of his service career, and in a consequent bitterness of spirit which knew no discrimination as to its object.

Down that river Sheldon knew he was bound to travel. India held nothing for him, as a white man, save the eternal shame of the pointed finger and the whispered reference to his affairs. He was young enough to be sensitive. He could not face life in the East. He shrank from the ordeal of traveling home by one of the regular mail steamships, where home-going Indian officials of his own race would recognize him, and would knew his story.

Douglas Sheldon was not a bad man, although some people might have thought him a foolish one. His crime, in the eyes of society, was that he was unsuccessful. Like many of his brother officers, he had gone the pace, but, in his case, the cards had turned against him. Gambler's luck!

In accordance with time-honored custom, an army officer who could not pay his gambling debts must resign. Gambling of itself was considered one of the pastimes of an officer and a gentleman. Society would applaud a winner, but it tabooed a loser, especially when he had plunged beyond his depth.

Douglas Sheldon was now experiencing the pangs of remorse, and in his hypersensitive state of mind he was inclined to rail against the society from which he had been shut out and the temptation to which he had succumbed.

It seemed to him that there was little left in life. Without money, friends, or reputation, his future presented a cloudy prospect in his distorted imagination.

"Pride of race!" he muttered, flipping the stub of his cheroot into the yellow water. "Pride of race! For two *pice* I'd paint myself with furniture polish and go 'fantee'!"

"Going fantee" was, in Sheldon's case, merely an expression fitting his mood of the moment. His real desire was to get out of Calcutta as fast as ship could take him, and his choice of ships was limited. There were vessels aplenty in the river, but when the mail steamers and other steamers bound home by way of Suez had been discarded as possibilities for reasons before stated, his selection narrowed down to the occasional sailing ships with various destinations.

Aimlessly he took the road leading to the Kidarpur Docks. He had a hazy idea of having at some time read of somebody in much the same situation as himself, who had shipped for home before the mast in a square-rigger, survived the experience, and found material for a vivid book dealing with the sea and sailors. This book, written from the inside, brought its author sufficient fame to persuade him to make further literary efforts. By grasping at such a straw, this soldier-sailor-author carved out a new profession for himself and became a man again.

"Who knows?" mused Sheldon, his eye involuntarily becoming critical as he sent an inquiring glance over a tier of four great clippers in the river. "At any rate, there's romance in the reek of the cargoes going into those ships. Tea, indigo, jute, shellac, silks — going where? On the winds, sure enough; and when they drop their pilots out in the bay, they're out of the world for months, until they suddenly pop up somewhere flying the pilot-jack for home."

He continued on to the end of the docks with less aim than before, but his mind was made up for a passage somewhere in one of those clippers. He wandered past other ships now, merely for the purpose of seeing them all, before making his final choice. Reaching the last one loading, he suddenly found something which nailed his interest.

Here was a ship indeed — a great, full-rigged ship of two thousand tons, smart as paint could make her, yet without that trimness aloft, either of furled sails or idle gear, that had characterized the other sailing ships he had seen. Sheldon stood beside a lumbering wagon, full to capacity with all sorts of personal baggage, and stared with wonder at the teeming life aboard the big ship.

The strange goods going into the yawning holds puzzled him. Where other vessels had gorged freights of country produce for use in the white man's land, this ship, the *Orestes*, engulfed vast tonnage of native food-stuffs, native cloths, mats, rugs, pots, and the hundred other things necessary to the support of a native community. As he watched, from behind him came the indescribable babel of sound that accompanies a gang of coolies. The sound of pattering bare feet dulled the voices, and, rank upon rank, an army of brown men surged along the dock to halt, at a harsh command, at the foot of the gangway. Other brown men, but of commanding aspect, appeared at the ship's rail and directed the horde below.

A silence fell, and presently the crowding coolies filed in orderly procession up the sloping gangway to the deck.

For all his years in India, this was Sheldon's first sight of a coolie ship. In a vague way he knew that some of his people, whose incomes were drawn from the West Indies, professed a keen interest in the health and prosperity of the Hindu working man; but it had never occurred to him that there was any regular traffic in coolie labor from the East to the West Indies.

As the brown men filed upwards in seemingly endless procession, another point was forced upon his notice. He turned to the stolid driver of the baggage wagon for enlightenment.

"Where are they going?" he asked. "Why do they take their women? Don't they ever come back?"

"If Allah is good, perhaps, *sahib*. Who knows?" returned the native indifferently, shrugging his shoulders. "Ship, he go for Demerara — very bad place, *sahib*. Some coolie die; some run away; some stay many years and no want come back. Maybe some came back. I not know, *sahib*."

"Demerara!" muttered Sheldon under his breath, "The land of Roraima and El Dorado; of gold and of diamonds; impenetrable jungles teeming with game; the country of the Caribs and Arawacks; the land of discontented negroes and renegade Portuguese."

A wild, romantic vision flashed through his brain. His eyes were busily scanning every detail of the ship and her thronging passengers; he sought in vain for a crew, as he understood the term. Of white men he had seen eight at most, and four of these might better be called boys.

He heard the shrilling of a *serang's* pipe, and followed the sound, for he expected to see sailors appear in answer. But a swarm of linen-clothed Lascars responded to the pipe. Clambering like monkeys into the rigging, they took up stations in the tops and along the yards, while other brown men on deck proceeded to send up some of the lighter sails which were still not bent.

"A Lascar crew!" he mused. "Three hundred coolie men and two hundred of their women; there must be thousands already in the country; and not a dozen white men all told in the ship. Lord, what possibilities! A determined man might seize that ship and found an empire — if only he had a few rifles!"

II
DREAMS OF EMPIRE

SHELDON LAUGHED outright at his own conceit. The notion had flashed upon him, and he had unconsciously put it into words. His first thought, in the reaction following the brief dream of empire, was of the absurdities of the dream, and he glanced at the wagon driver, half expecting to find the native staring amazedly at him.

Apparently his wild murmuring had not been sufficiently loud to reach other ears, for the native sat stolidly on his perch, his whole attention fastened upon a fat Babu at the head of the ship's gangway. He evidently was awaiting orders from this Babu.

But Sheldon's brain refused to cast out the flashed impression. The harder he strove to forget it, the more insistent it became, until his mind resembled a mental mosaic, in which the pattern consisted of the ship and her voyage, her people and their uncertain ultimate fate, his own situation, and, by insidious degrees, his own reawakened bitterness against society.

"By Jupiter! *Is* the thing preposterous?" he ejaculated at length, as he moved away from the wagon and seated himself upon a pile of rice bags. Then he proceeded to give his fancy free rein. The rumble of the big wagon aroused him; he looked up to see the heavily loaded vehicle draw close to the ship's side. A turbanned *serang* stood on the rail, holding on by the fore-royal backstay; a *tindal* and a score of Lascars overhauled a tackle; other seamen swarmed over the wagon to sling its contents.

The fat Babu directed operations from the gangway, and Sheldon hated him violently for the oily importance of both voice and mien. The Babu, too, evinced far greater solicitude in the shipping of the baggage than he had in the safe embarkation of the five hundred coolies.

This circumstance did not escape Sheldon's keen notice; he looked closer at the baggage and found further food for reflection. The baggage was assuredly not that of coolies, nor yet that of superior servants or overseers. It was not the kind of impedimenta that one associates with the traveling European; but often, in his journeys on army service, Sheldon had seen similar gear.

"Native officers' kits," he decided immediately. "But where in thunder are native army officers going in such a ship?" A shrill outpouring of Bengali imprecations rushed upon the Lascars from the fat Babu superintending, and at the same moment a large packing-case slipped from the heap and crashed on to the deck. The Babu evinced all the signs of imminent frenzy and rushed halfway down the gangway, as if to chastize personally the delinquents who had dropped the package.

The Lascars sprang to the ground and adjusted the sling, sending the big case aboard on the tackle. Smartly and quickly as it was done, Sheldon has seen enough of its contents to startle him.

A very few moments before he had gazed upon a dream empire, the materialization of which was only obstructed by a trifling difficulty in regard to arms. And here, among the baggage going into the ship's hold, precisely where he would need it, if he made the great hazard, a broken case revealed rifles; how many, he did not know; but, assuredly, more than one, two or three. And on the wagon were many other such cases, each a potential arm chest for the new empire!

Carried off his feet by the dazzling vista opened up to him, he started towards the gangway, determined to sail in the *Orestes*, even though he had to stow away. He had little money; ample to purchase a passage home, if necessary, but, with no further available resources, he felt the need of economy. Furthermore, to foment the necessary feeling among those coolies (he had no doubt but that he could foment it), he must mingle with them on the passage, and that could be accomplished with greater ease if he were a humble member of the crew.

Brushing unceremoniously past the fat Bengali whose suavity did not prevent his throwing a viperish look at his back, Sheldon mounted to the poop. A boy, an apprentice, was the sole occupant of that part of the ship. To him Sheldon applied:

"Is the captain on board, old fellow?"

"He's below with a passenger just now, sir," replied the youth, willingly leaving his job of plaiting a ball-lanyard to talk. "D'you want him?"

"I'd like to see him about a passage. I'll wait," replied Sheldon. He turned an admiring look over the stately clipper, which even among the disorder of loading, fascinated an appreciative eye with her sweeping sheer, her spacious decks and her graceful cobwebbery of glistening black rigging supporting her three sturdy, yet tapering, masts.

"Passage where?" the boy broke in. "We don't go anywhere a white man wants to go. This is a black man's hooker with a black crew and a cargo of black ivory going to a place where people are blacker still. That's why I don't savvy what on earth —"

Sheldon heard the first part of the boy's speech. The rest trailed off, so far as he was concerned, into a dying mumble. Another matter had claimed his attention. A string of gharries had arrived at the dock and now swung around and pulled up by the ship. They set down a party of six stalwart, bearded natives and six veiled, heavily bejeweled ladies, all of so obviously superior a caste that even the fat Babu salaamed with beaming politeness.

Repressing an exclamation of astonishment, Sheldon stepped behind the mizzen-mast and, hidden by the hanging screen of cordage, tallied off the new arrivals as they ascended the gangway and stood in a group at the companionway doors.

"Every one of them!" muttered Sheldon cryptically. "Their women, too! But why Demerara I wonder?"

In the six new male arrivals Sheldon had recognized half of the native officers' mess of a famous regiment of native cavalry, men whose names were being mentioned just then in Army circles in much the same way as was his own. What their offences had been he did not know; he simply realized that they must have been pretty serious.

Every one of these men knew him, knew of his disgrace. They would feel that he had lost all claim to that deference which they were forced by custom to pay to one of his race.

As the native officers filed down the cabin stairs he stepped from his shelter to go ashore. It seemed unthinkable, now, for him to travel in the same ship with these men and women.

But with his foot on the first downward step of the gangway he halted with a start. A new angle had presented itself to him. If these men were so desperate as to embark in a coolie ship for the other side of the world, why should they not prove good material for the furtherance of his own wild scheme?

A heavy step clanged on the brass sill of the companionway door behind him and a gruff, honest voice hailed him.

"Anything you want, sir? I'm the chief mate."

Sheldon decided swiftly now. He gave up all thoughts of asking for a job; his money must carry him as far as it would. Then —

"I want to see the captain, Mr. Mate," he stated briskly. "I want to engage passage to Demerara."

III
PREMONITIONS

The effect of the double awnings over the *Orestes'* poop was to render the spacious cabin beneath a retreat of deliciously cool shade, in which moving figures lost their individuality and became vague shapes to the new arrival, fresh from the outside glare.

Sheldon followed Mr. Scott, the mate, down the companionway, heard his own name announced, and stood dazed for the moment by the sudden plunge into comparative darkness. Gradually he was aware of other people near him. Out of the faint rustle of garments and of the sibilance of soft voices, in a brisk, capable tone, came directions for his guidance.

"Two steps to the left, Mr. Sheldon, and then straight ahead. Rather bewildering at first, stepping down here out of the sun."

Sheldon went confidently forward, and presently he felt on his arm a strong hand, guiding him to a chair beside Captain Horner. As he sank into the seat he sensed, rather than saw, a dim white shape sitting across the table from him. A subtle fragrance of heliotrope warned him that he was in the presence of a lady, a member of his own class.

"Want to engage a passage, eh?" inquired the captain, as soon as Sheldon was seated. "We're not bound for London, you know. It's Demerara we're going to."

"I know it, captain," replied Sheldon, peering hard across the table in an effort to see his *vis-à-vis* clearly. "I want to get to British Guiana. Aside from the destination of the ship I need a sailing voyage to hem up my nerves. I'm all frazzled to strings. Have you a berth left? I saw a lot of passengers come aboard."

"As a matter of fact, sir, there is no berth left," stated the skipper. "I've got twelve native ladies and gentlemen this trip, though what they want to sail in a ship like this for beats me. But, if you're keen on coming along I shall be very glad to make room for you, for Miss Royce is a bit nervous at the idea of being the only white passenger among so many natives, particularly as we have a native crew as well."

"Any sort of berth will suit me, Captain Horner," Sheldon assured him. "I have very little baggage and I don't expect to spend much time in my bunk, anyhow. I need sea air."

"Well, then, I can fix you up, Mr. Sheldon. We carry no regular third mate. The senior apprentice is acting in that capacity. He can go back into the half-deck for the passage and you can have his berth aft here. He won't mind. You can make him some trifling acknowledgment for the accommodation, if you like, and I'll allow it out of your passage money. A fiver would appeal to him, for he expects to take his examination next time home, and he will need every cent he can scrape up to engage a crammer."

The bargain was struck. Sheldon was introduced to his fellow white passenger, Miss Eunice Royce. Carrying with him the impression of a small, cool hand, a beautifully poised figure and an indistinct memory of a face, to the loveliness of which he was prepared to attest because of the vibrant sweetness of its owner's musical voice, he hurried ashore to collect his baggage.

As the gharry rattled along to his rooms, Sheldon permitted his thoughts to dwell upon Miss Royce to such a degree that he was startled when the memory of his true business with the *Orestes* occurred to him. The presence of a lady of his own race promised complications which he had not allowed for, and he was still in a brown study when the pulling up of the gharry recalled him to the material present.

"Let me get started first," he muttered, as he swept together his belongings and sent the gharry-walla down with them.

"She takes her chance with the rest," he decided, as he reentered the gharry. "At the worst, she'll have the experience of a ship's going ashore. At the best" — he laughed bitterly — "who knows? A new empire should have an empress, and it is as well that she should be of the same color as the emperor."

In the early morning the *Orestes* followed her tug out into the stream, and Sheldon was on the deck to take a cynical farewell of the City of Palaces. Not one of the other passengers apparently cared to brave the early morning air, with its reek of river mud and its clammy warmth, yet undried by the sun.

The great hatches were open and stirring coolies swarmed in and out of the 'tween-decks in their before-breakfast preparations. Sheldon gave them scant attention. He was vaguely conscious of disappointment that Miss Royce had not joined him, but preferred to remain below and put final touches which were to transform her restricted quarters into a refined woman's habitation.

With the exception of the chief mate and the carpenter, who were stationed on the forecastle, the entire white staff of the ship were aft. The captain stood apart with the important-looking pilot whose gorgeously brass-bound assistant, shielded with a canvas apron in the forechains, hove the lead in person.

One of the ship's apprentices was posted on the fore-and-aft bridge, a sort of human telegraph for the conveyance of messages between poop and forecastle. The second mate directed a gang of Lascars unshipping the awnings in order that the decks might be clear when the real business of sailing should be reached.

Sheldon was mildly surprised to see the same fat Babu who had tallied in the human freight still on board. Knowing little of the ways of outward-bounders, he evinced slight interest, except, perhaps, to wonder what business such a man could possibly have with coolies who would, in all probability, never see the Hugli again.

That the Babu commanded deference was plain; he passed among the coolies from group to group and, if they ignored him at first, they gathered around him as soon as one of their own older men spoke to them in swift, subdued harangue.

Sheldon dismissed the man from his mind and turned again to his contemplation of the awakening river and its teeming folk. But, long afterward, he recalled the circumstance that, while the Babu was going among the coolies, one of the native passengers from the cabin passed along the deck, ostensibly to enlist the aid of a sailor in some matter pertaining to the handling of baggage, and that some of the older coolies who had taken no notice of the Babu when he passed forward made a sign of homage as he returned aft.

The native passenger departed from and reentered through the maindeck doors. Thus he and Sheldon did not meet. Indeed, it was not until the *Orestes* was slipping past the James and Mary Sands, with Hugli Point just ahead, that Sheldon's presence in the ship became known to the native passengers. At breakfast, hoping to see Miss Royce, Sheldon made an early appearance, before any one else was at the table. He scarcely expected to have the company of the ship's officers and he, therefore, hoped to enjoy a quiet *hazri tête-à-tête* with the only white passenger on board except himself.

He was doomed to disappointment. The silent Goanese steward bade him be seated and rapidly repeated the bill of fare. In reply to a query he stated that the *sahib* would breakfast alone, for the *mem-sahib* was taking her breakfast in her stateroom.

While he was scowling with disappointment, one of the native passengers came to ask something of the steward. As the man passed him, Sheldon involuntarily raised his eyes. The man stopped short with astonishment vividly portrayed on his face. The look of surprise gradually changed to a smile of half-recognition, and Sheldon felt a flush rise in his cheeks. The man's smile had been that of a man, hitherto an inferior, who all at once realized that relations were changed and that the white man was now merely an equal.

Mastering his inclination to berate the man for his changed demeanor, Sheldon was mindful of his future plans and started at once to ingratiate himself. He forced himself to nod familiarly and gave the man, "Good morning!" with a pleasant smile.

"You are sailing with us, *capitan sahib?*" asked the native, with a trace of mockery in his oily tones.

"Yes, but I'm plain 'Sheldon' now, old chap," Sheldon forced himself to say. "Drop the *'capitan'* and the *'sahib,'* if you don't mind. I am just one of yourselves now."

"Very good, *sahib,*" said the man, his parted lips revealing two perfectly fitting sets of strong white teeth. "We shall take care of her, and it is well."

Sheldon quickly finished his meal and returned to the poop. He was impatient for the ship to pass outside the Sand Heads and to lose sight and touch of land.

There was a note of impatience in the captain's orders, too. This seemed to grow more intense as the hours dawdled by. Following up sundry clues, Sheldon thought he detected the reason for this and he wondered into what kind of a mess he had pitchforked himself.

The fat Babu, after breakfasting with the men of his own race, now stood beneath the break of the poop in deep consultation with the six native passengers. They spoke rapidly in Bengali — much too swiftly for Sheldon to follow all that they said — and many a nod of the head upward and then forward, seemed to indicate that the subject of conversation included both Sheldon and the coolies.

However the captain's irritation, though indirectly attributable to the affairs of that group, was only concerned with that portion of the Babu's activities which concerned the ship's company.

From time to time the fat Babu left the group and shuffled along to where the *serang* and the *tindal* — or the Lascar boatswain and his mate — were busy at their duties. At such times all ship's work ceased, for the crew left their stations and, in attitudes of keenest attention, gathered around the *serang.* Sheldon intercepted from the crew many a covert glance, which even he, landlubber as he was, knew was entirely out of place in a ship whose white crew was out-proportioned by some fifty to one, without counting women.

There was a decided lightening of the atmosphere enveloping the

Orestes when the pilot-boat hove in sight outside and took off the two pilots and the fat Babu. Sheldon's last impression of the Babu was a greasy face wearing an oily smile and a fat, blubbery body that quivered and shook, as if with a convulsion of internal mirth.

The ship was assuming her snowy garments, frisking to be free of the land, and Sheldon cast the Babu out of his thoughts in rapt contemplation of the wonderful transformation that came over the naked masts and taut yards.

With the great top-sails sheeted home, the Orestes leaned to the breeze with a powerful outfall of bow-wave. To the weird singsong of the Lascars' piping voices, in obedience to deep-throated orders from the capable mates, snowy sail after snowy sail fell from the yards, billowed out and up, restrained by the stretching of hoisting yards and hauled-in sheets, until, from chess-tree to trucks the towering fabric was a resplendent pyramid of deep-bosomed canvas, booming with unleashed power.

Sheldon became conscious of a presence near him. He snatched his gaze away from the fascinating complexity of the ship's motive power and turned to greet Miss Royce.

She was looking as cool and fresh as if no such thing as temperature existed. Sheldon, knowing full well what the cabins were like at that hour of the day after awnings had been stowed away, complimented her upon the wonderful results she had achieved in her own person.

"I think that this breeze is the magic worker, Mr. Sheldon," she laughed, and her laugh thrilled him through and through. "I did not dare to appear before. I have been unable to get rid of a most unpleasant feeling. Do you know, all last night and this morning I was so foolish as to fancy that there was a queer atmosphere about this ship — a sort of tensity which seemed as overpowering as the multitude of shippy odors one gets when the steward opens his little storeroom. But if it had nothing to do with this ship, it was still an indescribable feeling — something akin to the one I experienced when I looked down the Memorial Well at Cawnpur, where all those bodies of women and children were thrown."

Sheldon laughed in the attempt to appear at ease, but the attempt was quite an effort. He sought out a couple of deck-chairs, placed them on the shady side of the companion deckhouse and conducted the girl thither.

"That's a shivery sort of comparison, Miss Royce," he said. "I think that the feeling you mention will soon pass off with this fresh gale blowing the land-tang overboard. We'll hope so, anyhow, for one needs an easy mind in order to get the best out of a sea voyage.

"You've probably been used to traveling in steamers. This would account for your early uneasiness. There's an air about sailing ships which is entirely their own."

"I hope that my feeling is caused by that alone, Mr. Sheldon," replied the girl, settling back in her chair and flashing a dazzling smile at him. "I'm not at all inclined to be needlessly scared at things, but I am tremendously relieved to find that I'm not the only white passenger aboard. Perhaps the fear that I was going to be the only one had something to do with that queer sense of something impending,"

IV

THE RAJA'S LADY

THE BAY of Bengal was in one of its vacillating moods when the *Orestes* plunged into it. For three days of whistling wind, succeeded by a like period of baffling airs and greasy calms, a shipload of brown misery floated under a blinding sun which drew from the harassed vessel odors of staggering variety and stupendous pungency.

Sheldon and Miss Royce were left alone because of sheer necessity. The captain and mates, the three junior apprentices and the cockney carpenter — all of the white portion of the ship's company — were too busily occupied in driving service out of laggard brown sailors to be able to waste time with passengers. The twelve native occupants of the best staterooms were as busily concerned with their own dire physical tribulations. No amount of persuasion would suffice to coax them out into the sunlight.

The 'tween-decks resembled the cattle deck of a Plate River ship in a *pampero*; its unhappy denizens, five hundred simple-minded coolies whose only mental quality seemed to be a hair-trigger tendency toward panic, tumbled and surged from side to side in the giddy lurches of the becalmed ship, sending up through the hatches a volume of terror-stricken sound that reverberated eerily in the volleying canvas aloft.

An occasional swirl of curry fragrance mingled with the awful reek of bilge water, as if grotesquely to remind the groaning sufferers that at least their European custodians were not to be frightened from their meals. Through it all Sheldon solicitously watched his fair companion. He was anticipating the moment when she would surrender to the atmosphere of misery and would beg to be escorted below. But on the second day of the calm, in the zenith of the ship's inquietude, Miss Royce's face shone just as fair and wholesome as when she had watched the tug swing back for port.

Sheldon tried to hide his astonishment; it was a matter of pride that he did not show his own discomfort; but it was impossible wholly to conceal his feelings when, in a matter-of-fact tone, Miss Royce suggested that she would like to visit the coolie quarters.

"I think, Mr. Sheldon, that something should be done for those women," she said, searching his face with a cool, level glance. "I would have gone to see them before, but I found out only at tiffin that they have no stewards or any one else to attend to them."

"But Miss Royce," expostulated Sheldon with a scarcely repressed shudder, "you must not venture down there. You will find things in a frightful state. Those people are accustomed to receiving no consideration. They are born to such a state. They do not expect to be waited upon, and no white woman ever thinks of bothering about them."

The girl rose from her chair. She stood for a moment swaying easily to the heave of the vessel. She looked down at Sheldon with a smile at the same time whimsical and contemptuous.

"I'm afraid I haven't been properly coached in what a white woman is expected to do, Mr. Sheldon," she said. "Do you think that a white person who refuses to help a fellow-being of another color is a superior being? But don't you bother, anyhow, sir, I'll ask that club-footed sailor with the gold earrings to help me down the ladder. He looks as if he might have a heart concealed somewhere."

Miss Royce turned her back on Sheldon and started towards the sailor of whom she had spoken.

"Wait a moment, Miss Royce," pleaded Sheldon, springing up. "Of course I'll come with you, if you feel that way about it! I simply wished to apprise you of the conditions that you might expect to find, and to advise you that white women do not usually set out upon such errands of mercy, and that you take the risk of having your motives misunderstood."

As Miss Royce looked at him appraisingly he hastened to add, "Can't I fetch a smelling-bottle or salts for you? It's bound to be a bit thick down below."

"Please don't be so solicitous about me," retorted the girl somewhat petulantly. "I've nursed hundreds of plague cases, and I'm used to unpleasant sights and smells. However, get my smelling-salts for yourself, if you are going with me. You will be far more likely to need them than I will."

Sheldon colored with embarrassment as he preceded her down the main deck to the hatchway, where an improvised deckhouse gave access to a rough timber ladder.

During the last few days his dream of founding an empire in Guiana had occupied but a small place in his thoughts; his association with Miss Royce had given him other food for dreams. Yet he had by no means abandoned his project. Whenever he did permit his thoughts to settle upon his former dreams he saw the difficulties perceptibly diminishing. Just now, as he led the way to the dark, noisome 'tween-decks, his thoughts were of his dream empire and of Miss Royce. They seemed to go together, somehow.

Together the two passed around the gloomy 'tween-decks, Sheldon meekly obeying Miss Royce's orders. At her command he picked individual women out of groveling heaps and laid the most helpless ones in regular rows, with their heads on the midship line of the deck, thereby minimizing, so far as possible, the effect of the ship's motion.

Many times he longed to rush up the hatchway and fill his choked lungs with sweet air, but his softly speaking, entirely self-possessed companion went serenely on her way and pride forced him to stick to his job.

Everywhere that they passed he heard whispers of awed appreciation and reverence for his fair companion. It puzzled him, for he had never heard quite that tone used with reference to an ordinary white *mem-sahib*. Miss Royce's reception by the natives seemed to be accompanied with the homage such as the natives are accustomed to pay to their rulers.

As they stepped to the ladder, in preparation for ascent to the deck, a small knot of coolie men followed them. The fervor of the salaams and the deep obeisances prompted Sheldon to inquire of one of the men if Miss Royce was known to them.

The fellow's reply made Sheldon gasp. He hurried after the girl and stared at her in a manner far from well-bred. As he came to a stop beside her chair she asked him, with a pretty assumption of offense:

"Do you usually stare at a lady in that manner, Mr. Sheldon?"

"I beg your pardon, Miss Royce," he stammered shamefacedly, "but the remark which I have just heard was so astonishing that I have lost my wits for a moment."

"What can you ever have heard to make you behave so much like a yokel?" she inquired curiously and with raised brows.

"Why — er — Miss Royce, you see I noticed that all of those coolies treated you with such deep reverence that I was anxious to know the reason for it. I inquired if they had known you before. I hardly know what you will think and it is most embarrassing to have to tell you, but the fellow that I asked stated that you were his 'Raja's lady.' "

Miss Royce threw back her head and laughed merrily.

Sheldon, relieved that he had not incurred her anger and puzzled much more, added, "I thought that it must be a 'spoof,' but what object had he in saying such a thing if it is just buncombe? Could he have mistaken you for somebody else? The queer thing about it is that the whole crowd of them seem to have the same idea."

"I am sure I don't know,"' smiled the girl. "Though to be sure I had an unpleasant experience in regard to being somebody's 'lady.' It was just before the *Orestes* sailed; in fact, it was the cause of my sailing. Did you happen to notice that I remained in my room until after the pilot left?"

"Yes," replied Sheldon, anxious, but not daring to tell her that he had noticed everything she had done since he had met her. "I thought that you were fixing up your quarters."

"No, that was not the reason. The real reason for my staying below went ashore with the pilot, Mr. Sheldon."

"What reason? I must be dense, Miss Royce, for I fear I do not understand you."

"Well, it has become a joke now, so I don't mind telling the experience," replied Miss Royce, as a faint flush stole over her animated face.

"I was governess in the family of a big official in Calcutta. It is not necessary to mention his name. I don't know what evil deeds I must have been guilty of in a previous existence, but they must have been deeds meriting dire penalties, for my employer tried his best to force me into marriage with the fat Babu who was checking in those poor coolies."

Miss Royce shuddered at the recollection, before she continued her recital with a smile:

"There was some business connection of a character unknown to me between my employer and my corpulent lover. I often thought that it must have been some financial interest in these coolie ships, through which the Babu received favors in the way of irregular permits or legal eye winkings, and the great official received gratifying cumshaw in the shape of cash.

"Whatever was the connection, it was sufficiently close to make things most uncomfortable for me. My refusal of the Babu brought all kinds of pressure to bear upon me. I was given to understand that my future depended upon my acceptance, and my suitor was encouraged to maintain a siege of the most annoying character. My employer told me bluntly that, quite apart from the great material advantages of the match for me, he absolutely could not afford to offend the Babu.

"At last the situation became so unbearable that I was, for very self-respect, forced to resign from my position. They could not prevent my resigning, but they took pains to point out to me that, by voluntarily resigning, I broke my contract which had two more years to run, and absolved them from all necessity of paying my passage home.

"I realized the seeming justice of what they said, but I could not endure that oily black man for another moment, even though I feared that I did not have sufficient money to carry me back to London, and so might even have to ship as stewardess in order to reach home. I left the official's house with only barely enough money to carry me halfway home. In vain I sought another position. The influence of the official was sufficient to render that impossible.

"As I was ready to give up in despair of being able to stay in Calcutta, and was trying to arrange for some kind of a passage home, a strange thing happened. The Babu came to my hotel and in the most respectful manner begged permission to bid me 'good-by.' I reluctantly consented to see him. The man's delicacy astonished me. He never even referred to his suit. In the quietest, kindest way, he expressed his regret for what had happened, and handed me an open letter which he requested me to read.

"It was a personal introduction to the governor of British Guiana, and a high recommendation of my services as governess. While I was reading the note the Babu said that the *Orestes* was sailing for Demerara. He offered to arrange a passage for me at a price which came just within my means.

"As you may imagine, I was glad to accept his offer, which was made, I believe, through remorse at having so inconvenienced me. I felt that as I was paying my own passage I could afford to accept the letter in the spirit in which it was offered. I did so and boarded the ship.

"After I had booked my passage he tried to hang around my hotel, but I succeeded in avoiding him. When I discovered that he was coming down river with us, I decided to remain out of sight until he had gone."

Miss Royce ended her recital by smiling at Sheldon and saying, "No, by no means a 'Raja's lady' and, thank God, by great, good luck, not even a 'Babu's bride!'"

As the girl finished she regarded Sheldon quizzically and rallied him on his preoccupied expression. He was trying to connect the Babu and his infatuation for Miss Royce and the native officers and their women and their queer destination.

Suddenly he sat erect and stared forward. The girl followed his gaze and saw three of the native passengers hurrying through the main hatch into the 'tween-decks in great haste, as if unwilling to be observed.

V
OTHER DREAMS

A SPARKLING fair wind boomed out of the northeast, as the sun sank behind the pink clouds. The unrest of the ship was lulled until at an early hour in the first watch sleep cast a soothing spell upon her people, and her officers, free from annoyance, kept their vigil.

For the first time since leaving Hugli, the rosewood case of the old-fashioned piano in the main saloon had been opened and Miss Royce's slim fingers attempted to coax some semblance of Moskowsky's "Valse Brillante" from its jangling strings. She had laughingly closed the lid after several such attempts with the remark that the glasses and decanters in the swing rack over the table made much more musical notes. She retired to her stateroom, leaving Sheldon undecided whether he was regretful or pleased.

He concluded to be pleased in view of the fact that the native cabin passengers had, that evening, evinced signs of throwing off the blue effects of the trials of the past few days. At various times since he had seen three of them slipping down to the 'tween-decks, all six of the men had come out on deck, seemingly for a breath of air, and they were all beginning to take an interest in the ship and her affairs. Miss Royce's absence made it an opportune moment to accomplish a little sounding out of views in general. He lit a cheroot and stepped out on the main deck by way of the forward doors. A great white moon hung low in a sky of silky smoothness. Beyond the immediate sheen of the moon the blackness of the heavens was resplendently bejeweled with clear-weather tropic stars.

A few of the watch on deck paced silently in the waist about the galley; above him, and aft, Sheldon heard the soft pad of jute-soled shoes, as the officer of the watch paced from the wheel to the rail and back again.

He stood for several minutes, drinking in the fascinating beauty of the moon-bathed ship, his ears pleasurably assailed by the myriad sounds accompanying the swaying of the tall spars. One side of the broad deck was in black shadow. Where the moonlight poured over the tall bulwarks the planks shone like silver, shaded with each gentle roll of the vessel by the quivering leaches of the sails as they swung across the face of the lunar beams. Every glistening spar, each bar-tight weather stay and shroud, straining sheets and twanging braces — all insistently whispered a demand that their work be noticed. And, lest the beholder should ignore them in his appreciation of the scheme of things, swinging blocks far up aloft and tapping reef-points on the bulging courses drummed an accompaniment to the demands of their coworkers.

Sheldon's thoughts rapidly became far too poetical for a man with his prospects and his intent. He was brought back to earth, however, with a jolt for which he gave thanks. Before he had quite recovered his more practical thoughts, soft sandaled footsteps approached, and a soft, vibrant voice at his shoulder murmured:

"Sheldon Sahib is looking into the future, yes?"

Sheldon swung sharply round. He dissembled his surprise and assumed an air of friendly greeting when he saw that he had become the center of a group composed of the six native cabin passengers, each wearing a smile which might mean anything from affection to murderous intent.

"Yes," he replied softly, "I was. I was looking into the future of this great ship."

"And what of the ship's future, Sheldon Sahib?"

The question was but a whisper — a whisper in duet, but, in the smooth harmony of the Bengali voices Sheldon fancied that he detected a note such as the hunter often hears, down near his legs, as he steps over a rotten log in the jungle — a noise like the hiss of a poisonous snake.

Assuming an air of nonchalance which he was far from feeling, he answered evenly, "I was thinking that we have here a complete world in itself; for many months the outside world will know nothing whatever of us. Suppose that this vessel should run upon some unknown coast or upon some solitary island, bearing sufficient subsistence for so many people — eh?"

"Well, *sahib?*"

The hint to proceed was again but a whisper, but it came from six mouths now and it was much nearer Sheldon's face.

"Oh, it was merely a passing thought," replied Sheldon carelessly.

He threw a world of meaning into his voice when he said next: "It might occur, you know. For example, suppose something happened to the white officers of this ship and she took the beach on British Guiana soil, just a little south of the Venezuelan border. There is everything aboard this vessel to form a colony, or —"

"An empire, *sahib?*"

Sheldon stared, frankly amazed at this voicing of his own thought. He stared into six dark faces, each lit up by a pair of glittering black eyes, each now rendered more expressive by parted lips revealing flashing white teeth, and each shaking with silent laughter.

The ship's bell struck four bells — ten o'clock — and the fo'c's'le bell was struck in answer; a shadowy figure detached itself from a shadowy group forward and came aft to relieve the wheel, as the lookout on the fo'c's'le chanted musically, *"Hum — dekta — hai!"*

The relieved helmsman descended the poop ladder on the lee side. As he passed the group in the waist one of Sheldon's companions spoke softly to him, received a soft reply without the man's pausing in his stride, and the big, black-bearded Bengali who appeared to exercise some influence over his fellows turned back to the Englishman.

"Sheldon Sahib," he said, soft as a lover's whisper, imperative as a woman's wish, "our circumstances are known to each other. We shall not foolishly waste time. You will please walk forward without haste to where the anchors lie. We shall join you there in five minutes. The man who takes the lookout now for two hours is a man of ours."

Sheldon smothered a gasp. He turned away and strolled along the shady side of the deck. He was tingling at every digit and at every hair root at this sudden taking shape of his plans. He had not the least doubt but that the suggested meeting, out of sight in the ship's bows, had as its object the discussion of the project over which he, too, had dreamed.

Some of the old caste spirit asserted itself in him as he mounted the forecastle head. Accustomed to receive deference from such people as Lascars, he was almost shocked into punitive action by the assertive quality with which the lookout accosted him and grinned into his face. The saving remembrance that such men as he might eventually be factors in his scheme, alone enabled him to reply to the man's presumptuous greeting with any semblance of civility.

He took up a position on the shank of the starboard anchor, which was to leeward, and consequently hidden from aft by the foot and lower part of the lee-leech of the fore-course. The steady roar of the lee-bow wave beneath him promised immunity from eavesdroppers when the others arrived. He swiftly mapped out a line of argument against their coming.

As they had said, it was unnecessary to waste time.

The six Bengalis sauntered silently forward in pairs and as silently grouped themselves about Sheldon. The big fellow who appeared to be a sort of leader took up the duties of spokesman. His companions grunted their attention by nods, shrugs and occasional grunts.

First assuring Sheldon that nothing was to be feared from the lookout, the spokesman said, "Now, Sheldon Sahib, we talk freely."

Sheldon began: "Well, as you hinted, we are aware of each other's status and can speak plainly. Why need this ship ever go to Demerara?

Now, my plan was, when I took passage —"

"Yes, yes, Sheldon," interrupted the other quietly, "you have plans, as you suggested; that is why we are talking to you here. But it is not of *your* plans that we will talk. We have our own plans which are better than yours. You have said enough for us to be sure that we need not fear you; perhaps you may even join us. It may be necessary that you should, when you have been made a confidant in our scheme. Listen!"

Another shadowy figure appeared from the fo'c's'le and took up, at the rail, a position where he could readily see any one approaching from aft. A look of understanding flashed in the glinting eyes of his companions, and Sheldon had a shivery feeling that, instead of being the prime mover in a tremendous plot, he was but a pawn in a game immeasurably greater. The harmony between native passengers and native crew was surely too absolute to be accidental.

Fixing his black eyes full upon Sheldon's face, the Bengali spokesman resumed:

"Your plan is good, *sahib,* but you are too late. Have you not wondered why we, men of family in India, should take passage in an uncomfortable sailing ship and expose our women to such discomforts to reach such a port as Demerara?"

Sheldon nodded. He saw a light.

"Then why proceed there?" resumed the other softly. "Do you know that, for such a community as you hinted at to be self-supporting, many things are needed which, for such a ship as this, would cause suspicion? And how long do you, a soldier, think such an enterprise could exist under the noses of British officials such as swarm in the West Indies?"

"Not long, I suppose," replied Sheldon. "What do you think of trying, then?"

The group about him stirred slightly and he felt an electric intensity in the air that rippled his scalp as the reply came back; "We do not *think* of trying, Sheldon; we are going to *do.* We have every detail perfected, even to connections in Calcutta. Our new empire is as assured as yours is visionary. Further, since you are of one mind with us, and since you could do nothing by yourself, we shall not permit you to change your mind, now that you must realize that you cannot command in this thing. You are either with us, or against us now; and you must decide which it is to be before anything else is confided to you. If you agree, your army training will stand you in good stead and will recommend you to our absent chief for a high place."

"Absent chief?" thought Sheldon, feeling as though he were poised over an abyss full of chilled air. "This is a dangerous plot, and no mistake about it!"

Aloud he said: "Suppose I need time to think about it? Suppose I want to know more about your plans? What could you do if I simply walked aft and told your plans so far as I know them to the captain? He wouldn't believe it if you told him that I had suggested a similar thing and I denied it. He is a white man, and he would prefer to believe a white man. In short, what if I refuse to play the subordinate to you?"

Patiently the men listened to his words. Each sat motionless until he had finished. Then six rows of shining teeth gleamed in six black faces, and the spokesman gently waved his hand and made a sharp clicking sound with his tongue.

Swift as a panther the lookout leaped upon Sheldon from behind. A silk scarf was slipped over his mouth and he saw a slow smile sweep simultaneously across six faces. He could still hear distinctly, and the big Bengali said, without heat:

"You speak rashly, Sheldon Sahib. Over the bows is silence for babbling tongues. Not one of this ship's crew — except the Englishmen — would see you go if you passed before all their eyes.

"Time to consider I will give you, for I know your disappointment at finding your dream a chimera. I know, too, that your given word will bind you. Therefore you will nod or shake your head to this question: 'If you are freed, will you say a word concerning these things to any man?' If you promise this, you are to avoid open communication with us; but you are to come to this place at this hour tomorrow night with your final decision.

"Now, Sheldon Sahib, a nod will release you; a shake of the head will be a signal for your departure from this earth. Which shall it be?"

Sheldon's brain was whirling. The face of Miss Royce kept persistently before his mental vision. He considered her possible fate if he were out of the way, and he was man enough, regardless of his own peril, to base his reply wholly upon his certainty as to the probability of her fate.

He nodded.

VI
THE EMPIRE'S KING

THE NIGHT found Sheldon sleepless. For the first time he now realized the visionary nature of his own foolish plans. When the idea had first flashed through his mind it had seemed so simple to utilize four months of sailing in spreading his views among the coolies. He had entertained no doubt but that, long before the passage was up, they would be so heartily weary of the ship that any proposition holding out promise of freedom would be more than welcome.

Yet here were his own plans met by the cool assurance that he was "late" with his ideas; that what he had idly dreamed about was all but an accomplished fact; that an absent chief with puppets in Calcutta pulled wires of tempered steel!

Then again, his own plans, vague though they were, had called for the ultimate safety of the vessel and of her crew. He had never intended to wreck the ship utterly and murder her white officers, except in a life-and-death struggle between them and his fellow conspirators.

Even Miss Royce, since he had unexpectedly found her aboard, was to remain in the vessel unmolested, unless she expressed her willingness to follow his fortunes. This latter contingency Sheldon had begun to hope might come to pass.

He spent the day in moody isolation. Captain Horner and the different watch officers chaffed him, accused him of concealing an affair of the heart and rallied him in their bluff fashion. Miss Royce laughingly tasked him with neglect of her. Failing to secure his attentions by this ruse, she thereafter appeared to be offended and openly avoided him.

For this he was devoutly thankful, for it left him free to wrestle with his problem and to decide what answer he should give when night should come and bring the end to his hours of grace.

Throughout the day he saw nothing of his fellow passengers. They occupied quarters across the stern of the ship, and after they had taken possession at Calcutta, no member of the *Orestes'* company had been able to enter their quarters. They ate together in the largest stateroom and their own *bearahs* cooked and served their own food. The women were attended by their own *ayahs*. They had brought their own food.

Captain Horner apparently saw nothing worthy of comment in an arrangement which simply meant that he received full passage money from twelve people who asked a bare passage without food and attendance, yet paid for both.

Sheldon watched the companionway clock until four bells struck. Then he sauntered forward. He had stood in the waist of the ship for more than half an hour before the time came and had seen nobody emerge from the cabins. Yet when he arrived on the fo'c's'le-head there were the six conspirators already sitting about the big anchor.

He told himself that there was something uncanny about it as he strolled up. Resolved to carry himself confidently until he could glean more intimate details of the plan under discussion, he took his place with a friendly nod of greeting.

He was received with a silence which amounted to a direct command for his decision. He noticed that an unusual number of Lascar sailors had decided to sleep on the fo'c's'le-head that night.

A cool backdraft of air poured down upon him from the fore-top-mast-staysail; the rumbling overfall of the bow-wave reminded him of the previously thrown-out hint of his possible destination if his answer should chance to be unsatisfactory. Altogether he felt chilled to the marrow as he took a seat on the anchor shank.

Stiffening himself, he put his case boldly.

"Look, here, Tewarra," he began, addressing the spokesman. "I have kept my promise. I have spoken to no one since last night and I have thought over your proposition. That same promise will bind me until I ask you to release me from it, but it will be more conducive to good feeling between us if you will give me a clearer idea of your plans."

"Have you acquaintance with the *mem-sahib* before coming on board this ship?" inquired a soft voice beside him. Six pairs of glittering eyes snapped in the dim starlight.

"No. Why, what has that to do with the question?" demanded Sheldon, puzzled and wishing that diplomacy forbade his resenting the question, as he would have liked to have done.

"Then you are not her lover?"

"Certainly not!" laughed Sheldon, beginning to see light.

In low, level tones that yet gave a hint of conscious power, the spokesman went on: "Have you ever heard of a small group of islands called Pona Mobubque?"

Sheldon shook his head.

"There is such a place, Sheldon Sahib. They lie between the Maldive Group and the Chagos Archipelago. They are as immune from intrusion as an undiscovered land, and they bear, within the limits of the group, all things necessary for the support of a community.

"This ship will pass within one hundred miles of those islands. One week after the date of our departure from the Hugli, a fully equipped steamer followed us. She carries everything necessary for the establishment of a court and materials by which the low-caste people may support their superiors.

"Modern arms and coast defense appliances are in that ship. There are looms for weaving, seeds for planting, materials for building, and sufficient supplies of all kinds to ensure subsistence for one year, after the cargo of this ship is used up."

The speaker paused, and his eyes seemed to bore into Sheldon's.

"Our chief, he who will be our king, comes in that steamer, *sahib*," he went on. "He will be there to greet his subjects. When the *Orestes* comes in sight of the new kingdom, she must not hold a single life which is not sworn to the service of its king."

The completeness of the whole scheme staggered Sheldon. He felt the necessity of sparring for more time. At the same time he realized that the situation resembled a dynamite charge with a mighty short fuse.

"I bow to the great intellect behind this thing," he said at last. "But tell me more. What of the coolies? Are they sworn?"

"Their elders — yes," came the quiet answer. "For the rest, they are slaves, they count for nothing, they will follow where they are led, or go where they are driven. But even the slaves know who will be their king. He has seen them and spoken to him."

"And what of the officers of this ship, Tewarra? I understand you have secured a hold over the Lascars, but the white men? What of them? And what of the ship?" pursued Sheldon.

"The ship will be anchored near the island until all her goods are taken out. Then she will be sunk in deep water and her owners will, doubtless, grow rich on the insurance money," was the reply, given with the suspicion of a smile.

"But the officers?" persisted Sheldon.

"They will not see the island, *sahib*. The *serang* will find out from one of the white boys when the ship is to be nearest to Pona Mobubque. Then the white men's wives or families will draw consolation from the insurance."

"You mean to murder them?" ejaculated Sheldon, for once off his guard.

"'Murder,' *sahib*? That is an ugly word that does not become your lips. Say rather that the white men will probably 'die.' Doubtless, being Englishmen, as you are *sahib*," he continued, in a warning tone, "they will die fighting."

"They are too few to give much trouble," replied Sheldon, "and half of them are boys. It ought to be easy. Now, tell me what becomes of the *mem-sahib*. Does she die, too?"

A note of respect was distinctly audible in the Bengali's reply.

"The white lady will be our *ranee*. She is here under the protection of our king, who will be her lord."

A great lump rose in Sheldon's throat and all the stars were gathered into a whirling ball of points of fire. Vaguely he knew that an ominous rustling was going on around him; dimly he saw five lean brown hands thrust into five white linen jacket breasts. He heard a restraining murmur from Tewarra and the five hands remained motionless. Then, throwing off the choking sensation with a mighty effort of will, he smiled into the scowling faces around him and asked:

"Tell me, who is to be our king?"

Five voices grumbled protestingly. Again Tewarra soothed the unrest of his fellows. He replied, still in his even, low tones:

"There is no single man who can change our course, now. The most any one could do is to hasten the stroke. Ward it off you cannot, so I will tell you who is to be our king. Then you will know all. The man who accompanied the ship down to the sea and who returned to Calcutta with the pilot — he will be king of Pona Mobubque, *sahib!"*

VII
THE PART OF A WHITE MAN

SHELDON WAS staggered by the sheer audacity of the plot to which he now felt himself a party. His overwhelming sensation was that of homicidal hatred for a certain fat Babu whose kindness in procuring passage to Demerara for Miss Royce had by no means been disinterested.

For many pulse-beats after the announcement of the king a great silence enveloped the group around the big anchor. Sheldon knew that he was expected to break it by the announcement of his decision.

Many thoughts rushed through his mind. He was by no means in love with life. Suppose he refused to join the conspiracy and thus invited his own end? What of it? So far as he was concerned life or death seemed equally attractive to him.

But after his death, what of Miss Royce? If he became one of the conspirators temporarily, he might find opportunity to save her from the dreadful fate awaiting her. If he refused to join now — much as the man in him revolted against aiding a band of an inferior race in an offensive movement against men of his own color — her doom was sealed. If he consented, there was one chance in a thousand for her, a chance in which death probably lurked for him.

Consideration of these points took but a brief moment, for he knew all too well that even seeming reluctance would mean death now.

So intent upon their business had been the entire group that the poop-bell had struck unheard. Now the fo'c's'le bell struck five bells close behind them; the notes crashed on the air like a volley of musketry, as they echoed weirdly back from the bulging foresail. The Lascar lookout raised his thin musical cry to indicate that all was well.

Silence fell again. Even the roaring bow-wave took on a deeper, more slumberous note that seemed to be part and parcel of the manifold voices of the straining ship's fabric.

"Oh! There you are! I've looked all over the ship for you, Mr. Sheldon!" rippled a voice full of interest from the fo'c's'le ladder.

Miss Royce stepped up to the group and laid a small hand on Sheldon's shoulder.

A movement and a muttering among the men might have meant, to any one else, that they resented being taken by surprise, but Sheldon knew it to be merely the confusion of men faced by one to whom they felt that they owed homage, but to whom they were not permitted to pay it — yet!

"Did you want something, Miss Royce?" questioned Sheldon as he rose in token of respect. "What can I do for you?"

"Won't you please come aft?" the girl pleaded breathlessly. As she spoke, she pulled at his sleeve in an impatience which she took no pains to hide. "It's most important! I'm in a great hurry, too!"

"Just a moment, please," courteously replied Sheldon.

He turned from her to his companions and spoke in swift Bengali.

"Tewarra, I fight on the side of the new *ranee!*" he said.

Before the black had time to reply he hurried his fair companion down the steps.

"Now, what can I do for you?" he asked, as they hurried along the moonlit main deck.

"Oh, I need your cabin. You will give it up to me, won't you?" rippled the girl, and Sheldon now saw that she was very much excited.

"Certainly," agreed Sheldon with a grin at her eagerness. "Of course, since you want it. Anything you like. But tell me the news. What's happened?"

"I can't stop to tell you much now, there is such a lot to do. A little coolie woman in that awful hold has just had a baby and I have asked Captain Horner to let me bring them into my cabin. He says I may, if I can persuade you to give up your room to me."

"Bully for you, Miss Royce!" exclaimed Sheldon admiringly. "Go right ahead with your preparations. I'll pitch my things out in five minutes. You need not have asked. You might just have taken it."

Miss Royce smiled her thanks, as she hastened away to make her charges comfortable.

The tiny cabin was soon cleared. Sheldon hastily dumped his things out and then helped Miss Royce transfer necessary things from her cabin to his. He stood on guard over his own bags and holdalls as a party of coolies, bearing the mother and the newborn babe came from the 'tween-decks. He saw the brown faces as the little party entered Miss Royce's stateroom and as they came out.

Right there he caught the real meaning of devotion. The humble coolies simply glowed with a doglike loyalty for the *mem-sahib* who had treated one of their women as if she were a human being. Sheldon needed no other proof that fighting the *ranee's* battles might not be so hopeless after all.

While he was considering where to place his belongings, Captain Horner came out of his stateroom. The ship was already full to capacity. Unless Sheldon could make shift on a transom sofa, there was but one thing else to do.

"Here, Mr. Sheldon," said the captain after a moment of thought. "We'll turn out the steward and you can have his bunk for the time being. He's a Goanese anyhow, and he can bunk with the native cook."

The captain called the steward and gave the necessary orders. The steward said nothing and at once removed his belongings, but the expression on his face was not good to see. It boded no good, either for Sheldon or for the captain.

At the captain's second order the steward carried Sheldon's gear inside. Then with a scowling visage he betook himself and his belongings forward, to lose several degrees of importance among his fellows because he was now compelled to live among them.

It was midnight before Miss Royce had finished making her charges snug to her satisfaction. All of this time Sheldon waited in the main saloon, for he was anxious to be on hand in case she needed any help. When her labor of love was finished for the time being, and a coolie woman had been installed as nurse, Miss Royce came out and asked Sheldon to take her on deck for a breath of fresh air before she retired.

He led her to the poop and over to the lee side, thereby avoiding contact with the watch officer, for he had made up his mind to tell her of his problem. He so hated even the semblance of double-dealing that only the fate mapped out for Miss Royce could have induced him to break his given word. Knowing what he did about the rascals' plans for her future, he soothed his scruples by telling himself that he had only promised not to speak of the conspiracy to any "man."

He arranged a coil of the main-braces for a seat. When his companion had seated herself, he sat cross-legged on the deck before her and said quietly:

"Miss Royce, I have a confession to make to you. Try to be a lenient judge."

Beginning at the beginning of his army career, he proceeded to tell the girl everything. He told her the full circumstances of his quitting of the regiment in disgrace; he laid bare his own wild dreams of founding an empire; he spared himself not one jot. Then he told of the plot.

When he had finished, Miss Royce's face was deeply flushed.

"So the cunning Babu set this trap for me?" she whispered, and her face paled and then flushed a deeper red, as she thought of what might happen to her — even now.

"My cheap passage to a port which I was never destined to reach! My letter of introduction to an employer whom I was never destined to see! Mr. Sheldon, tell me! Is it the fat Babu who is to be the king of their colony?"

"Yes," replied Sheldon.

Miss Royce sat silent for several minutes, with her chin resting in her hand. Her sparkling eyes were steadily bent upon the scintillant seas racing past in the moonlight. She shuddered, tore her glance from the waters, and faced Sheldon. When she spoke, he felt as if he had reached the limit of what a man can endure — and still remain a man.

"And — you — *a white man* — you thought of doing the same thing!" she uttered in low, horror-stricken tones.

"But Miss Royce, I never even dreamed of harming you!" he stammered. "When the idea first struck me, I did not even know that you were on board."

"You — *a white man* —" she persisted in a whisper, as if unconscious that he had spoken.

"Punished for ill-luck, you would have dragged five hundred simple coolies into a conflict with your own race! The Indian mutiny should have been example and memory enough for you of what that would mean!"

"Oh, damn!" exploded Sheldon. "Excuse me, Miss Royce — that slipped out unawares. You are perfectly right, of course. It *was* a rotten thing to think of doing, wasn't it? But we face another problem now. What shall we do in the present circumstance?"

Miss Royce gazed straight into his own brooding eyes, her own cool and level once more.

"There is only one thing that a *white* man can do," she stated positively. "Advice is not needed as to that course."

"Wait," he muttered, rising to his feet.

He joined the officer of the watch on the weather side and walked a few turns with him. He spoke with him as soon as they were out of hearing of the helmsman.

In a few moments he rejoined Miss Royce.

"The second mate tells me that the ship passes as close to these islands as she ever will late tomorrow afternoon," he remarked. "I think that we will lose nothing, and at the same time avoid suspicion, if we wait until breakfast time before consulting with Captain Homer. You apparently have it in your power to work wonders, if you will."

"*I* can work wonders? Why, what do you mean, Mr. Sheldon? What can I do?"

He told her briefly of her standing with both native passengers and coolies, and added:

"I saw the look upon the faces of those men as they carried the woman and her baby into your cabin. It is only the elders among the coolies who have been taken into confidence in the plot. If you will speak to the husband of that little woman and explain what you want done, he will make every single coolie understand that you are in grave danger. Then, no matter what happens, you can be sure that there will be three hundred men on board who are lost to the fat Babu's cause. But you must see that they do not chatter about it until after the time comes to strike. You can do this, Miss Royce, if you will."

"And you — you who are in the confidence of these plotters — can you reconcile your conscience to playing them false?" Sheldon looked full at his fair questioner and laughed harshly.

"Miss Royce," he said, "when a man has resigned from his regiment under such circumstances as I did, he is black-balled to perdition. What matters it what he does? If I must choose between playing false to a crowd of murderous rascals and playing the scoundrel toward my own people, and to a white woman at that, there is but one way open to me, if I still hope to call myself a white man. I shall try to play a man's part in the game, and, long before this ship makes port, the clean, wholesome ocean will have cleansed my system of all bitterness."

VIII
THE ATTACK

AT BREAKFAST Captain Horner and Mr. Scott, the mate, sat opposite Miss Royce and Sheldon. The second mate had the watch. While the steward was forward, bringing dishes from the galley, Sheldon briefly and quietly outlined the state of affairs.

A dynamite bomb dropping through the skylight onto the table could hardly have created more open-mouthed amazement than that which followed Sheldon's words.

Early that morning Miss Royce had taken into her confidence the husband of the coolie woman whom she was nursing. He, in turn, had carefully carried out her directions in regard to his fellows in the 'tween-decks. The man was now in the *mem-sahib*'s cabin with his wife and new baby, awaiting the *mem-sahib*'s pleasure.

"See here, Mr. Sheldon," said Captain Horner, a troubled look in his frank blue eyes, "you're making a very serious statement. It needs backing. If it's true, there are scores of lives in danger; if it is just suspicion on your part, I suppose you realize how serious a false move on my part might be for all of us? A shipload of coolies is like a cargo of gunpowder, you know."

Miss Royce rose and stepped to her room. In a moment she returned with the coolie husband of her patient.

"Tell the captain *sahib!*" she commanded softly.

The steward had placed the dishes on the table and now hovered between his pantry and the captain's chair. His movements indicated a growing nervousness.

As the coolie began to speak the steward shot a swift glance toward the doors of the staterooms occupied by the Bengalis and sidled up to the captain.

"Captain," he said, "the Bengali gentlemen wish to get clothes from their baggage. "They ask for sailors to break out their baggage from the hold."

The captain, impatient to hear the coolie's story, waved the steward away with the order, "Tell the *serang* to take what men he needs and break out the luggage the Bengalis want to open."

Then he turned to the coolie and commanded him to speak.

While the man was recounting what he had gleaned while carrying out Miss Royce's instructions, the staterooms aft and to starboard opened, and the six native passengers, with their women, emerged and, taking no notice of the white people at the table, filed silently through the forward doors out onto the deck.

Sheldon was more closely concerned in those passengers than he was in the coolie's corroboration of his own story. He remembered suddenly what he had seen when the baggage was being shipped, and he broke in upon the coolie's concluding sentences.

"What arms have you, captain?" he questioned abruptly.

"Six revolvers," laconically replied Captain Homer. "The carpenter has an adz and a broad ax."

"And we are nine whites, counting three boys?" pursued Sheldon.

"You must count me, too. I can shoot!" Miss Royce interrupted eagerly.

"I don't think we'll have to call on you, miss," interposed the mate with a short laugh. "If this thing is true, I don't think the niggers have much in the shape of firearms. Haven't seen any, anyway."

"Man alive!" gasped Sheldon, springing to his feet and glaring at the unconcerned chief mate. "Those fellows have stacks of arms — rifles, or I miss my guess! In their baggage! I caught sight of some rifles when a case slipped and cracked open on the deck!"

Through the open forward doors came a sound like the buzzing of a million bees.

It rose through the open hatches and grew louder in response to the angry shouts of several Lascar seamen stationed at the hatch-coamings.

The group about the cabin-table started up, and Miss Royce's quick intuition enabled her to size up the situation.

"Here!" she whispered to the coolie woman's husband who stood by her in respectful silence. "Quick! Leave the care of your wife and baby to me. Get down among your people and stop their noise. Make them stay below, at all costs. If the old men who are with our enemies make too much bobbery, jump on them *hard!* If you can make them understand that everything is all right, it will be soon; but, if they keep up that racket, somebody will start to shoot down on them. Now go quickly!"

The man fled on his mission, and the girl hurried to her cabin at once to reassure her patient and to secure from her dressing-case a small revolver. Then she went up to the poop where the captain and officers were mustered at the rail, with pistols plainly in evidence, much to the discomfort of the Lascar at the wheel. "Now, Chips," ordered the captain, "take a couple of the boys and fasten up those saloon doors. So long as an attack must come by way of the poop ladders, we can hold it. And you" — to the smallest of the boys — "relieve the wheel! Send the Lascar forward!"

The carpenter's progress could be followed by the clang of iron, as he screwed into place the stout storm battens inside. A cry of anger burst from the baggage room hatch, and the six Bengali passengers scrambled on deck in answer to the warning. It was their first intimation that the little band of whites had taken the initiative.

The Bengalis left their women below decks and sprang on deck, armed with service rifles. Other arms and cases of ammunition were being passed up by the Lascars in the baggage room. From the belt of every Lascar on deck flashed a gleaming knife.

These things were a matter of seconds. Captain Horner led a move toward the deckhouse companion, which offered a vantage point for defense. Before his feet had crossed the doorsill a scream of terror rang out from the wheel, and, turning aft, they saw the helmsman leave the wheel, whip out a knife and spring savagely at the boy who had been sent to relieve him.

"Help! Help!" yelled the boy, plunging away from the wheel with arms tightly wrapped around his head.

Captain Horner and Sheldon ran around the deckhouse at the cry, and a scattering volley of rifles crackled out from the fore-hatch. Sheldon was fumbling with the jammed cylinder of his gun when his eardrums were racked by a smashing explosion at his shoulder and he saw the Lascar crumple into a heap at the flying boy's heels.

"Catch hold of her, Sheldon!" snapped the skipper, as Miss Royce swayed a little, a trifle dazed at the result of her first shot at a human being.

Sheldon took her inside of the deckhouse and the mate dashed aft, whipped a turn of small line around the wheel spokes after righting the helm, and then picked up the scared boy and hurried into the companionway with him.

The carpenter and the two apprentices completed their job, and joined the party in the companionway. Miss Royce paid a hurried visit to her patient, now nearly frantic from the noise of the shooting, and returned to the others, in spite of all efforts to persuade her to seek shelter below.

The ship plunged on, with no hand at the wheel, but keeping her course by virtue of Mr. Scott's expert adjustment of the wheel lashing. From the windows and open door of the deck-house the little party of defenders watched for their lives, but in the period immediately following the first scattered discharge a lull fell in the activity forward.

The second mate stuck out his head and shoulders. The crack of a rifle sounded and he felt a wasplike sting, where a nickeled bullet had ploughed through his neck.

"Oh, they're clever, all right!" ejaculated Sheldon, as he watched the erstwhile army officers. "They're using real siege tactics on us! Lord, but we've got a tough proposition to handle, skipper! If only we had one good rifle!"

His observation was correct. Instead of an armed rabble of Lascars, led by a half-dozen more intelligent ones, the attack was being developed along scientific lines that promised badly for the defenders. Ten Lascars swarmed aloft to the maintop. Ten rifles, with cartridge belts, were sent up to them on the bight of a buntline.

Six of them started to climb, monkey fashion, up the mizzen-topgallant stay, helped by hanks of the stays'l. At the main-hatch ten more Lascars were being formed into line. They were led by four of the native passengers, while the remaining two leaders mustered the rest of the crew at the companionway leading to the 'tween-decks.

"Chips!" shouted Captain Horner. "Run down below and shut the half-door leading into the sail-room from the hold! They're going to pile onto us from there."

As the captain spoke he cast a doubtful glance aloft at the swarming, patient figures, climbing upward to the mizzen-topgallant mast, from whence they could slide down to the mizzen-top and pour a murderous fire into the deckhouse through the skylight.

Sheldon and Mr. Scott saw that glance, and responded by sending carefully aimed shots aloft. But a revolver is but an exceedingly poor weapon for long-range shooting at a swaying object from a swaying platform.

The Lascars swarmed steadily upward. Their shots were replied to by rifle shots from the maindeck. Sticking a head outside was a risky business. The danger was serious.

The second mate saw one desperate chance and took it He slipped to the deck and crawled over to the coil of the stays'l halliards.

Far aloft the mizzen-topgallant-stays'l flapped. Then a big coil of rope shot upward, snaking out as it went. The weight of climbing Lascars, acting as a downhaul, brought the sail thundering and crashing down the stay. Two seamen lost their hold and plunged headlong to the deck.

But the second mate's bold attempt was bound to fail. The fate of their fellows gave the other Lascars a moment's grace. They started again to climb; others joined them; and now there was no sail to let go and stop them.

The group at the 'tween-decks hatch disappeared. At the same moment Chips rushed out, purple of face and perspiring as if from a stoke-hold, and announced:

"Can't barricade that door, sir! It's all jammed with gear. I've pitched about a ton of stuff up against it and 'twill stay 'em for a while, but they're at the door now!"

Now Lascars were sliding down the mizzen-topmast. As the first man stepped into the top, sharp commands rang out on the main deck. A steadily aimed volley crackled along the line in the waist, the file of Lascars advanced several paces, halted, and fired again. From aloft spat six rifles, hurling their leaden death through the deckhouse skylight.

Sheldon took in all phases of the attack, his face grim and white and seared with a ragged furrow where a shot from aloft had all but finished his career. His voice was cold and level as he drew Miss Royce down into an angle of the deckhouse, out of the line of fire, and whispered fiercely in her ear.

"It's our only chance!" he finished. "Can you — dare you — do it?"

The girl returned his gaze with a glance in which there was a consciousness of danger but no fear. Her smile was one of approval of the man, as well as of his plan.

"I both can and will!" she said. "Good luck, Mr. Sheldon, and, if it is to be, good-by!"

With a hasty handgrip, Sheldon darted down the stairway leading to the saloon.

IX
FIRE AT SEA

SHELDON'S FIRST care was to find the father of the little brown baby. That was easy. He found him standing sentry over Miss Royce's cabin, anxious and bordering on panic, but still steadfast in the carrying out of the *mem-sahib's* instructions.

Coolie nerves, unused to control, were not proof against the rattle of rifles and the patter of lead on the deck above. There was a hair-raising suggestion of peril, too, in the thudding blows resounding through the saloon from the imperfectly barricaded sail-locker.

Time was precious. Sheldon forcefully convinced the man that his life, that of his wife and baby, were in no danger if he did as he was told. He assured him that the *mem-sahib* was in great danger and would need his assistance in a few moments. This last argument was a master-thought. The kind white lady's need outweighed the man's own fears, and Sheldon saw that he could be depended upon.

Loading his revolver as he went, Sheldon made a hasty round of the cabins and pantry, collecting all the available water vessels. These, filled with water, he carried, one after another, to the sail-locker, which opened out of the saloon compartment by way of the second mate's room, and thence by the half door into the hold. Access to the decks was to be had either by way of the 'tween-decks or by the booby-hatch forward of the poop.

The half door, with its hastily piled barricade of sails and canvas, was quivering under the assault of the party in the hold. To gain possible breathing space, Sheldon fired thrice at the widening crack in the door, thus warning the assailants that they must not expect a walk-over. He almost choked in the fumes of his own powder in the restricted limits of the locker.

Then he made another swift search of the cabins and returned to the sail-room, laden with rags, paper, a can of oil, and the velvet cloth from the saloon table.

He piled these in the middle of a coil of running gear, which was plentifully soaked with water. While he worked he fired his pistol at frequent intervals. Savage voices outside took on a note of desperation, and the attack was redoubled.

Matches in hand, he took a final survey of his work. As he stood erect a moment, for ease after long stooping, a sound behind caused him to turn. Outside in the saloon another sound broke on his ears; he sprang aside to avoid an unknown but present danger.

Through the swirling gunpowder smoke he saw the malignant face of the Goanese steward. The man's piercing eyes had in them an expression of understanding. He sprang at Sheldon. His mouth opened wide in a yell which was to tell the attackers of Sheldon's ruse, as he attempted to frustrate it. A blow with his pistol butt glanced from the man's head, and Sheldon grappled.

Already, the firing on deck had reached the height of a fusillade; the pounding on the sail-room door grew more hollow as the crack widened, and a lump rose to the white man's throat with the thought that he was too late.

Faintly he heard the voice of Miss Royce calling from the main saloon, and he tried to shout to her. His foe's clawlike hand was over his mouth; his own fingers strove to choke off the cry that would ruin all. A brown figure like a cat out of a thicket hurtled through the door. There was a clash of teeth, a gasping cry, and the steward's grip relaxed.

Sheldon dimly saw a swift, writhing struggle, and the coolie husband rose to his feet and spat upon the motionless figure of the Goanese. Miss Royce called to ask if all was ready, and the coolie sprang to meet her with a growl of affection.

A match was applied to the piled materials in the coil of rope and a piece of canvas fanned them into flame. Shreds of the torn velvet table cover were added, and frayed ends of rope, together with balls of loosely crushed paper. These nursed the fire into a volume of pungent smoke. A swirl of the reek from the flame swept through the now half-opened door of the hold, and a doubtful note crept into the voices outside. Then Sheldon called our to Miss Royce in the saloon:

"Now, Miss Royce! Quickly, please!"

He heard the girl and her coolie at his back. With a whispered, "Good luck!" he snatched up a mass of smoldering rags and a flaming torch of paper and thrust both at the crack in the door. The draft drew flames and smoke through the aperture into the faces of the attacking ones.

Asiatic courage was not proof against Asiatic panic. A howl of terror which the officers leading the attack did not attempt to hush pealed through the hold and the Lascars stampeded for the booby-hatch ladder.

That howl found an echo in a rising murmur of fear from the half-crazed coolies, and it gave Miss Royce her cue. Sheldon snatched back his flaming materials and tossed them back onto the heap. Then he peered out through the smoke and hurled the door wide open.

Without hesitation Miss Royce and her coolie attendant stepped into the 'tween-decks and hurried along to the main-hatch. The retreating Lascars with their leaders had slammed the booby-hatch shut upon reaching the deck. Already cries of panic were heard from above.

There was a sudden cessation of rifle shots, while the sharp crackling of revolvers continued. Crashing home the half-door to prevent more smoke from going among the coolies, Sheldon sprang to the saloon, leaped upon the table and flung the skylight wide open. He stepped swiftly back to the sail-locker, listened for a moment and was reassured by sounds showing that Miss Royce's mission of pacification was succeeding, and that there was an even chance against a panic among the coolies. Then he darted up the stairs and burst in among the now almost desperate defenders of the deckhouse.

Smoke poured up from the skylight; the companionway was thick with the pungent reek. Out on deck the alarm had been taken, and six scared Lascars, with white, gleaming eyeballs, were swarming down from the mizzen-top. On the poop and in the waist frenzied seamen tore and wrenched at boat covers and gripes. Lascars whose fingers trembled strove to rig tackles by which to swing the boats out. Every moment a crash of wood on iron announced one more rifle cast away by the terror-stricken mutineers.

Crouched in corners inside the wheelhouse were the three boys with white, drawn faces and set, uncomplaining lips, reloading revolvers for their seniors. The small companionway skylight was riddled by a hundred bullets and the woodwork inside hung in splinters. Not a man from Captain Horner to the carpenter lacked shot or splinter wounds to testify to the reality of his peril.

The thickening smoke was an added source of danger. Though Miss Royce had begged the captain to remain in and hold the deckhouse until Sheldon's return, in spite of what might develop, the sight of the boats being swung out was almost too much for the fortitude of the defenders.

"What's happened, Sheldon?" demanded the captain, turning his face away from the port-hole for an instant. "Where's Miss Royce? We'll have to fight for one of those boats by the look of things!"

"Miss Royce is all right!" panted Sheldon, his lungs full of smoke. "Don't worry about the fire. That's only a ruse, and I have control of it. Just keep potting away at the men lowering the boats so that they can't stop to get water and provisions and so as to hurry them off. As soon as they are all afloat, come out and fetch Miss Royce from the 'tween-decks. I'll have the fire out and be up myself by then!"

Before going back to the fire, he peered through the portholes around the deckhouse. The column of smoke rising through the main skylight became thicker and blacker, and he knew that his hurriedly-damped fire was breaking out afresh. Haste was imperative, yet he saw something which could not be passed by.

On deck, by the mizzen rigging, lay four rifles and four cartridge-belts, flung down by the Lascars in the mizzen-top. He glanced swiftly through the door, saw that the deck on that side was clear save for the toiling sailors at the gig-falls, and with a snapped command to hold the door, he rushed out. He gathered up the precious rifles and ammunition, turned and plunged back for cover, just as a Bengali officer saw him and fired his revolver at him from the hip.

He was half conscious of a burning stab along his ribs, and stumbled. Hands grabbed him and his booty and hauled him inside. He heard the deck-house door slam and Mr. Scott's gruff voice:

"That settles it, Mr. Sheldon! I had my doubts about you, when you ducked below out of the shooting, but I apologize. If we see port, it's due to you!"

Muttering some vague acknowledgment of the mate's speech, Sheldon flung down the last of his own revolver cartridges from his pockets — for he knew full well the desperate work he faced — and leaped in two jumps down into the saloon.

He ran to the sail-locker. He had to fight his way through black clouds of stifling smoke that rendered breathing torture. Through the black reek he saw tongues of flame, red and yellow, blue and green, and he heard the ominous crackling of woodwork. Urgent though the need was, he ran first to the half-door, opened it six inches and looked out along the coolie deck to make sure of the safety of the brave girl who had made his own task possible.

Through the open hatchways the sunlight poured a yellow flood of brilliance, now only faintly dimmed by eddying smoke. Far forward, the center of a reverent group, Miss Royce soothed fast-dying fears by pointing with eloquent gestures to the lessening smoke and to the increasing sunlight and by bidding her hearers listen to the diminishing sounds of conflict.

Her coolie attendant was in command of a group of his own fellows. For a moment, Sheldon could not discern the center of their interest. Then, at a word from Miss Royce, the group moved aside and revealed, bound, gagged and scared nearly to death, all of the elders among the coolies — all those who had been in the confidence of the conspirators.

"Not an empress! A goddess!" muttered Sheldon, shutting the half-door again and plunging into the task of subduing the fire. The wooden racks which separated the sails and prevented mildew had caught fire, and tiny streaks of the destroying flame had crept up and flickered among the laths.

Setting his teeth grimly, Sheldon tackled the wood first. He tore down huge, rolled-up sails far above his strength to handle and tried to beat out the flames with wetted canvas.

The big heap of smoldering rubbish in the middle of the floor was growing hotter and redder while he toiled. Every fling of his stumbling feet scattered the mass and admitted air to the fire at the core of it. Gasping in torture, his eyes smarting and half-blinded, a pail in each hand, he staggered out for water. He could still hear, as if far above him, the crash of revolver shots. From somewhere, miles away as it seemed to his strained hearing, came the sound of tackles running through blocks and the shouts of frenzied men.

In a daze he groped to the pantry. The place was dark as Erebus, but his hands found the pump. It was dry. Choking down a sob he lurched back with his empty buckets and, in rage, flung them at the fire. His feet tripped in a wet, opened sail. One of the barricading places which had been soaked when first he wetted down the surrounding canvas broke out in flame.

With his chest bursting from blazing fumes and his legs refusing to support him longer, he seized the wet sail as he pitched forward. Dumbly fighting to he knew not what end, with an instinct that reached immeasurably above self-preservation, he rolled and rolled, and thrashed and flailed with body, arms, legs and wet cloth, across the blazing pile.

Then he began to realize that the smoke had got him. Vaguely he knew that the fire was quenched. Vainly he tried to escape, but his brain reeled and he felt himself sinking into a bottomless pit, the sides of which revealed, to his distorted imagination, a quickly revolving panorama of his whole life.

The remembrances of early childhood incidents, his playmates and school-chums, his mother and father in their quaint Devonshire cottage near the moorland, the college friends and the old martinet who ruled the destinies of Sandhurst cadets; his brother-officers and regimental life, the social whirl, the dice, the cards, the racetrack, and, at last, his fall from grace — all had their place in the vivid panorama.

He was dying, and he knew it. Soon, the visions would fade. With one supreme effort he raised himself and saw, at the mouth of the darksome pit into which he had fallen, the face of a girl who smiled and held out her arms to him.

"Ah!" he thought, "it is pleasant to die with the thought that someone cares for me!"

And then — blackness and oblivion.

X
REWARDS OF MERIT

WHEN SHELDON came to himself it was under very different conditions from those under which he had lost consciousness. He found himself lying between cool sheets in a large room. His surroundings apprised him that he was no longer at sea.

The cool air was stirring through the apartment, and he detected a trace of spicy fragrance, very unlike the noisome smoke of the sail-locker where he had died — or believed in perfect good faith that he had died.

When he tried to move he became aware that his stiffness was occasioned by many bandages in which he was encompassed. He succeeded in raising a hand to his head and was surprised to find that his cranium was bare.

"I wonder where I am?" he muttered to himself. "Thought I was dead and buried!"

As if in answer to his muttered exclamation, he detected a light footstep. Opening his half-closed eyelids, he found himself gazing full into the eyes of Miss Royce, now standing beside his bedside attired in the cool white cap and gown of a nurse.

"Ah!" he ejaculated, waking up to at least a part of the situation, "we have escaped, Miss Royce, but what of the others? Tell me all about what happened."

"Not just now, Mr. Sheldon," replied Miss Royce, smiling. "You have been very ill and the doctor has ordered that, when you awoke, you should refrain from bothering your head about anything for a while."

"Hmm!" grunted Sheldon, discontentedly. "I seem to be all right. Why not tell me now?"

Then he tried to smile engagingly and expectantly, only to receive from his nurse the laconic reply, "Nothing doing, sir!"

A light knock at the door announced a visit from the doctor, who, after a few whispered questions to Miss Royce, nodded his head approvingly and remarked to the patient: "You're doing fine, Mr. Sheldon! Keep very quiet and in a few days we'll have you on your feet."

TEN DAYS later, Sheldon was reclining in an easy chair on the piazza of the Oriental Hotel at Colombo. He had been conveyed here, unconscious, as soon as the ship had reached port.

Captain Horner sat beside him. Miss Royce fluttered around, performing all those little attentions that only a woman can for a convalescent.

Taking from his mouth the unlighted cheroot which he had been chewing, the captain congratulated Sheldon on his rapid progress towards health.

"Now tell me all about it!" demanded Sheldon of him. The captain commenced the recital of events.

"Yes. Everything panned out just as you had planned. We hauled you out of the half-burned sail-locker, just in time for you to escape suffocation. You had succeeded in extinguishing the fire, although, as you know, you were badly scorched and burned. Such a bundle of half-burned rags and tatters, arraying a half-baked, smoke-dried piece of humanity, I never saw before! We hardly knew whether you were dead or alive when we laid you on the deck, but Miss Royce decided in your favor and took charge of your mortal affairs which she has conducted ever since. And," added the skipper, quizzically, "Doc says she knows her business.

"You've had brain fever for several weeks, and that, and the fire, account for the depleted condition of your thatch." Sheldon laughed.

"Now, tell me all the rest of what happened," he begged.

"Well," replied the skipper, "that smoke-fest of yours worked wonders. It did the trick, all right! It scared that ugly bunch to such an extent that they stampeded for the boats. A few of them got drowned in the getaway, and," he added grimly, "if the whole bunch had been drowned, it would not have been much loss. However, they were pretty nearly as scared when they got away in the boats as when you played that smoke trick upon them. So after pulling aimlessly around for a while in a lumpy bit of a sea and getting good and hungry and thirsty with no supplies at hand, they were glad enough to come aboard again, wet and bedraggled, sans guns and pistols and knives and without an atom of a desire to found an empire or any other kind of a place. A very humble bunch!" continued the captain, sententiously.

"We made sail on the clipper and reached here in a couple of days, and turned the rapscallions over to the tender mercies of the British Government. They deserved to be hanged, but the authorities were merciful and shipped them back to Calcutta and they are now distributed in the various government jails. I hope they'll stay there for a long while," added the skipper grimly. "As for the Babu, he and his following ship were seized by a gun-boat while waiting near Pona Mobubque.

"Now, Sheldon, this is the first opportunity I've had of thanking you for the leading part you took in frustrating the designs of those pirates. You are a noble fellow and a brave man, sir!"

And the captain's eyes showed moisture as the bluff old salt clasped the least-injured hand of Sheldon.

Just then the lithe figure of Miss Royce appeared at the end of the long veranda.

"The mail steamer arrived from Calcutta a couple of hours ago, Mr. Sheldon, so I have brought you your mail," said she.

Sheldon noticed how winsome she looked as she advanced lightly and laid the letters, three in number, upon the arm of his chair.

"Well, by-by Sheldon," said Captain Horner, rising. "Now I'll leave you to look over your mail."

"Please don't go, Miss Royce," said Sheldon, as she rose to follow the captain's lead.

The girl reseated herself in response to Sheldon's invitation, and he asked, "Do you mind if I open these letters?"

"Certainly not," she replied. "I know that you must be anxious to read them."

She settled herself back in the easy-chair beside him and gazed dreamily out across the breakwater and the ships at anchor in the road-stead and into the great beyond.

"Ha!" ejaculated Sheldon. "This one is from the agent of British Lloyds in Calcutta!"

And he hastily slit open the blue, official envelope. There was a tinge of satisfaction depicted on his face as he scanned the contents of the letter.

At length he remarked: "I suppose that some men would say that this letter is very satisfactory, but," he added drearily, "money is not everything in this world."

He looked thoughtfully at his companion as he spoke. His words brought the girl back from her daydream, and she turned and faced him.

"Miss Royce, British Lloyds has seen fit to believe that I have done them some service."

He handed her the letter's enclosure, a bank draft for twenty thousand pounds. Yet somehow the possession of this large amount of money did not afford him any great satisfaction.

"Ha! This looks important!" he exclaimed, as he tore open an envelope which bore the seal of the British India office, and scanned the letter's contents.

This time he wore a quiet smile as he turned to Miss Royce and said: "The government has seen fit to thank me for my slight services and, in token of appreciation has sent me a draft for five thousand pounds."

And he laid that, too, in Miss Royce's lap.

Picking up the third letter he gazed fixedly at a handwriting which he knew well. He paused a moment as if reflecting, and then remarked, dryly, "This letter is from my old colonel, Miss Royce."

His hand trembled as he unfolded the sheet; and as he read its contents his eyes moistened. As he divided a smiling glance between his companion and the letter, "This is the best of all!" he almost shouted in his enthusiasm. "Listen, Eunice — I mean Miss Royce," and he read aloud the colonel's warm invitation to return to his regiment and his warm expressions of congratulation on his bravery.

"'Our fellows say you have upheld the honor of the regiment. Come back,'" he finished.

He glanced at the three letters with a pleased but puzzled expression, and then turned a wistful look into the eyes of the girl beside him.

"Awhile ago," he said hesitantly, "this would have meant a lot to me, because I could have paid my debts of honor and then regained my station and the good opinion of my fellow officers. But now," he continued, "things are different. To return alone would hold no charms for me. Will you go with me?"

Miss Royce flushed and said, "Are you sure you want me?"

Leaning over, Sheldon placed his arm about her shoulders as he said, "More than anything else in this world! Without you, life holds for me but little charm. Could you learn to care for me, Eunice dear?"

A deeper, softer glow rose on Miss Royce's cheeks.

Her eyes glowed as she replied, "I will not have to learn. I think I have always cared."

As he gathered her in his arms, "What about your dream of empire?" she questioned mischievously.

"I have found my empire!" he replied as he folded her as close as his least injured arm would permit and bent his head to give her the first kiss, that of betrothal.

"WATSON!"

"WATSON, my dear fellow, this inaction is maddening. I am *ennuied*," drawled a lanky, cadaverous individual reclining lumpishly in a long deck chair, a black cigar in his teeth, his brows drawn down, and his fingertips touching in approved Sherlockian fashion. A ripple of mirth passes around the small circle of which he formed the centre, and his expression darkened in outward resentment.

The man addressed as Watson glanced at the amused ones with a faint smile on his own face and replied indifferently, "Better take a dose of dope, my dear Holmes. The steward uncorks a rippin' brand of Scotch. Shall I call him?"

Holmes unfolded himself out of the chair without a reply and stalked away in the direction of the smoking room.

"He's on the scent!" chuckled a fiery-haired youngster.

"That's a scent you all can follow!" replied a merry-eyed girl, seizing the red one and dragging him off to play shuffleboard. Watson remained in his chair, and behind lowered lids his eyes glittered shrewdly.

Percy Anstruther's big steam yacht *Vagrant* never went to sea without a happy, careless party of youth aboard.

Percy himself was of the type dubbed porcine. Finding himself tremendously wealthy quite early in life, mainly by dint of ignoring the Golden Rule and playing up the Rule of Three — which he interpreted to mean, one for the firm — of which he was head — and two for Percy Anstruther — holding no scruples which might prevent profits accruing through some such idiocy as consideration for others, he soon decided, on retiring, that a steam yacht was the thing to gain him entry into the society of the exclusive set he desired to adorn. Percy knew enough to refrain from attempting the impossible; he paid high salaries, not wages, to the best of secretaries, the cunningest of chefs, the very paragon of stewards, and he possessed that native shrewdness which prevented him offending by any vulgarity of speech in select company, no matter how free he might be among his own kind. No amount of shrewdness could warn him of the bad taste, or inadvisability, of loading himself with costly, bizarre jewelry. He saw ladies and gentlemen of the class he envied, each wearing such gems as they possessed when occasion demanded. In his small mind there was only one reason for their not wearing more — the lack of possession; only one reason for limiting the times of wearing what they had — fear of losing them. And since neither fear of losing them nor limited possession applied to himself, Percy Anstruther's fat fingers were ever loaded with flawless diamonds, his fat neck glowed from the fires within a great single ruby in his scarf, his fat watch fob scintillated like a cluster of stars against his fat little paunch.

"I've got 'em, why shouldn't I sport 'em?" he had demanded many times in answer to suggestions from his friends. "I can afford to wear 'em, and the crook isn't born who'll take 'em away from your Uncle Percy. No, sir!"

Which all brings us back to Holmes and Watson; for it was the long, lean, cadaverous Holmes who first expressed entire agreement with Percy's ideas on the subject of fashion in gems. They had met, and become acquainted, at the great Casino of Ocean View, off which the *Vagrant* lay anchored while her owner and his guests disported in a dance or two, a turn or so at the wheel, or a little chopping, according to individual taste. Percy, furthermore, strongly desired to become acquainted with somebody who would accept his hospitality without making him see and feel that he became a debtor by receiving the honor of the present company. He was gratified by the celerity with which he attained his object. There could be no doubt regarding the desirability of Mr. Holmes or his friend Watson. Those names appeared on the register of their hotel, and by them they were known and introduced to Percy by the croupier of the roulette table. There could be no cavilling at friends secured through such a sponsor. And, best of all, they quite certainly did not seek his acquaintance merely to have a finger in his pocket-book, for they politely insisted upon buying wine themselves; and their taste was proven when they ordered a brand which Percy always hesitated about, though he knew it was quite the thing, simply because he wasn't sure how to pronounce the name.

"I say, you chaps must come for a cruise with me," he had said eagerly at the third bottle.

"The ocean's rather a bore, old man, but perhaps we could endure it for a few days, ah, Watson?" Holmes had replied in a drawl which seemed incongruous with the sharpness of his big, steady eyes.

"Oh, just for a week, perhaps," Watson had conceded, with similar lack of eagerness, and the thing was done. They vacated their hotel that same day; the *Vagrant* steamed just beyond the blue skyline in the cool evening.

WITH a young party on board, it was inevitable that Holmes should speedily acquire the name of "Sherlock." For Dr. Watson to be dubbed "Doctor" followed as naturally as night follows day. At first they mildly resented it, although, queerly enough, Holmes rather deserved it than otherwise, for he was forever reading the detective books in the yacht's well-stocked library, and he could easily be led on to expound the methods of the famous sleuth of fiction. But soon they accepted the titles bestowed on them, and gradually Percy, seeing the fun the others got out of the little pleasantry, and seeing that his new guests suffered nothing actually by it, fell into the mood himself, and often cast out bait in the hope of getting Holmes into a tangle of explanations over some really trivial circumstance. Such as the time, for instance, when the crew's cook, who looked after the fowls carried to supply the owner's table with fresh eggs, reported the best layer missing, and the boatswain, at the same time, pointed out to the chief officer chicken tracks up the side of the freshly painted smokestack.

"You let the bloomin' chicken loose yourself while washing down decks," was the mate's emphatic decision. "You scared her trying to chase her back, and the bally thing flew up against the funnel before she volplaned overboard. You want to be more careful, bo'sun."

But Percy, urged on by his young friends, suggested to Holmes that there might be another solution to the missing chicken mystery. Holmes placed the tips of his long, white fingers together, drew down his brows, and nodded sagaciously. From the stokehold grating came the merry whistle of a happy fireman whose spirits were proof against the discomfort of his work. A windlass clanked, and two firemen just off duty drew up a can of ashes and dumped them down the lower-deck shute; from the galley door a sculleryman emerged, staggering under the kitchen garbage pail. Both containers discharged their waste into the blue sea at once, and tigerishly Holmes darted to the rail and keenly scanned the floating refuse. Then he resumed his chair, lighted a huge briar pipe filled with strong plug, and placed his finger-tips together again, while Percy Anstruther and the merry band of youngsters waited for his next utterance.

"You are right, Mr. Anstruther," he said crisply. "There is another, very different answer to that seemingly simple riddle of the chicken."

"Oh, surely you have not solved the mystery so soon?" protested Percy. His young friends giggled.

"My chain is almost complete, sir," Holmes replied. "You hear that peculiar whistle emanating from the fire-room? I dare say it is the first time you have noticed it. But I, who note the meanest trifles, can assure you that there has been, is, method in that whistle. Where are the poultry pens? Right beside the stokehold ventilators, are they not? Very well. The messmate of the whistling fireman slyly opens the cage, the whistler pipes up a cunning note, the chicken creeps out, the cage is once more fastened, and the miscreant who opened and closed it darts below to join his fellow criminal. The whistling goes on, the poor deluded chicken follows it, and now it takes on the quality of ventriloquism. It seems to emanate from the funnel. The silly fowl walks up the smokestack, the fumes overcome it when it gets to the rim, and it falls down into the hands of the hungry pair waiting for its advent, singed and cooked ready to devour. That, gentlemen, is the solution of an apparent mystery. Quite simple."

A roar of merriment pealed out across the sea, and Holmes appeared annoyed.

"Fine!" laughed Percy, with the conscious superiority of having discovered a palpable flaw. "But tell us, old chap, how these awful criminals got the chicken out of the furnace? It would be burned up long before it reached the bottom of that chimney."

"You may amuse yourselves unravelling that point, gentlemen. I will give you a tip, though. I stepped to the rail just now. You imagined I did so idly, or simply to knock out my pipe. It was not so. I examined the refuse thrown over at that instant. Feathers, some burnt, some whole, floated away on a mass of ashes. It is the trifles which count in detecting crime. Now, Watson, I think we will investigate a rumor that the steward was seen breaking out a new case of Scotch this morning."

There was a medley of voices in the group he left. Some actually wondered if he really believed in his own deep cunning, since he was never seen to smile even while expounding his most outlandish notions. Others were only disgusted. There were two who warned Percy without reserve that before the cruise was up he would be touched for money by the Sherlockian Holmes and his friend Watson.

"Oh, I don't think that," objected Percy. "He's rather idiotic, of course, but I think the chap's only fooling himself. They're both gentlemen, anyway, and we're having some fun with them."

"Why not let us make up a real mystery, Percy?"

"Oh, goody!" cried a merry-eyed girl, dancing joyously. "Oh, let's! You can have a tremendous robbery, or something, and have all the clues point to all of us, and all of us have an alibi, and you can scatter my hairpins and combs about, and —"

"That's the identical scheme!" chuckled Percy, shaking like a jelly in his mirth. "Let's dope out a plot."

"Presently!" interjected the red-headed youth, intensely. "Here's the Watson chap. Not a word!"

Watson strolled along the deck, having left Holmes in the smoking room, and he wore a grimace of mingled boredom and contempt. He glanced around the little group inquisitively, then addressed Percy.

"Holmes begins to irritate one, doesn't he, Anstruther? A little of his nonsense is amusing; too much is sickening. I wonder what he'd do if faced with a real case. Sometimes I think he's really keen on scientific investigation of problems, at others I feel disgusted at his childishness. The chicken twaddle, for instance."

Percy hesitated for a minute, then, smiling fatly in justification of his resolve, he said.

"I say, Watson, you must be a thought-reader. When you came along we were discussing playing a little joke on your friend to see how far he would dig into a real puzzle. You won't mind if we keep you out of it, will you? Might drop him a hint, you know, and spoil —"

"Not at all," replied Watson quickly. "Make your plans and start him going. I'll have my fun looking on, I assure you. I hope you concoct a real mystery, though, with something far deeper than vanishing poultry as a motive. Good luck."

THE first outcome of a long and close secret confabulation was the sudden increase of Percy's jewelled embellishments. That evening at dinner he simply blazed with light from gorgeous gems, and in place of his customary offering of big, sleek Cuban cigars in a handsome snakeskin case after dinner, he preferred still choicer weeds in an amazing gold case on both sides of which his monogram leaped out at one in diamonds. Then, under pretence of showing the men some intimate curiosities, he took them into his great stateroom where, obviously through oversight, a stout cash box stood open on his table, crammed to the top with bank notes of high denomination.

"Confound that man of mine!" he exclaimed, closing the box, but leaving it on the table. "He's always leaving valuables about as if they were pebbles."

While exhibiting the trivial curiosities he had brought the men in to see, he shot keen side-glances at Holmes, and chuckled shakily as he led the way out to the after deck, omitting to reprimand his valet, however, for his carelessness.

"It's a gorgeous night," he remarked, when the space under the awnings resounded with tuneful music from an excellent machine.

"Let's have a bit of dancing, hey, folks?"

IN THE quietest hour of the most silent watch, about two o'clock in the morning, the yacht rang with sounds of dire mis-happening. A pistol shot shattered the stillness on deck, a heavy splash was heard over the side, and in a minute the decks were alive with alarmed seaman and excited officers; a huddle of sleepy guests milled about each other in well feigned panic. Watson was there, as panicky as the rest; and Holmes, true to his assumed character, took up the burden of discovering the meaning of that midnight alarm.

"Where is Mr. Anstruther?" he demanded, peering around like a scrawny hawk. "Find him, steward. Fancy him sleeping through such a racket! He's getting far too fat."

While Watson looked on in silence from the companionway door, and a little giggling group nudged each other delightedly, Holmes flashed a pocket torch about the decks and rails. On hands and knees at times, he nosed along waterways and peering overside into the silken blackness of the smooth sea. Presently he brought forth a huge magnifying glass, and the red-headed youth laughed outright. The sound seemed creepy in the darkness and quiet, broken before only by swish of water and that flickering circle of light from Holmes' torch. But the steward's sudden appearance and agitated announcement diverted attention again.

"Mr. Anstruther's — Oh, his room, it's horrid!"

Prepared as they were for such an announcement, it required all their self-control to prevent the conspirators uttering little gasps of sheer suspense, so vivid was the steward's terror. Watson glanced keenly toward the absorbed figure of Holmes, who was scrutinizing the steward pitilessly, every inch of the man's outward aspect coming under the inspection.

"That will do, my man," snapped Holmes at length. "You may show us the way to Mr. Anstruther's stateroom. Come, Watson, I may need you." The steward led the way trembling, and the muffled giggling burst forth again as the youthful jesters saw the Sherlockian one tumbling into the trap they had set for him. All the details of the plot had been left to Anstruther, and they were sure he had done a good piece of work, for he had outlined most of what he intended to do, but none had anticipated the perfection of theatrical setting which seemed to leap out at them through the door of Percy's room.

"Ooh!" cried the merry-eyed girl, and shrank back with fright which was more than half real. Her companions too, playing out their hands, peeped inside, drew back, gasped and stared in simulated terror.

Watson looked in, then stepped inside, his ruddy face wearing an enigmatical expression. Holmes alone maintained an utterly expressionless air as he waved everyone back from the threshold and took from his pocket a tape measure.

Well indeed had Percy done his part. The bed was upset, and the coverings strewed the carpet. One curtain flew loose through the wide porthole, the other hung by one hook, torn in halves. The table and writing desk in a corner were bare; the drawers, both hanging open almost out of the slides, lay empty. The stout cash box was on the floor, empty but one forlorn note of small denomination lay pinched under one corner of it. Across the room, near the bed, which was a four-poster and not a bunk, was a woman's hair comb, broken; a yard away lay a pyjama button, still a yard further a red and green grass bath slipper, obviously far too small for Percy to have ever worn. And, stabbing the dim light like a spear, a great red smear ran from a dark stain on the bed-head clear up to and through the open port.

Watson stepped over and touched the red smear with a finger, smelling it and peering at it under a light globe. A queer curl wreathed his lips, and he glanced curiously at Holmes who was on his knees with tape and lens. Afterward, when talking over the events of that night, some of the young men recalled that queer glance of Watson's, and remembered, too, that he contrived to get into the foreground quite as much as Holmes, yet without in the slightest degree seeming to want to. Anyhow, in all the after pictures of that night which rose up before any of the guests, the short, heavy figure of Watson loomed as large as the long, thin, stooping figure of Holmes.

"What's happened, d'you think?" whispered somebody. The merry-eyed girl giggled hysterically, and rejoined, "Give Mr. Holmes time. Don't you all see there's been a horrid crime committed, and that poor Percy has vanished? Don't breathe. You may disturb something, mayn't they, Mr. Holmes?"

For answer Holmes suddenly appeared before the little group in the door, his eyes ablaze.

He seemed to arrive from the other side of the room without, motion, like a shadow; and without warning he plunged his hand into the tumbled mass of shining hair over the girl's startled eyes. In the other hand he held the broken parts of the hair comb he had picked up from the floor.

"Same color," he muttered, matching comb with hair. "Where is your comb, miss?"

Confronted with the very thing she had suggested herself, the girl looked less happy than she had expected. Confusion seized upon her, and her saucy tongue failed her. She stammered, sheepishly enough, "That is it. I er — I lent it to Percy to, er — to —"

"That is all, thank you," Holmes interrupted her sharply. "I will ask for you when I require your statement. You may retire." A tiny murmur of protest rippled around at sight of the girl's crestfallen air as she turned away toward her own room; but then the hugeness of the joke struck all concerned, and they crowded close to hear what was coming next.

Holmes closely examined the carpet, the bed, the curtains; he even measured the length and breadth of the red smear on the side panel. He sniffed at some dust he scraped up, he struck his head through the port-hole and peered up and down, fore and aft, like a raw-necked vulture seeking prey. Then, stepping to the centre again, he looked for a moment at the faces before him and at the red and green bath slipper. Suddenly he went to his knees before the red-headed youth and forcibly lifted his right foot knee-high. He flung aside the leather Romeo the young man wore and clamped the grass slipper to the foot.

"H'm! You, too, I shall know where to find when I need you," he remarked. "You may retire, sir; and I warn you that this very serious occurrence may lead into unpleasant places. If you wish to tell me any-thing, you may do so in the morning. That is all, thank you."

Now he held out the pyjama button, scanning the sleeping suits before him. One jacket lacked a button, and one only. Like a tiger Holmes sprang before the wearer, clapped the button to the vacant place, and glared terribly into the young fellow's face. "B-but, Holmes, it isn't the same pattern!" giggled another bystander, scarcely able to talk for re-pressed mirth.

"Married?" Holmes jerked out abruptly to the man who lacked a button.

"Surely," laughed the youngster, recovering his nerve.

"Pattern doesn't matter then," was the unexpectedly sophisticated reply. "You will be called in the morning, sir. That will do."

"Say, Holmes," put in the last onlooker, who, except for Watson, alone remained unspotted by suspicion. "I don't lack a shoe, nor a button, nor even a comb. Can't you discover some clue which indicates me as the brutal murderer?" There was a keen note of sarcasm in the man's sugges-tion. Holmes looked at him gravely.

"I shall permit nothing to escape my notice which bears on this mon-strous mystery," he said. "Place your left hand here, please."

With excessive care he pressed the man's hand down into the nap of the thick carpet, and scrutinized the edges through his powerful lens; then released the man and told him to go, but, like the rest, to hold himself ready to be questioned.

"Meanwhile," remarked Holmes, "we shall turn in toward some port. This is a matter for the regular police, to whom I hope to be able to deliver the criminal."

"Sure you can't find something which incriminates Watson?" gurgled the young fellow just released. "This is such a scream it would be a shame to keep him out of it."

"You will kindly keep your witticisms for a more suitable moment, sir," was the dry retort, and the guest departed, leaving Watson gazing thoughtfully at the stooping back of Holmes.

"My dear Watson," the sleuth said presently, "pray ring for the steward." The steward answered the bell, and Holmes told him, without turning around, to go and order the captain to change the course for the nearest port, and to notify him immediately which port it would be. In answer, the captain appeared in person, and a very angry, irritable person he was. He opened fire at once on the sleuth.

"What's the meaning of this?" he demanded warmly. "Why am I not called in to be consulted about this? And who are you, to order me into port, I'd like to know. Where's the owner?"

"Mr. Anstruther has disappeared, captain. There has been some foul play. That is why I suggest running into port —"

"And this is the first I hear of it!" bellowed the captain. "Shooting goes on aboard my ship, somebody tells me my owner has gone, and I'm not asked for an opinion but told to run —"

"Just a moment, captain," Watson put in quietly; "I will explain a lot to you if you'll give me a moment outside. There has been mischief, certainly, but not so serious as might be. Come, let Holmes continue his investigation. I'll tell you about it."

He led the mollified skipper out to his own roomy cabin, and Holmes flashed a look of appreciation after them as he shut the door.

AN EXPECTANT party gathered about the table at breakfast in the morning, for daylight brought back all the brightness of the farce which night and its gloom had almost made to seem like tragedy. They awaited Holmes, who presently appeared looking haggard and pale after an obviously sleepless night. He crushed up a white pellet and stirred it into his coffee, which he drank before eating anything; then coldly, and with an incisiveness worthy of a graver situation, he plunged into a bald recital of his discoveries and decision. On deck, listening through the skylight, a

gleeful yacht captain chuckled hugely, slapping his leg, utterly recon-
ciled to the temporary loss of his employer.

"We shall be in port in a few hours now," Holmes began. "The culprit
in this brazen piece of villainy will be taken ashore then, I promise you.
You all heard the shot in the night, and —"

"How about the shoes and buttons and other haberdashery?"
grinned the red-headed youth maliciously.

"I shall come to that, my young friend," replied Holmes, glaring
fiercely. "You heard the shot, I believe. You all saw the scene of the
crime —"

"That shot was on deck!"

"The scene of the crime," the sleuth proceeded as if no interruption
had been offered, "and even my friend Watson could discern the obvious
signs of violence there. You saw the odd slipper, the pyjama button, the
broken comb, and the gory smear on the wall. Now there is one chance
remaining for the guilty one to make reparation, and thereby perhaps
gain leniency. I shall run over the facts, and on our arrival in port I shall
summon the police to take the criminal, unless meanwhile he confesses.

"Now that slipper would fit only a child or a woman. That button
might have come from a lounge pillow. The comb could easily have been
picked up broken somewhere else and dropped in the cabin by the owner
himself. I have some little skill in reading signs, and I say that pistol shot
was fired out through a porthole, sounding thus as if it were on deck; the
slipper is one of a heap of about fifty pairs of all sizes, kept by Mr.
Anstruther for the use of guests who may have forgotten to bring bath
shoes. The button assuredly came from the cushion in Anstruther's own
arm chair, and the comb was probably dropped by him when he returned
from the deck."

"Why, Holmes, you might be accusing Percy himself!" roared the
party in mirth. Then, realizing suddenly that they ought to wear more of
an air of gravity, since Percy was apparently murdered in his own yacht,
and they were all more or less under suspicion, their faces fell, and they
leaned closer to Holmes in deep attention.

"Making due allowance for youth and frivolity," Holmes proceeded
coldly, "I will bear with you. Here is a tip, which you may find useful.
Pray try to assist the course of justice, rather than hinder it because you
do not see things as I see them. You would find the assassin and thief?
Very well then. Look for a person of this description: A tall, lean man,
rather stout, and about five feet eight inches high; he is florid and pale of
complexion, and wears a number seven or number ten shoe. On one hand

he has a crooked finger, which he can straighten whenever he wants to."

As one man the party got up from the table, and on every face was a sneer. They had expected something far better than this, else Percy would surely never have submitted to many hours of discomfort in order to play out the jest. The merry-eyed girl lingered behind to state, forcefully, her opinion.

"Mr. Holmes, I think you are a beast! If you are such an idiot as your silly words seem to indicate, you should at least have decency enough to refrain from uttering such nonsense at a time like this!"

She flirted out, and a slow, deep smile overspread Holmes' lean face as she disappeared. The captain, on deck, turned away to face a stammering, pop-eyed steward at his elbow.

"Mr. Anstruther, sir! He's down —"

"S-sh!" the skipper warned the man sharply. "Keep your mouth shut, steward. This is all right. Don't say a word."

"B-but, sir, he looks —"

"I tell you it's all right. It's a game he's playing. Keep quiet, I tell you."

Watson was having a similarly difficult time persuading his fellow guests to let the joke go on a little longer. They were, to a man and girl, for seeking out Percy and telling him it was useless to remain in hiding any longer.

"Why, Watson, it's too darned silly to be funny," cried the red-headed one. "It's simply idiotic to let old Percy sweat himself sick down in some dark hold just to draw this faker Holmes. I never heard such rubbish, even from half-witted kids."

"Don't spoil it," Watson advised quietly. "I know Holmes rather better than you, and I tell you he's only trying to scare you off while he makes out a case. If you leave him alone, say until we get to port, he'll have something amusing to tell you, even if it is all wrong. At any rate it will be a logical sequence of points comparing perfectly with all the clues."

"But how about poor old Percy?"

"I'll see him myself. He'll be agreeable, I know, since he arranged the joke himself. I'll take him down some wine and see what else he wants."

"Oh, then you know where he's hiding? He didn't tell us."

"I know, yes. Just keep quiet and watch awhile. You'll have something truly interesting to talk about soon, I promise you."

The yacht ran into harbor before noon, and as she steamed up the sail-dotted bay Holmes came on deck in town clothes. Every eye fastened on him, and smiles were carefully concealed.

"I am going on shore to bring the police, gentlemen," he stated sharply. "There is little time, but still time enough, for the culprit to reveal himself."

He turned away and stood at the rail. Behind him muffled giggles and chuckles broke out, and the merry-eyed girl chirped recklessly, "Oh yes, let him go! It'll be bully sport seeing the real police tear his silly old theories to rags."

Holmes seemed to notice nothing that was said, but presently the steward appeared absolutely dripping with the perspiration of fear, and in a moment all was changed from farce to earnest.

"Captain!" the man yelled to the bridge, "I've found Mr. Anstruther, and he's hurt! He ain't fooling, no, sir! He's been tied —"

Watson stepped forward, laid a hand on Holmes' arm coolly, and jabbed a pistol muzzle into his ribs. He faced the group with a smile.

"The steward is right, gentlemen. You thought to play a joke, but Long Holmes here turned it into a real game. That is, he almost succeeded. But I have been keeping tabs on him for a long time, and I've got him now with the goods. Yes, I'm a detective. You might see after Mr. Anstruther. I shall come back and report to him as soon as I've placed my prisoner in safety."

Holmes twisted his neck and glared down at Watson with murderous eyes; but the smaller man kept his pistol pressed to the other's side until the yacht docked, then put it into his pocket, warned his prisoner, and marched him ashore and into a taxicab.

Percy was brought up from the darksome depths of the storerooms, blinking and furious, but more than a little frightened. He shook a fat, abrased fist after the disappearing taxicab when the captain told him who was in it, and launched into a feverish recital of his adventures.

"By the Great Horn Spoon!" he gabbled, reddening up like a turkey's wattles. "That chap's smart, but he ain't a patch on the quiet Watson. There's a sleuth for you! Followed his man, he has, for months, I'll go bail; why, I'll bet he made his acquaintance at Ocean View just to keep right after him until he pulled something.

"And nobody suspected him all the while Sherlock was turning our little game into a damn nasty reality. I knew something was wrong—kind o' felt it, y'know—but it was too late to do anything when the suspicion grew to certainty. I was hobbled then.

"Oh, I give it to Holmes, fellows, he fooled me nicely! I came into my stateroom as we arranged, scattered those fool clues about, and was just ready to gather up the loot and blow off the gun out of the porthole, when in comes Sherlock like a ghost, slams me up against the wall and busts my nose, wraps me up in my own bathrobe and ties it with the cord, and carries me down below. Then he passed up again, and I heard the pistol go off, and there I've lain ever since until just now."

"By George! It was a clever bit of trickery," exclaimed a wide-eared listener. "Lucky it failed, eh?"

"Yes, thanks to Watson. I knew that chap was the real thing," vowed Percy, dabbing tenderly at his swollen nose. "You got to hand it to him, though he didn't deceive me for a minute. He had just the look of a real, clever crime-hound. I'll do something handsome for him when he comes on board."

None of the party wanted to go ashore until Watson had returned. They lounged under the awnings, sipping long cool drinks and chatting over the affair. About half an hour after Watson had taken his captive ashore, a wide-winged flying boat flew overhead close down, circled once or twice as if inspecting the fine yacht, then flew swiftly seaward in the general direction of a long line of islands belonging to many different nations, lying far down over the horizon. Flying boats have ceased to be objects of intense curiosity, and nobody took more than a fleeting interest in the low-flying machine, until it had almost speeded out of sight in the sea haze and the radio man suddenly appeared in obvious excitement and handed Percy a message. Percy read it idly, re-read it with staring eyes, dropped it on deck and sprang to the rail, gaping into the blue sky for that vanished speck which was the flying machine. The merry-eyed girl picked up the message, smoothed it out, and with a hesitating glance at the stupefied Percy read it aloud to the shocked company.

"Thank you, Percy," it said. "We've had a lovely time and bear you no malice for your friends' ridicule of our methods. We'll write you from Mars, or Venus, or some place. Ta-ta, old boy. Sherlock and the Doctor."

Faces gaped into faces in utter amazement, then all turned to Percy. But Percy was already taking the companionway stairs six steps at a time, bound for his ravaged stateroom from which a treasure in gems and cash had all too surely vanished.

www.ingramcontent.com/pod-product-compliance
Lightning Source LLC
Chambersburg PA
CBHW051922240626
47153CB00004B/1325